PRAISE FOR *A FORTY YEAR KISS*

"Nickolas Butler is at the top of his game with *A Forty Year Kiss*. The characters are so real, I feel like they are family. The story is absolute perfection and a romance for the ages. From the first sentences, the reader is placed right into the pages, and I didn't want it to end. I have been waiting a long time to read a book like this, and Nickolas's writing will forever live in my heart."

—Mary O'Malley, Skylark Bookshop

"Nickolas Butler sets the page on fire in *A Forty Year Kiss*. This is not an out-of-control wildfire of a love story—it is, instead, the slow burn of mature people who know love. *A Forty Year Kiss* understands the peaks and dives of a lifelong romance and illuminates them gloriously on the page. Charlie and Vivian are complex, fallible, and very real. Let yourself fall head over heels for the new novel by this remarkable author."

—Pamela Klinger-Horn, Valley Bookseller

"An unforgettable love story that transcends time. Nickolas Butler has crafted a stunning portrayal of new beginnings that is raw, honest, and deeply moving. *A Forty Year Kiss* inspires hope and proves that it is never too late for a second chance at love. I couldn't put it down!"

—Maxwell Gregory, Madison Street Books

"Life-affirming and straight-up beautiful. Will stoke the good fire in your chest. I absolutely loved it. A must-read."

—Matthew Quick, *New York Times* bestselling author of *The Silver Linings Playbook*

"A big-hearted, comforting novel about second chances—at love, at recovery, at forgiveness and redemption. Butler treats all his characters with dignity and affection. When we die, we'd all be lucky to come back as a character in a Nickolas Butler novel."

—Ash Davidson, author of *Damnation Spring*

"Nickolas Butler only writes good books, but this is the one that sticks most tightly in my brain and heart. While Nickolas dedicates the novel to Nora Ephron—and indeed it's deftly written and should translate seamlessly to the screen—it might be more evocative of Kent Haruf in *Plainsong* or *Our Souls at Night*. Its Midwest is weathered and described with affection and restraint; its people are presented whole and in context, the seldom-seen brought into vivid focus, their yearnings and failings intact. *A Forty Year Kiss* has the courage to suggest it's not too late—for romance or transcendence or just to be better. It's a book for the midnight optimist that is waiting inside us all."

—Leif Enger, bestselling author of *Peace Like a River*

"Thank you, Nickolas Butler, for writing a love story that feels so powerfully real, a story that captures the hope, grace, and joy of new love—but also the mistakes, scar tissue, and regret of past love. It's a wonder to behold, a novel capable of such breadth. This is the kind of book that makes me a better human."

—Nathan Hill, *New York Times* bestselling author
of *The Nix* and *Wellness*

ALSO BY
NICKOLAS BUTLER

Shotgun Lovesongs

Beneath the Bonfire

The Hearts of Men

Little Faith

Godspeed

A
FORTY
YEAR
KISS

A FORTY YEAR KISS

A Novel

NICKOLAS BUTLER

Published by Sourcebooks Landmark, an imprint of Sourcebooks
P.O. Box 4410, Naperville, Illinois 60567-4410
(630) 961-3900
sourcebooks.com

Library of Congress Cataloging-in-Publication Data

Names: Butler, Nickolas, author.
Title: A forty year kiss : a novel / Nickolas Butler.
Other titles: 40 year kiss
Description: Naperville, Illinois : Sourcebooks Landmark, 2025. | Summary:
   "Charlie and Vivian parted ways after just four years of marriage. Too
   many problems, too many struggles. When Charlie returns to Wisconsin
   forty years later, he's not sure what he'll find. He is sure of one
   thing-he must try to reconnect with Vivian to pick up the broken pieces
   of their past. But forty years is a long time. It's forty years of other
   relationships, forty years of building new lives, and forty years of
   long-held regrets, mistakes, and painful secrets. An accomplished
   exploration of starting over and sunset triumph, A Forty-Year Kiss is a
   novel in the tradition of Kent Haruf's Our Souls at Night. This is a
   literary valentine that promises to become a love-story for the ages"--
   Provided by publisher.
Identifiers: LCCN 2024019326 (print) | LCCN 2024019327 (ebook) | (hardcover) | (epub)
Subjects: LCGFT: Romance fiction. | Novels.
Classification: LCC PS3602.U876 F67 2025 (print) | LCC PS3602.U876
   (ebook) | DDC 813/.6--dc23/eng/20240429
LC record available at https://lccn.loc.gov/2024019326
LC ebook record available at https://lccn.loc.gov/2024019327

Printed and bound in the United States of America.
LSC 10 9 8 7 6 5 4 3 2 1

For Nora Ephron (1941–2012), the patron saint of love stories

For Tom Waits, the heart of Saturday night

And for Rob McQuilkin

Come let us kiss. This cannot last—
Too late is on its way too soon
And we are going nowhere fast.

from "Variations on an Old
Standard" by A.E. Stallings

1

He sat at one corner of the bar, in the pale pink glow of a neon light in the window advertising beer. Not much of an angle to view the television, just the long narrow room before him, just the stretch of the bar, a skyline of backlit bottles, glowing amber or emerald, all of them waiting and beautiful. He was nervous. As nervous as he could recall feeling in years, maybe decades. He'd have to reach back into his memory, all the way to middle school or high school, to some time in his life when he still cared, really cared, what people thought of him. When he still cared about grades and teachers, about his parents' approval. He landed on it now and knew that he hadn't felt this nervous since he was a boy, or maybe just a bit later, as a teenager, when he started to notice girls. When he started to care if a girl found him attractive or witty enough to talk to. Funny, though. Now it wasn't a girl, but a woman. A sixty-four-year-old woman. God, he was nervous.

He wanted to light a cigarette, but that would mean leaving his place at the bar, and it was cold outside. Cold and drizzling.

The neon smudged across the slick of the sidewalk, raindrops dripping down the window, down the windows of nearby cars. The smoke of recently discarded cigarettes curled out of the tall plastic outdoor ashtray and lent the scene a kind of dreaminess.

He hadn't imagined returning to this town, this little town, but here he was. Sitting at the rail of the Tomahawk Room on Bridge Street in Chippewa Falls, Wisconsin. It was only the first day of October, but it felt like winter wanted to arrive early. Like winter was standing on the porch, uninvited, banging loudly on the screen door with one fist, a bottle of whisky all wrapped in a brown paper bag clenched in the other hand. He didn't like that persistent oncoming cold—he didn't care for winter as much these days. It seemed to sink through his clothes, past his skin, and settle right into his bones. But this was Wisconsin. He'd have to toughen up. Buy some warmer clothes. He remembered growing up here, all those early-autumn softball games he'd played without so much as shirtsleeves. All those football games he'd played in winter without even a jacket, his hands pink and raw with the sting of snow and wind. And how as a kid, on a dare, he'd peel off his clothes, right down to his socks and underwear, then fall into the soft new snow to make the shape of a fallen angel. He couldn't do that anymore, he thought; it would kill him. Would seize his heart right up. That kind of cold.

Anyway, he was an hour early. It was silly, he knew, foolish. What if she were to pass by on the street and see him here? It didn't seem likely though. Besides, would she even recognize him now? They'd been married for four years, but that was some forty years ago. Married in '80; divorced in '84. So long ago it felt like a separate life. He tried to imagine where she was right now, in her bathroom, perhaps. Taking a shower or doing her hair. Staring at her own face in the mirror to apply makeup or lipstick. She never needed any of that stuff, he thought, but she wore such things on dates. At least, back then she did.

Three years ago, he became haunted by her. Haunt is a strong word, but that was the only word for it. Haunt. His memories of her. His regrets. Of course, she'd never left his mind, not completely. You can't love someone the way they had loved each other and then just forget, forget everything. But over time, he'd come to think of her less and less until, instead of thinking about her every day or every week, she flitted through his mind maybe once a month, once a year. Then, after decades of not visiting her in his imagination, she was back at the forefront of everything. Like an ache.

After their divorce there were times of anger, and bitterness. Unstable years when he chased other women, even marrying two more of them, both mistakes. Not the women; it wasn't their fault. The mistakes were his, he knew now, with chagrin. He shouldn't have married them. Shouldn't have married anyone. He should have spent time working on himself, going to therapy or something. Living in a monastery, even. But he didn't. Always he'd been lonely, and women seemed to fill that essential loneliness, that quiet loneliness that shadowed his days. God, he loved women. But now he understood that, really, he had only ever truly loved this one woman.

He was nervous. So nervous, he suspected, he was keeping other patrons from filling the stools closest to him as he fidgeted and readjusted, then glanced out the windows and then towards the back door. Like he was looking to score or something. Maybe that was okay, though; okay he was so twitchy. That way there would be a stool for her when she finally walked through that doorway. And they'd have some measure of privacy. This was a small town, after all, and even if he was something of a ghost, unknown to the bartender and patrons, she most likely was not. Maybe she had friends or relatives who stopped off at this bar after work, for happy hour, and they'd recognize her and come over, wondering who he was, this man, looking goofy as a teenager, pie-eyed for her. Lovestruck for Vivian, for Viv.

He'd overdressed, that much was for sure. The weekend before, he'd traveled to Minneapolis and bought new shoes, designer jeans, a black cashmere sweater, and a black blazer. No one in this bar was wearing a blazer. So, he shucked it off. Spread it on the stool beneath him and troubled the salt-and-pepper whiskers of his face, these days mostly salt, and then peered down at the black sweater and gave the cashmere a swipe. Now he moved the blazer to the stool beside him, where he imagined she might sit. Saving her a seat. There. Good. He found himself sighing. Sighing with impatience, with excitement.

He wondered what she looked like. Oh, sure, he'd found her on Facebook. Signed up for an account just because of her, because he wanted to find her. So, he'd seen her pictures, and to him, she looked beautiful. Still looked beautiful. Just the way she always had. Didn't look like she'd aged a day. Maybe that wasn't quite true, no, he admitted. Forty years had gone under the bridge, no two ways about it, and it was true, he supposed, that she had wrinkles around her eyes and the skin of her throat was not so tight anymore, but then, he had his own share of wrinkles, didn't he, and sagging skin? And scars. Her hair was still red, probably dyed, he figured, but he liked that. She was still trying. Still taking pride in herself. In some of her pictures, she wore chunky red glasses that he thought were cute. He imagined them adorning her bedside table. Readers, probably.

All these things he could see and imagine, but she wasn't there beside him. He couldn't see, for example, what might have been airbrushed for social media. If the pictures were old or even truly hers. He didn't trust anything on the internet. The account he'd found of hers was actually a business. A little business it seemed she owned—Violet Vintage it was called—and he'd searched for the actual brick-and-mortar but…no dice. Anyway, that was how he reached out: a Facebook message of all things. He remembered the minutes and minutes he had strained and stressed over each word in that message before hitting send, and then holding his breath. Days he held his breath. Waiting. Like a pearl diver. And then she replied. He could hardly believe it. Back and forth they messaged, right up until this evening. A few phone calls mixed in for good measure. Even now, he felt like he couldn't quite exhale. Like only she could give him permission to resume breathing.

He realized his fingers were tapping at the bar as if a row of piano keys. His right knee seemed unhinged, too, bouncing like an old spring. He finished the beer he had been ignoring, and the bartender was there in a nonce, asking, Want another?

No, he said quickly. Then, wait. Yeah, sure.

Same thing? the bartender asked. Leinie's?

Yeah, he said.

The bartender set the beer in front of him and turned to the register, added the drink to his tab. He drank the beer quickly and cautioned himself, Don't get drunk now, you fool. Don't overdo it.

It was what broke them up, drinking; led to their divorce. Or one of the things anyway. One of the things that led her to ask for a divorce. God, I was stupid, he thought. Then, don't do it again. Drink this one down but then take a break for Christ's sake. Do not blow this now.

He took another long, delicious drink. The beer was perfectly cold, and he felt the bubbles explode across his tongue, like magic, warming his throat, warming his stomach. It was chilly there at the corner of the bar, near the window. When the door opened, the cold jetted right towards him. And there was a draft from the windows. But it was quiet here. He knew that if he drank too much, he often grew loud. Too boisterous, too excited. No, he'd drink this beer down and then take a glass of water, or even a root beer. There was no shame in ordering a root beer. He finished the beer easily, and said to the bartender, I'm going outside for a smoke, can you watch these two stools?

Those two? the bartender asked.

Yeah, he said, I've got a friend coming soon.

You got it, boss, the bartender said, with a casualness that might have called that friend's arrival into question. Fine—he let it go. Beer sometimes did that to him, he knew. Caused that irritation he had with other men, especially. That itch, that temptation to throw down, to pick a fight. Silly, he knew, immature. This, too, had undone them. He had a temper back then, a bad one, though he hoped all that was behind him now. He was old now, too old to fight. And old enough to know better. Calm down, he said to himself and quietly, Take a deep breath. That was something his mother always said to him as a child, Charlie, take a deep breath. Good. Now another. And another.

No one smoked anymore, or almost no one smoked anymore, so he stood outside alone on the sidewalk, cupped his hands around a Camel, and drew the hot smoke into his lungs. Toasty. He always liked that word. Especially with cigarettes. Toasty meant comfortable, meant waking up in the morning and dropping two pieces of sourdough bread in the toaster and waiting, and then, spreading butter to melt on that bread, and spreading marmalade over the melted bread and then leaning against a counter, munching, and munching, a hot cup of coffee beside your knuckles... Or the woodstove at deer camp. Waking in the middle of the night, out in the deep, deep woods of northern Wisconsin, and knowing that the fire had gone out in the woodstove, and now, in the complete darkness of that shack, the wind rattling the roof and the windowpanes and the stovepipe, now you'd need to kindle a new fire. Kindle a new fire, and then, as the flames caught and took, you'd stand there and keep feeding; keep feeding until the heat spread across your knees and thighs and the old floor, and you'd crawl back into your down sleeping bag, and then you'd surely know and understand that word—toasty.

He was toasty as could be there, even in the determined drizzle. The neon light was pink and inviting, and traffic went by on Bridge Street in a pleasant blur of rubber tires over rainy asphalt. It was quiet. Ninety percent of the businesses were closed, lights off, doors locked. Even the restaurants in this small town closed early, maintaining strange hours—eleven to three, eleven to two, three to six. That was why they were meeting here, at the bar. The bar stayed open. You could count on it. People here took their drinking seriously; the whole state did. Drink Wisconsibly, they bragged.

He stubbed the cigarette out into a plastic container full of sand and then returned to his stool. No one had moved in. If anything, the bar seemed to be dying down a bit, happy hour droning to a halfway happy close. He held a finger in the air, and the bartender returned.

Can I get a root beer? he asked.

Sure thing, boss, the bartender said.

He looked at his watch and felt his stomach seize and roll. Ten to six. She could be here now, he thought. Or any minute. His bladder twitched, and before the bartender could set a glass in front of him, he all but jogged to the bathroom.

It was quiet in the bathroom. Clean. He tried to pee, but it came haltingly. Frustratingly. He rose up and down on his toes, trying to get something to happen down there, finagle a few drops, but nothing came, which made him all the more anxious. What if she came now? What if, even now, she was standing there in the little entrance, and he wasn't there? Would she even wait? Or was this all she had ever needed? This excuse. That he wasn't there, or that he was late. And here she'd gotten all done up, all dressed up; she'd risked this, chanced this, and now—sure enough. What a deadbeat. Worse yet, he was there and had been for over an hour, but now here he was in the men's room, all but hopping up and down trying to convince his sixty-four-year-old bladder to unclench itself. All the Facebook messages, all the emails, all the texts, and lately, all the telephone calls—all of that maybe for nothing. Because he was waylaid in the bathroom, like an understudy too nervous to take to the stage.

He flushed some water, and even that didn't help, so he just zipped up and washed his hands in the sink and stared at himself in the little mirror. I don't look too bad. That was his first thought. He was whiter now, no denying it. His goatee was white, or mostly white, a few stray black whiskers still hanging on, and the yellow around his lips from a lifetime of cigarettes. But his teeth were good somehow; he'd always had nice straight, long white teeth, nicotine notwithstanding. And his skin was burnished ruddy from all the years on the railroad, all the hours outside. Also, truth be told, a few beers put some color into his cheeks to suggest a certain confidence, a certain happy roguishness. He still had his hair, or most of it, though that was trending white, too. He wasn't fat either, he thought, as he cinched his belt up, and that was something. He dried off his hands with a piece of paper towel. There was a bowl of red-and-white mints, and he took one, unwrapped it, and immediately crushed it between his teeth. Starlights, that was the name of the mint, a nice name, a nice image. Starlight. He liked this bar. Too bad his best drinking days were in the rearview.

He returned to his stool. The root beer was there, a nice sweat on the glass, but it only made him want to pee again, so he didn't drink more than a sip. It was six o clock now, and she hadn't shown. Did that mean she wouldn't? He checked his phone. No messages. 6:01, now. He sighed deeply and closed his eyes.

2

She turned the ignition off and just sat there in the old sedan, watching the rain race down the windshield. Her heart was beating rapidly. So rapidly, she closed her eyes and unzipped her jacket to slide a hand over her chest. Concentrated on her breathing. Deep breaths. This doesn't have to mean anything, she thought. This can just be a nice reunion. A drink with a man you once knew in a different life.

You don't have to put too much into this. She had to think of it like that. Like a very small high-school reunion. Dwelling too much on their marriage—all the ways he had frustrated her and eventually broke her heart—that wouldn't do. The secret she still harbored from him, her beloved secret, through all that time...no expectations, she told herself. One drink, maybe two. That's all this is. She opened her eyes, glanced at her reflection in the rearview, and then left the car, rain already beading in her hair. Meeting him like this, she realized, was allowing him as close to the secret as he'd ever been. As close as one misstep in conversation, one detail, one pronoun, one aside that betrayed decades of omission. One drink, she said again, aloud.

Her head was down, focused on the sidewalk, or she would have seen him right there in the window. Sitting there, staring at her. She was walking towards the front door, thinking about the last time she had been to this bar—ages ago. Memories went skittering through her mind—second thoughts, regrets, doubts— all tumbling against one another in a maelstrom of confusion. She reached for the door and pulled, only to squint at all that greeted her. She saw someone waving in her direction, though it was difficult to focus through the darkness and the rain and the gauze of cigarette smoke drifting towards her from that outdoor ashtray. And then, just as she was about to pass the threshold, a man seemed to be trying to leave the bar. He was blocking her way now, like a lummox, and without looking at him, she tried to move around his strong, wide body, but he was standing still, like a statue, in front of her, and she said, Excuse me. And then she looked at him.

He was just standing there, like a boy. Like a boy grinning on his birthday, or Christmas morning. And now she focused on the images of only a few moments ago. The man waving. She realized that it must have been him. She must have seen him, waving, and then standing up from his stool and then sitting back down. Then awkwardly rushing to the door. And now here they were. Standing within inches of one another. As close as they had been in forty years. All of this she processed very quickly, and yet, she still could not believe it. That it was happening.

That he was here, standing in front of her, smiling expectantly. He looked extremely happy to see her, his cheeks red with what looked like joy.

He was handsome, she thought, but then, he always had been handsome. Still, she was pleased to see he had not let himself go. Of course, they had exchanged photos through Facebook, but she knew that didn't guarantee anything. Yet, here he stood, dressed very smartly in expensive-looking clothing. Even his haircut looked fresh. And they were standing so close that even in the dim light, she could see that he trimmed his nose and ear hairs. That was something she hated with older men. Older women, for that matter.

Oh wow, she said, it's you. She was laughing. I didn't expect you to be, you know, right there like that.

I'm sorry, he said, I was, just trying to, uh—he gestured behind her—you know, get the door.

Yes, well, she chuckled, you definitely got it.

Well, anyway, I was sitting over there, he said, indicating the mug of what looked like Coca-Cola or root beer at the corner of the bar. I saved you a seat, he said, gesturing with his arms as if he were a maître d' at some fancy restaurant. But of course, what did she know about fancy restaurants? She couldn't remember the last time she had eaten out at so much as a Red Lobster or Applebee's.

She walked towards the bar, and just before sitting down, he was beside her. Can I give you a hug? he asked gently. Would that be okay?

13

She sighed and smiled, Yes, I'd like that.

And then his arms were gently around her, squeezing her lightly, and her arms were around him, too. She was aware then of the smell of his cigarette; it didn't smell bad. And of his soap and his cologne, spicy, woodsy, clean. His chest had broadened since he was such a much younger man. He was like hugging someone else entirely now. A bear, she thought. Or a tree. Like wrapping her arms around a tree. She closed her eyes again and imagined that: hugging a very specific willow tree on a bright early summer afternoon when the sun had warmed the deep, gnarly bark. It felt good, she admitted. He was strong and smelled good, and he was excited to see her, though she suspected he had already been drinking. Well, she thought, we'll see how this goes. It had been a while since anyone seemed so excited just to see her.

She gently pulled away from his embrace, and he sat down, a bit dolefully, it seemed; he did not know what to do with his eyes, where to put them. Or his hands. He was a sixty-four-year-old man now, but he was frightened of her; she could see it, plain as day. No, he was nervous, she thought. Very nervous. Like he did not want to break her, though, of course, he already had, so many years ago.

Thank you for seeing me, he said, finally meeting her eyes. I didn't know if you would come.

She didn't know what to say. You're welcome? No. She didn't want to give him too much, too soon. Didn't want to raise his hopes too high, though she could see a kind of optimism had risen in him, right past his heart, perhaps to his shoulders. His posture was of a man with considerable promise. Like a man interviewing for a job he very much wanted.

It's nice to see you, she said truthfully enough.

You look beautiful, he began suddenly. I'm sorry, no, I mean, I'm not sorry. It's just—there you are, and…you're beautiful. So. Thanks for seeing me. For coming out. He gestured towards the rain and the darkness. God, it's awful out there.

The bartender came just then, which did something to break up the awkwardness. She glanced down the rail at all the liquor bottles, but the truth was she didn't drink very much. She spotted a box of red wine in the corner, like an afterthought, and ordered a glass. The bartender slid a paper napkin onto the bar and set the high-necked glass of Malbec on the napkin and said, Six dollars, and then, looking at Charlie, at her ex-husband, asked, On your tab? and then turned away from them and made a note on a paper pad near the cash register.

Cheers, he suggested, holding his glass up.

Cheers, she said, touching his glass with her own.

They both took sips and then set their glasses down. Both cleared their throats at about the same time and then looked up into each other's eyes to stifle uneasy laughs.

So, you're back in town, she tried again.

Yeah, he said. Well, you know some of the story. I was living in Albuquerque. Working for the railroad, and I, uh, I don't know. I guess I wanted to move back. I wanted to… He paused. Well, I suppose that I wanted to, or that I hoped to, reconnect with you, for one thing. So—here I am.

Wait a minute. You moved back here just for me? she asked, leaning away from him ever so slightly.

Well, he stumbled, yes and no. I mean, my uncle passed away and left me his farm. Outside Spooner. So…I'm fixing that place up. Spooner's a good town. Great little bookstore there. And across the street there's a wonderful brewpub. We should go sometime. Out to dinner, I mean. Up there.

She could see that his hands were trembling, that he was biting his lip. She felt compassion for him, and curiosity.

I don't mean to—I don't want to scare you off, he said. But I guess it's true. Mostly I came back to see…well, to see if there might still be something between us.

Now he was glancing down at the bar, and she wondered how this evening would go. He was moving fast, it seemed, already thinking about another meeting, another date. Was this a date? She supposed it was. And was this new Charlie a conversationalist? Was he interesting? If he was interesting, would he be interested in her? And what would she even say? She tried to think back, to remember who he was exactly, all those years ago?

If she was being honest with herself, it wasn't that they'd married because they shared so much in common, or because they had dated for months and months, talking and talking before finally their relationship evolved into something more. No. They were kids driven by attraction. They were in love. In lust, more to the point. Oh dear. The thought of it made her blush. She could feel the warmth, the blood in her body rush to her chest, to her neck, to her face and ears. She imagined someone shaking a champagne bottle just before the cork exploded.

You live in town? he asked.

She nodded, relieved by his question, though not quite sure what to share. That she lived with her daughter? Her poor daughter, raising two young kids with no help from either of the fathers, and no savings or worldly possessions. Just an old minivan, all rusted out above the wheel wells with a muffler that dragged below, scraping sparks along the road. An old minivan full of stale Cheerios and half-empty juice boxes. What else? That they rented a tiny little house? That she herself didn't have much to call her own. A 401k with about thirty grand. A Saturn Ion with over two hundred thousand miles and four bald tires. About two thousand in the bank, and another two in cash, which she kept hidden and just for herself, stowed in the ceiling above her closet. A business that never quite got off the ground. A life that wouldn't fit the contours of anyone's typical family photo above the mantle. She thought now of the many photos she just didn't have. She turned away from Charlie, and collected herself, steadied herself. How she dispersed information tonight mattered. Not just what she told him, but how much, and when. She didn't have to lie, exactly, but did have to withhold, and protect. She sighed and began.

I've been living with my daughter, Melissa, she said at last. She's got two young ones, so I do a lot of cooking and babysitting. This younger generation, she said, trailing off...

You're a grandmother, he exclaimed, like she'd won the

lottery. That's wonderful. Amazing. Then, more calmly, I bet you're a wonderful grandma.

He was sipping from a glass that definitely looked full of root beer. She eased up a bit. Felt the gravity of her stool. Allowed herself to relax. She hadn't been out in many months. Maybe years. Certainly not on a date, not with a man, not like this.

Was this a date? She found herself returning to this question. It mattered to her, defining this moment, and perhaps his expectations. Did the hug suggest that is what it was? That they were on a date? Maybe this was all commonplace for him, maybe he was still going on dates with other women—how could she know? And did it matter? Could she ask? Suddenly, she found herself wondering if everything went well—if this new Charlie could somehow sweep her off her feet—where exactly would they go? Not to her house—or rather, her room in her daughter's house. There were kid toys strewn everywhere, and she hadn't tidied up—no, no, no. That wasn't what she wanted. Not yet. Way too soon. And there were details in that house she wasn't ready for him to see, particulars of her life. He didn't need to see them now, anyway. This was just their first meeting. And she couldn't quite imagine where he lived, this man, or how he lived. Only those quick, sudden memories of their marriage, and how much beer he drank, how many cigarettes he smoked, how he liked to cook bacon in their kitchen, splattering grease everywhere, not just on the stove, of course, but also the walls and the counters and the floor. Grease everywhere, and he never, not once, cleaned it up. In the end, on the day when she walked out, that was the tipping point: an empty scroll of white butcher's paper with the word bacon scrawled on the paper and a kitchen stinking of smoke, grease, and cigarettes. She couldn't take it anymore.

But it was curiosity that had brought her here tonight. Curiosity and, truth be told, boredom. Charlie reaching out through the ether of time had disturbed the humdrum of her days with an unpredicted excitement. When they messaged at night, she felt an old electricity, a connection. There was nothing forbidden in what they were doing—as far as she knew—but there was something unexpected. Something sweet about his messages and phone calls. When she thought about it, the messaging had been like dates, had been like flirting. Which made this evening feel all the more woozy, all the more surreal.

No, no, no. It wouldn't come to that. This evening would end nicely. It would end like—a polite date. No hanky-panky. There was no need for that. Not even, she thought, any real desire. No, we'll just move slow. If we move at all. Slow and steady.

I keep busy fixing up the farm. It probably doesn't make much sense, a guy my age taking over a farm. But I don't think I'm built to move into a condo or town house and wave the white flag like I can't chew the fat anymore. Anyway, it wasn't even in such bad shape. Mostly it just needed someone to throw out the old, you know? Fresh paint. New windows. The old furnace gave up the ghost, so I'm replacing that. New air conditioner. You should come out sometime. Maybe I could, um, make you dinner.

She laughed. Covered her mouth. Laughed again.

19

What? he laughed.

You, she said, cooking. You never cooked a thing. The whole time we were married. She remembered the bacon. No, that's not true, she admitted. You could cook bacon. You just couldn't clean up after yourself. Oof, what were those sandwiches you used to make? Bacon and pickles and mayonnaise on white bread?

Well, he said, that was true then. Now I can cook a little bit. Clean up, too. I'm actually tidy. I guess that happens when you live by yourself for long enough. A place for everything and everything in its place.

Like what? she asked, distracted by the thought that she'd never once lived alone, now that she thought about it. She'd never known the peacefulness of an immaculate kitchen, or the silent austerity of a home without children.

What do you mean?

You said you could cook a little bit. Like what, exactly?

Oh, plenty of things, he said, pinched into a corner. Now he smiled, or maybe winced. Glanced at her like a student who does not have ready the proper answer to his teacher's question.

Okay, she said, I'll make it easier for you. Name three. Three meals you can cook.

Spaghetti, he said.

She shook her head. That doesn't count. Boil noodles. Heat sauce. Anyone can cook spaghetti.

Okay, he said. I like to grill. Steaks. Chicken. Fish, sometimes.

Any idiot can grill, she said, instantly sorry for saying so.

Maybe, he admitted, smiling.

I'm sorry, she said. You can grill. That's good.

Fine, I like making fajitas, he said proudly. I have this old cast-iron pan that I like to sauté onions and peppers in. I warm my tortillas up in a colander, between two layers of kitchen towels over boiling water. Sometimes—all right, I know it's not cooking—but I'll open a can of beans or rice, too. Right? And I'll grate a nice sharp cheddar cheese. Cold lettuce. Avocado. Thick sour cream. I got spoiled down in New Mexico. All the good restaurants. Still trying to shed all the weight I gained down there. What else? Oh—I'm making my own hot sauce, too. I could bring you a bottle sometime.

That sounds good, she admitted. She liked hot sauce on her eggs in the morning.

Oh, well, he said, holding that glass of root beer. I guess I'm not much in the kitchen. Truth is, I've been on my own for a long time. Cooking seems like a waste when most recipes are for a family. If I make a proper meal, I'm eating it for a week at a time. Until I get sick of whatever it was that I was so excited about cooking in the first place.

Sometimes, she said, it feels like all I do is cook. Or assemble snacks. Prepare meals and wash dishes. Do you have any idea how many dirty dishes two little children can create? It's like they think they're at a hotel, you know? Just put it in the sink, and then—she waved her hands like a magician—presto. The dishes clean themselves. Same with the laundry. Oh, mostly I don't mind. But sometimes I feel like... I guess I don't mind. She laughed, took a sip of her wine. Did not wince.

That's all another world to me, he said, somewhat sadly, she thought. Never did have any children.

She felt pity for him then, because she knew something tragic, something beautiful, something secret that he did not, something she had never shared with him. Something she thought of every single day and wore like an elegant necklace of lead. A decision she'd made without him, so many years ago. All the decisions she had made to create her life, when she might have made other decisions that opened doors she could not imagine, to places and opportunities she could not fathom.

It was probably for the best, he said. Took a long time for the wild to leave me. I wouldn't have been much of a father, I guess, much of a dad.

She nodded her head, in perfect understanding.

Now he turned to her, their knees practically touching, a faint electricity there, or magnetism, between them, and he said, Vivian, listen to me—I'm sorry if I wasted those years of your life. I've been thinking a lot about who I was back then and the mistakes I made. But I loved you very much, and I'm sorry that I was a bad husband.

She stared at him, at this new Charlie, her mouth slightly open, but hidden behind her hand. She had no idea what to say. But he wasn't done.

I hear a lot of people these days say they have no regrets, but I've never understood that. They've never made a terrible mistake? I don't understand. Of course they have. I mean, I know I made bad mistakes. A lot of them. But the biggest mistake was losing you.

She could not seem to find her voice. It had been a very long time since anyone had apologized to her. And this was not because her life had been easy, or because everyone she'd encountered had been wonderful to her, because she'd never been wronged. No, quite the opposite. She swallowed and swallowed again. Wanted to suddenly tell him everything about her life, all of the disappointments and hardships. That he wasn't alone in his mistakes and sadness. But instead, she took a deep breath and then a small sip of her wine.

You don't have to apologize, she said at last. That was a long time ago.

They were quiet just then, very quiet, as the last of the happy hour crowd drifted out of the bar in a slow skein of jackets, hats, and gloves. Over-the-shoulder good nights and keys jinglejangling. The bar was quieter now. The bartender washing glasses. A man at the billiards table, rubbing blue chalk on the tip of his cue. Someone talking about the weather. About the weather making his joints feel sore.

I don't know how to say this, Charlie began, but I never ever stopped thinking about you. And lately—you're all I can think about. I want to spend time with you, Vivian. I want you back in my life. I want to learn all about you. What I missed. And I'm willing to just be your friend if that's what you want. I'll be the best friend you ever had. I'm retired now, so I have time. I can help you with your grandbabies, or your house—

Whoa, she laughed, slow down. Slow, slow, slow down. Easy, tiger.

She took a drink of her wine, pushed some hair behind her ear, and tried to collect herself, her thoughts. Tried to understand her own expectations for this meeting, this reunion, this man. The night was moving in a way she had not anticipated, and yet, she couldn't help feeling delighted by the developments. Everything was coming as a surprise, shining like a tremulous rainbow. A lost coin on the sidewalk.

Do you still love horses? he asked.

Always, she smiled. I've always loved horses. I should've married a rich man who could have bought me a dozen horses and a nice dry red barn. Funny to think about, you know? But maybe that's all I've ever wanted. She burst out laughing. Is that too much? Am I asking for too much? Some horses?

No, he said, shaking his head. Only he was serious. I don't think so at all.

Come to think of it, I don't need the rich man, she said, keeping it light. Just the horses. Horses never disappoint you. She closed her eyes and felt her forehead resting on the muzzle of a horse, her fingers scratching its thick, coarse hair.

I sure wish I owned some horses, he said. I guess we could go buy a horse right now. Does it have to be a specific horse? Or will any old nag do?

She ignored him. Sometimes I'll buy a lottery ticket, she went on. I like to dream about what I'd do with the money. I'd buy my daughter a house and a new car. Set aside some money for the girls' college, she said thoughtfully. Then I think I'd buy a nice piece of land with an old barn. And then I'd buy a few horses from folks who can't afford them. Can't take care of them. It happens all the time. People's hearts are bigger than their checkbooks, and those horses get left out in the lurch. I'd rescue old horses. That would make me very happy.

That doesn't sound like asking for too much at all.

Yeah? she said. What would you do? If you won the lottery?

He looked down at the bar, at his hands, and struggled to tamp down a smile. After tonight, I mean…what more could I ask for?

Oh, come on. Don't be silly.

No, I'm serious. You live long enough, you understand the value of a second chance. A new beginning. If you'd told me two, three years ago I could sit down at a bar and talk to you, be this close to you…how much money would I have paid for that chance, that time? I would have paid anything.

Really? she asked.

He nodded his head.

You're serious? she said.

Yeah, he said, easily, I am.

She watched his face. While he spoke, his eyes seemed fixed on just about anything but hers, nervous. She had never thought of him as an emotive man, not at all. Of course, they had been so young when they were married, so immature, both of them. But she could sense a kind of desperation in Charlie. All his cards were laid out before him. It was as if he felt there would never be another night like this one, another chance to somehow impress her, or at least make her curious. She felt nervous for him. Almost to the point of nausea.

Excuse me, he said suddenly, and made for the bathroom. And she was left there alone, sitting at the rail of a mostly empty bar, her glass mostly empty as well.

3

ehind the door marked Men, he stood at the urinal again, and this time, his water came freely. He closed his eyes. He could still smell her perfume on his garments, even in his own whiskers. Was it flowers? Maybe she smelled of flowers, wet tropical flowers like those he'd seen in Florida, just after one of those big storms swept in off the gulf. Flowers and salt water, the ocean. Maybe lemons or grapefruit. Or maybe a big city somewhere, some elegant metropolitan museum. He saw her face, lit by that pink neon light, and just outside, all of the colors of the night merged in the puddled rainfall. His heart was pounding very fast now, totally unreasonably. Please, he said to himself, don't screw this up. Please, he said to his heart, don't fail me now.

Of course, it was true—yes, he was back in town, or the area anyway. But why? Well, that much he knew. Knew that he moved here, straight from Albuquerque, because of her. But admitting as much, as he just had, saying it aloud, was it crazy? Was he crazy? Because it felt wrong to admit that all his kin were basically gone from the area, maybe a few cousins here and there that he never spoke to, but otherwise—no; no, he didn't have a damn person here to talk to, to attend to. That the farm he'd inherited was in rough shape, though he'd already made some major improvements. But that wasn't the draw, that old money pit, handsome as it was, not in the least. It was just her—Vivian, Viv—that he had pinned all his ridiculous love-crazy hopes on. And he'd admitted as much to her, only moments earlier. God, he thought, you're going to scare her away. She's probably already gone. Running towards her car, keys in her hand.

He wanted so much to kiss her ears, to bury his head behind her ear, in her hair, beside her neck. For some reason, he thought of the two horses that lived in a pasture not far from his new-old house. They belonged to a neighbor girl who had just learned to drive, a neighbor girl who he saw every day, driving the country roads, in an old pickup truck, one of her parents sitting beside her on that wide, truck bench, looking nervous as hell. Waving, quickly, like they were afraid to wrench either hand away from the door handle, the dashboard, or the seat—where it was soldered on for safety. He thought of that young woman's horses, how they stood beside one another, necks touching, silken bodies sharing heat. All that space and those two horses stood so close to one another there was hardly room for so much as a blade of grass between their two bodies.

At the sink, he was aware that his hands were trembling. No, shaking. He splashed water on his face and then wiped it away with a paper towel. He looked at his face in the mirror. Don't you dare botch this, he said quietly. Be cool. But not too cool. You don't have to say everything tonight, but you shouldn't hold back either. This is your chance. Your foot in the door. Then he looked at himself in the mirror again and nodded. If not confidently then a close enough approximation of it.

He returned to the bar where she seemed to have ordered another glass of wine. This pleased him. I'll have a pint of beer, he said to the bartender.

The same? the bartender said. Or root beer?

What I started with, he clarified, his face flushing briefly.

4

So, she thought, he hasn't stopped drinking. He was just putting on a show. He must be nervous. She took him in now, more thoroughly. The strong hands he held in his lap, like he was harboring a rabbit that might try to escape. The thick thighs. The mostly flat stomach. He accepted the glass of beer and seemed to focus on bringing it to his lips. He took a long, slow swallow, and then set the beer back down on the bar. He seemed to be collecting himself, focusing on his breathing. She just watched him. Felt nervous for him.

Charlie turned to her now, and his eyes were a soft medley of love and defeat. She could see it, as plainly as if he held a placard announcing his intentions. He was a different man from the one she had known. Instantly she felt sorrow for him, because she knew the same love and defeat. Knew all the accumulated years and decades, all the disappointments, dead ends, and wrong turns. She felt her throat constrict with sympathy and something more than sympathy. Some emotion she hadn't predicted, and it was like love.

I still dream about you, he said.

She felt her breath stolen away. She had not anticipated this from him. This unexpected poetry. This sweet candor.

I dream about the mornings when we were lying in bed. All those mornings. I can still see the curtains in our bedroom, the white lace, moving with the wind. I can hear the radio playing classical music. I looked it up, and the song I always think of is Clair de Lune. I've been dreaming about you for years, Viv. And sometimes they aren't even dreams exactly. They're—you're just—you're the last thing I think about before I fall asleep. When I'm lying in bed and I close my eyes. I think about you. I think about those mornings. I dream about kissing you. Can I? Can I kiss you?

She said not a thing, frozen in her delight, her surprise, and he moved ever so gently towards her, with the looming grace of a cloud approaching a coastline. Then he kissed her, as gently as she could ever remember being kissed. And she kissed him back, exhaling slightly through her nostrils.

This was not the kiss of a twenty-year-old man, or a thirty-year-old man. This was the kiss of a teenage boy. A teenage boy wary of girls, all but afraid of girls. This was the kiss of a man unsure if he might ever kiss again. His lips were wet with the sparkle of the beer, and the taste of mint, and when he pressed his lips against hers with slightly more pressure, she inhaled him, and pressed her own lips tight against his, and felt her tongue searching for his. They kissed like this for what felt like minutes, and she did not care one iota whether anyone was watching them.

Her heart was beating so forcefully she felt a little lightheaded. Like she was a lemon-yellow balloon on a string that had, only moments ago, been clutched in a child's hand but was suddenly released and now sent giddily soaring towards the afternoon sun. She felt extravagant. She felt desired. His right hand was resting on her left thigh, and she wanted much more of that, but also wanted them to move slowly. So much time had passed. Was there a hurry? Or were there years ahead for them to explore? Was this really happening? The rain was still falling outside, still streaking the glass.

Oh, he sighed. I missed that. I missed kissing you. You remember how much fun we used to have together? How in love we were?

She looked at his hand on her thigh, so delighted she could not say a thing. So surprised by this evening that she felt it was surreal. Her body was thrumming like a guitar string strummed hard.

I do, he continued. I remember all the little trips we took. To La Crosse. Eagle River. We used to just drive to the Mississippi without any plan. Do you remember that? Just drive north or south. Find a little motel. Or that camper we had.

God, I love you, he said. I'm sorry if it's too soon to say that, but I feel it and, well, there it is. I don't want to hide anything. I want you to know how I feel in case, I don't know, there isn't a tomorrow.

You used to always have chocolate for me, she said, laughing softly, remembering those times, how young they were. How free they were. She realized with a start that she hadn't felt truly free in decades; always there were some kind of responsibilities that kept her in place, that held her, like gravity. Suddenly, she longed for those days of chocolate and back roads.

I did, he said, clearly surprised that she remembered, then, it seemed, downcast, almost despairing that he had no hidden Toblerone in his pocket.

You would forget our anniversary. But you would remember chocolate. How much I loved chocolate.

His eyes were aimed at her thighs, where both his hands now rested. Thank you, again, for meeting me tonight. I didn't know if I would ever see you again.

She sipped her wine, aware that her hands were also trembling. Just a little. She was drinking faster than he was now. But she could not seem to help herself. She was so happy.

I'm going to a wedding this weekend, he said.

Oh.

Yeah, he continued. I got some new shoes in Minneapolis. A pair of navy-blue trousers. A nice checkered shirt. Pink. I like wearing pink. It throws people off. You should come with me. We could stay in a fancy hotel. Not like the places we used to stay at. Something much nicer. Hey, he said, touching her shoulder gently, a place with chocolates on the pillowcases. Would you like that? Would you like to come with me?

She smiled and trusted he could see on her face both the weariness and the hope, a hope she had meant to tamp down, the hope that he would not break her heart again. A hope that meant maybe she would give him a chance to prove who he was now. And maybe he'd see something else too. That she was poor. Actually poor. That she had never in her entire life stayed at such a hotel. That in her entire life, no one had ever pampered her, or made her life easier.

And she felt a sadness then, knowing he had contributed to her difficulty, that their marriage had not been an easy one, especially for her. She was embarrassed to admit to herself that perhaps she had always wanted someone to pamper her. Not every moment, mind you, or every hour, or even every day. But occasionally. Someone to lift the weight off her shoulders. Or share the weight. Or to absolve the weight altogether and to say it was okay for her to close her eyes and take a nap. That dinner was taken care of. That she didn't have to worry about every single dollar, every single dime.

Can I kiss you again?

She returned to the moment, to their seats there at the bar. To the sound of rain lashing parked cars.

Yes, she said softly.

Yes, what? Yes, to the hotel? Yes, to the kiss?

The kiss.

And so they kissed again, and this time his hand pressed patiently, warmly past her ear, to the back of her head, beneath her red hair, where he held her and pressed their lips together. Her life had been so ho-hum, for so many years, so vacant of surprise, this kiss felt like waking up in a rose garden just after a rain. It felt like a dream, like another woman's life. Maybe she wasn't quite trapped after all, no longer destined for the life she had been living. Maybe there was another path, lined with hotels and travel and dinners, a life with this man who made her skin feel splashed with benevolent fire.

When he pulled away from her, she was aware that her tongue felt ticklish, that her whole body was vibrating with desire. She wanted to kiss him again, and so she did—leaned right towards him and took his face in both of her hands. She felt the grit of his whiskers and the soft furring on the lobes of his ears; he had always had nicely shaped ears, like two beautifully soft old snails. She felt the hard hidden dunes of his cheekbones and the sudden give of his considerable nose. The bar was tilting and whirling very pleasantly, and outside a police car raced by, its blue and red lights suddenly breaking her reverie. It seemed that the rain had slowed.

God, I missed kissing you, he said.

Come on, she said, taking her purse and jacket. Let's go.

But, he said, I don't want to go anywhere. I want to stay here, with you. He sounded afraid.

Please, she said, reaching for his hand. I need a breath of fresh air.

Let's at least finish our drinks, he said. Look—it's still raining out there.

So, they sat quietly. The bar was empty now. Just them and the bartender, watching a baseball game on the television. He took a chance and reached out for her hand, squeezed it. He turned towards the window and the rain had abated, mostly.

Come on, she said. It'll be good. To stretch our legs a little bit.

5

They zippered their jackets and walked out into the night. It was cold, but not too cold, and the wet evening air felt good in their lungs. He reached again for her fingers, and she reached for his. They squeezed hands and held on, and if that was all the night was, he might have been thrilled. It had already been so much more than he could have ever expected, ever dreamed. If this was his last night on earth, it had been a miracle, and he could lie down in his bed and close his eyes and know a final complete happiness, a warmth and solace that could carry and guide him anywhere. She had already done that for him. But now here they were, out on a walk, strolling along Bridge Street down a slight incline towards the Chippewa River. He did not feel like a man over sixty years old. He did not feel any age. All he felt was love. Promise. He tried to tamp down his emotions, but it was almost impossible.

They passed over West River Street to a new park built right along the river. This part of the city had changed so much from his memories of it that there was a real moment of confusion, of cognitive dissonance. There was the river and the dam, and the dam was all lit up. Strobing lights of red and yellow and the electric company's logo above it all—NSP—also in yellow. These lights were doubled on the water where they blurred and rippled nicely. There were fishermen at the foot of the dam, talking, and smoking marijuana, but he could not quite hear what they were saying.

I'm sorry, she said, but I should probably head home soon. Melissa will wonder.

Melissa's your daughter? he asked. There was so much to learn about her, her path had branched off, again and again, leading to other generations, whereas he realized sadly, he had created nothing. No one would mourn him when he was gone. He felt some nervousness just then, about meeting Melissa and her children. He worried that even if he'd comported himself well tonight, there were still opportunities ahead to ruin everything, to ruin the perfection of this evening.

Yes. She's a good kid. Just a little lost maybe.

Well, we've all been there. Like I said, I never had any kids myself, but that's the advice I used to give the younger guys on the railroad. Be patient. Success looks different for different people. Folks find themselves at different times. It's not always so easy to know your purpose. To know what'll make you happy. Even if it's right in front of you.

That's true, she said quietly. Should we maybe turn back?

No, he said. Let's walk a little more. Just downriver a little more. A block or two.

Okay, she sighed. A little longer then.

They didn't say a word, but their shoulders were so close they were like two trees growing together. He didn't dare utter a thing, so afraid was he of ruining all this.

Finally, they stood in front of an old bar, the Sheeley House Saloon. There were three men inside, drinking, staring up into the blue of a television mounted above them.

Want to go in? he asked. We could have one more. For old times' sake. A nightcap?

This place is supposed to be haunted, she said, turning to smile at him. Do you believe in ghosts?

I don't know, he said. Then he said, Yes, I guess I do.

Really, she said. Why?

He looked up at the night sky. There were a few handfuls of stars, the brightest ones anyway, burning against the lights of the sleepy town. But he couldn't find the moon.

I guess, he said unsteadily, that I want to believe in spirits, in souls. I wouldn't have said something like that back when I was younger. When we were married, I suppose. But...you start to get—

Older? she put in.

Yeah, he said. You start to lose people. First your grandparents. And then your parents. Then it's your favorite musicians and actors. Athletes and writers. Then it's your friends. And you want to see those people again. At least I do. I miss those people. I hope heaven is a long party where I never get drunk. Someone just keeps passing me flutes of cold champagne, and I go from one room to the next seeing old friends, old relatives. But no one ever has to stop to clean the dishes. They just—disappear. A waiter brings you a new fresh cool glass. It would be like a reunion. One of those evening parties where time doesn't matter. Where it's dark as you walk into the party and dark when you walk out. I think that must be the trick of heaven.

When he was finished talking, he immediately worried that he'd gone on too long, said too much. He'd shared with her that his image of heaven was endless drinking, and now, he wanted those words back, even if it was his truth. He glanced at her face, but if she was bothered by what he had said, she betrayed nothing. Only the discomfort of the cold and drizzle.

The trick? she asked.

Yeah, the trick. There must be no time in heaven. No sense of time. Everything would have to feel like one scene. One beautiful scene. Otherwise, wouldn't it get old? Wouldn't you start to, I don't know, almost want something bad to happen? Something disappointing. Wouldn't you crave the mundane? Sleep? A rainy day?

Maybe there isn't any alcohol in heaven, she said, smiling mischievously. No coffee, no fattening foods, no cheese, no bread and butter. No fried chicken. No steak. No french fries.

Maybe, he allowed. Maybe.

This is heaven, he thought. Right here. The cold of the night made her hand feel warmer, encouraged him to squeeze tighter. He wasn't drunk, not even close, but the alcohol did take any edge away. The drizzle that fell to his face cooled his skin. Yes, this was heaven. There was rain in his eyelids. Rain tracing a path down his jawline. Rain dripping off the tip of his nose.

She smiled, squeezed his hand.

They began slowly making their way back in the direction of the bar. It wasn't dew, of course, but there were tiny droplets, tiny diamond-beads of rain in her red hair, and her cheeks were flushed red with wine and the cold.

When they reached the Tomahawk Room, right where they started, he asked, Where are you parked?

They stood there in the wash of pink neon light, faint music issuing out. Crimson and Clover. He could hear it, the reverb of the guitar, the plaintiveness of the vocals. It wasn't the song he would have selected if he could have soundtracked this moment, but there was something about the sound, the blurriness of the guitar, that fit like a missing puzzle piece, and he just wrapped her in his arms and breathed in her hair. He wanted so very badly to invite her back to his house, but knew that all of this should take longer, that he wanted both not to waste a second and to extend each possible moment as long as humanly possible.

He kissed her again and she kissed him back.

Can I call you? he asked.

You better call me, she said, smiling. Get a girl's hopes up…

He felt like his heart was a dam about to be detonated with happiness and promise, about to burst. He hadn't messed up, had in no way done anything to diminish the evening. He had said the things he felt. He had not drunk too much. He had been brave. He had been his best self, his best person. The man he should have been always. He wanted to be that way, for her, for the remainder of his days.

Good night, she said at last. She even blew him a little kiss.

He watched her open the driver's side door of an old baby-blue Saturn pocked with rust. One headlight was out, and he hoped she wouldn't be pulled over. He would replace that headlight the next time he saw her. In fact, he'd buy the light bulb tomorrow morning, before he could forget. The engine started and she checked her rearview mirror before giving him a wave and departing.

The instant she was gone, he wanted her back. He hadn't felt so alive in years. Knew that he would not be able to fall asleep that night.

He drove home slowly. Very, very slowly. About seventy miles separated Chippewa Falls and Spooner, but the driving was easy and there was something calming, something therapeutic about taking the highway with no rush, headlights swimming past him. Passing signs. The steady, soft hum of the engine. The warm air issuing from the vents.

He was reliving the night. Like rewatching a favorite movie or dropping the needle again and again and again at the start of a sacred song. Now the lightest of snows was falling. Falling through the throw of the headlights, and he felt it was a blessing, a sure sign of good things to come. The first snow of the year.

His father used to wake him up on such nights. He'd feel the old man's warm hand on his little-boy chest. The kind, easy command, Wake up, it's snowing. And he would stand on the front stoop with his little brother in their pajamas, bare little-boy feet on the cold, damp concrete stoop, their hands out like paupers, like street urchins begging alms. Their mouths open to taste the snow. First snows were a magical thing. A new season. Life on earth, resting, pulling a blanket over its shoulder before a long, dark sleep.

He turned into his driveway, parked the truck, and unlocked his back door. Blueberry, his dog, stood there, tail wagging, mouth open in welcome. He made for the living room, built a small fire in the woodstove and sat down heavily in his favorite chair, his hand resting on the gentle rise of his dog's head. He did not want to close his eyes. But he did. Minutes later his chin slowly sagged to his chest, and the dog turned a few lazy circles before slumping onto his shoes, there to fall asleep at his master's feet as the fire died down to orange-black embers, then white ashes.

6

The children, two girls—Ainsley and Addison—woke her
before dawn, as was their custom. If they knocked on her
bedroom door, it was too soft to hear. She just felt them
crawl into her bed, right beside her. Oh, she loved that feeling.
Their little bodies. The way they smelled. Their shampoo. Their
breaths. Their little hands in her hair. Nestled inside the coves
of her arms. In so many ways, Vivian's life amounted to a series
of detours. Detours through bad jobs, disappointing men, lonely
nights, anxious times when having money was like holding sand,
when everything in her life was broken or so worn down it might
just as well have been broken. But these children and these
mornings—how they loved her, and how she loved them back.

She could hear Melissa gathering her things. Her purse and
keys. Heard her faintly slip into her shoes, and then the door was
shut and locked, and Vivian closed her eyes, thought about last
night. So long since a man had kissed her. So long since she had felt
a man's hands explore her body. It was one thing for a man to touch
her, but Charlie's hands last night...they were not just touching

or feeling…but remembering. Remapping her. She blushed, just
thinking of him. Then it felt wrong to replay the evening with
her grandchildren wrapped around her, so she rose carefully and
quietly and drew a robe over her shoulders and walked into the
kitchen while the girls remained in her warm bed, asleep again.

Her daughter was thoughtful. In some ways, at least. She
always made them a pot of coffee in the morning, which was not
nothing. And the kitchen sink was always clean each morning.
There were any number of ways in which her daughter was less
considerate, but where mornings were concerned, there seemed
an understanding it was difficult enough to engage in it all
without any unwanted messes. Without any cleaning to confront
first thing in the day. She sat at the little kitchen table where
they took their meals. On her aged cell phone there was a text
from him: I had a lovely night. You looked beautiful. Dinner next
Saturday? I can pick you up.

Then her phone dinged again. Right there. In real time.
Another message: I can't stop thinking about you.

She felt like a teenager. Long before cell phones. When a
family was lucky to have more than a single landline telephone.
Back then, if she wanted to talk to a friend, or a boy, she had to
wait until after her parents were asleep before she could slink
down the stairs and sit in a chair, the cord wound around her
wrist, her finger fidgeting while she whispered into the receiver,
terrified that any second her mother would flash on a light and
ask her who she was talking to and did she know what time it was,
or how much those calls cost?

She held the phone in her hands and thought about her response for so long she almost didn't send the message: Saturday works perfectly. Six?

She wasn't sure Saturday would work perfectly. Wasn't sure what Melissa's plans might be. And, of course, every Sunday she was occupied. But Vivian had asked for so little. And now she was happy. Now this man, her ex-husband, had returned to her. A different man, it seemed. A better man. Oh, the things he said to her. The kind, kind words that came out of his mouth. No one had ever said such things to her. No one had ever told her they had dreamed of her. Not even Charlie himself, back in the day... She sat and stared out the window at the tiny backyard barely covered by the white of last night's snow. By what looked like the sheerest of old white bedsheets. Faded plastic toys nestled in the green grass and white snow. Her daughter's sad excuse for a vegetable garden, neglected tomatoes black on the vines. She watched as a tabby cat stalked a cardinal in the lilac bush, and then stood and drummed her knuckles against the window, causing the bird to alight.

Ainsley padded into the kitchen and walked right into her arms. Climbed up into her lap. She swayed the girl back and forth, back and forth. Heard herself humming. Felt her lips kissing the top of the child's head.

Can I fix you some breakfast? she asked her granddaughter.

Yes, please, the child yawned.

What would you like, my love?

Pancakes.

Pancakes, she repeated. I can do that.

One difference she found between being a grandmother and a mom was that she mostly did not mind being a short-order cook. Mostly. Easier simply to ask the girls what they wanted, than to foist and force food down upon them. No longer was she in the business of pushing vegetables or the venison her uncles gave her every autumn. She was too tired to fight. No energy for unnecessary screaming matches or battles of will. These were her grandchildren, and she'd feed them as she saw fit.

She set about mixing the batter from scratch. It was cheaper that way. And tastier. She thought about Charlie as she measured flour, sugar, baking powder, salt. As she cracked eggs and poured vanilla. As she sprinkled just a dusting of cinnamon into the works. As she zested the skin of an orange. As the pan heated and the butter began sizzling.

She was suddenly not just excited about the prospect of Saturday, not just eager, but desperate almost. She wanted to call him just then. They had only scratched the surface, she realized. She didn't really know anything about his life. She wanted to see his house outside of Spooner, and wondered what that old farm looked like. She wondered how he occupied his days. Had he ever married again? Was he now divorced? And, if so, since when? Was this, as her daughter sometimes said, a rebound? How much did he drink? He said he was retired. From the railroad, she assumed, but she wasn't sure. They had so much to work through, to talk about. That excited her. Those future conversations.

Grandma, Ainsley said, smoke.

She realized with a start that the pan was too hot. The butter was burned. She'd need to wash it and wipe off the char. Start all over.

I'm sorry, pumpkin, she said. Grandma must be a little tired.

You were talking to yourself.

Was I now?

The girl nodded and hid a smile behind her little hands. Her hair was a series of wicked tangles and knots, and they would have to spend time that morning brushing it out. Ainsley never enjoyed this, but Vivian did. It had a medicinal effect. Counting each stroke of the brush. Running her fingers through the sweet-smelling hair, as the little child, restless at first, finally started relaxing. Succumbing.

They would watch cartoons in the morning. The girls half playing with LEGOs or drawing. Half watching the television. After lunch, both girls took a nap, or at least some sort of quiet time, and most days, if she was being honest, so did Vivian. Just in the recliner. It felt so good. Because, at first anyway, she'd forgotten that exhaustion, that parenting exhaustion. How parenting seemed to suck the life right out of you. But now, she was often fatigued, more so than when Melissa was a child. She thought about that, children as vampires. No—too dark a thought for so early in the day.

She prepared almost all their suppers in a Crock-Pot that sat on the kitchen counter. Seasoned ground beef for tacos. The girls liked that meal. Or barbecue pork. Pulled chicken. She watched the sales at the grocery market, bought pounds of cheap meat. Cooked meals that provided leftovers her daughter could bring to work. Meals that created minimal cleanup, minimal waste. Lasagna was popular. Baked ziti. Homemade macaroni and cheese baked with a breadcrumb crust. Most evenings, she crawled into bed in her small bedroom and read romances. Mysteries. They lived within walking distance of the library. On Saturday mornings, when Melissa slept in almost to noon, she would gather the girls and meander over to the library and let them loose to roam the aisles. To read and explore. It was a safe place, and free.

Only now there was this man. This unfamiliar familiar man. She wondered what space he might occupy in her future.

She finished cleaning the skillet and replaced it on the stove. Melted butter. Poured the batter into pale disks and watched as they slowly bubbled. Dropped a small handful of blueberries into the batter before flipping the pancake. One batch of batter made about twelve or fifteen pancakes. Enough to feed her and the girls all through the morning until the grilled cheese sandwiches they would have for lunch.

The girls slept in Melissa's room, where two narrow mattresses paralleled the larger bed on the floor, jammed in alongside it. Though most nights, Vivian suspected, they slept with Melissa. Or on her bed anyway. Vivian kept the thermostat as low as she could. She knew that Melissa would sometimes sleep in the living room, on their secondhand couch, after a late night working at the bar, for instance. Or on a twin mattress in the basement, which sounded worse than it was. The basement was dry and quiet. The girls' toys were all down there, but they liked to be upstairs, so the women had created a little space for themselves. That mattress, a soft chair, a lamp, a shelf of paperback books bought at the library's annual fundraiser. It was the unspoken policy: if either Vivian or Melissa felt overwhelmed or tired or simply needed a break, they could go to the basement—no judgment.

The basement was also where Vivian stored all the clothing she had bought over the years for the business she had once imagined, Violet Vintage. Racks and racks of clothing, already cleaned and priced. Dreaming of the day she might open her own storefront, she'd even started by opening a Facebook page, which was, of course, how Charlie had found her. So perhaps, in some strange way, the business had succeeded. It had connected them.

She wanted to text him again, already. She was lonely for another adult to talk to. But she wasn't sure how things even worked these days. Were they dating? Was that what they were doing? And whether they were or not, would texting him again make her seem too eager, too desperate? She didn't care. Maybe she was desperate. For some change. Some companionship. She sent: Hey, I know it's a drive, but maybe you'd like to join us for lunch?

Almost immediately, he replied: Yes!

She smiled. Smelled smoke. Realized she had burned the pancakes again. Quickly lifted them up and out of the pan and presented a plate of three pancakes to her granddaughter, unburned side facing up.

Butter? she asked. Syrup?

The girl nodded her head.

Her phone dinged again and she all but rushed to it. Another message: Or I could take you all out to lunch.

Well. That sounded nice to her. But the car seats were in the minivan, with Melissa. She typed: We'd have to walk.

The phone dinged: See you at noon.

She smiled. Realized that, even as she was doing so, she hadn't smiled this much in many years. She felt tears forming and brushed them away. Don't be silly, she thought. Get it together. She was the type of person who cried when she was happy, which drove her daughter bonkers. But it was what it was. How she was hardwired. New tears formed again, and she felt a thrill of happiness coursing through her, of excitement. She hadn't been out to lunch in a long time. She would need to get ready.

Now Addison was awake too, chewing her pancakes. Grandma's going to take a quick shower, she said to the girls, and then later, we're going out to lunch. With a friend of mine. You'll like him. Her phone dinged: What's your address?

What's his name? one of the girls asked.

She typed the address.

Grandma?

Oh, Charlie. His name's Charlie.

Charlie? they giggled. They said his name, goofily, like a joke, Char-lie. Char-lee. Giggled some more.

Yes, Charlie. She found herself laughing lightly too. Why? What's so funny?

The girls must have sensed something. Something about the way she was acting. The phone dinging again and again with text messages. The burned pancakes. The smile she couldn't quite hide. Didn't want to hide it.

Is he your—boyfriend? Ainsley asked, giggling harder, laughter that rollicked her from her little belly up. She pronounced the word, boyfriend, in two long, long syllables. Boooyyy... fffrrriiieeennnddd.

Can I tell you a secret? she said, leaning down to talk to the girls.

They didn't say anything, went utterly silent. Only leaned towards her, their mouths full of pancakes and butter and syrup.

Once upon a time, she said conspiratorially, he wasn't just my boyfriend; he was my husband. We were married.

How can your husband also be your boyfriend? the girls said, doubled over in laughter.

Oh, how that tickled them. Sent them into unrestrained giggles. Addison dropped her plate onto the kitchen floor. Vivian didn't care. It could be cleaned up. They were all laughing now. Even the voices droning out of the TV suddenly sounded cheerful, less phony or canned. A dog barking a few houses over sounded playful, rather than annoying. What a day, she thought, taking in the sunlight just now shining on the bright new coating of snow on the ground. Icicles clinging to the gutters like blown glass. They were all going out to lunch.

She took a shower and dried her hair, then put on a little makeup and was just about to borrow a spritz of Melissa's perfume, before wondering if that was strange. If he was attracted to that smell, did it mean he would also be attracted to her daughter? She washed it off quickly. Fine. No perfume then. Just soap and shampoo. Her body lotion. Maybe after Christmas, she thought, I'll buy a new bottle of perfume.

She glanced out the window at eleven forty-five to find a big navy-blue truck idling beside the curb. It was snowing again, though lightly. Was that Charlie's truck? At eleven fifty, she looked out again, and could clearly make him out in the cab. It looked like he was talking to himself. She smiled behind her hand, wondered briefly if she should have her teeth whitened.

Just before noon, he rang their doorbell and the girls rushed to the entryway. Before she could say anything, they had allowed him inside. She didn't like that, didn't want that. It made her nervous. There were things she hadn't told him yet, and perhaps this house might yield those secrets. He was kneeling between them, a dozen roses beneath one of his arms. She drew closer and could see that he held a plastic bag filled with water and two goldfish. The girls poked at the bag. One of them had a small hand on Charlie's shoulder. All of this did not seem possible even a week ago. Twenty-four hours ago. And now, here he was. Here was Charlie, back in her life.

Hi, he said, smiling up at her. You look beautiful.

———

The girls were too smitten with their new goldfish to giggle, to notice. But oh, the things he said to her. The things he said to her that she didn't remember him ever saying when they were married. The things he said to her now, that she couldn't recall any man saying to her, unless they were drunk, unless they wanted something from her. Sex. Or money. Or to be taken care of. Coddled. But he didn't seem to want any of those things. Or maybe he did. Maybe he did but simply hadn't been entirely forthright with her... But she didn't think so. On the contrary, he seemed vulnerable, even to a fault. Still, the reality of him standing here, inside her house, before she had had the opportunity to clean...it filled her with anxiety. But hope and happiness seemed to trump her trepidation, at least for the moment.

She hoped that he was honest, but it seemed wise to tamp down her dreams. Not to get too excited. Though it was difficult. Difficult when he stood up to kiss her on the cheek, handing her the red roses. It had been decades since someone had given her flowers, and she didn't even know if she owned a vase. So, she just held the bouquet, felt the stems through the thin clear cellophane in her hands, and raised the blooms up to her nose to smell them.

I bought a light bulb for your car, he said.

What?

Your headlight. On that old Saturn of yours. It was out. So I, uh, bought a new bulb for you. I could replace it for you now if you'd like.

She allowed herself to laugh. She couldn't help it and held one hand over her chest. Not quite her heart. But the way people did in commercials for Publisher's Clearing House when they won a jackpot. One of those oversized checks. Gestures like this did not happen to her. What did happen to her was that she was always too distracted, too tired, too broke, too busy, and the headlight, if she knew it was out, would stay out, all the way until a cop pulled her over and gave her a ticket. A twenty-dollar headlight became a fifty-dollar fine. That was her life, the life she recognized. She did not know what to say.

He smiled. I'll just go ahead then, and replace the bulb, he said, producing it from his jacket pocket and holding it up like a good new idea—eureka. Unless you'd like to give me a tour of the place?

Uh, no. Not yet, she said, making her body wide to hide whatever lay behind her.

Girls, do we just let people into our house? she scolded, suddenly aware of how the house might betray her, what secrets hung off the wall in her bedroom or on the door of the refrigerator in the form of photographs, what letters and forms might be sitting on the counter, there for him to see.

But you said he was your husband, Ainsley said.

Ex-husband, she said quickly. Then, speaking to Charlie, Thank you for the flowers.

Of course, he said, peering around the cramped space. Would you be more comfortable if I waited outside? I didn't mean to intrude.

If you don't mind, she said. It's just—I haven't had a chance to tidy up.

No problem, he said, inching back outdoors, and closing the door.

She sighed with relief. Next time, she would take greater care. Allowing him into this house was as good as allowing him all the way into her life, and she wasn't quite sure she was ready for that, even if she was the one to invite him over. She just wasn't ready to reveal herself to him completely, not yet. She glanced at herself in the mirror that hung just inside the door.

Okay? she said. I'll just, uh. I need to find a vase or something for these.

———

They held hands and walked behind the girls. For the first time in days, the sun shone brightly, with water dripping off roofs and into the gutters. Old men were out with shovels, clearing the sidewalks and shaking salt onto the thawing ice. Downtown was busy and they ended up at a delicatessen—Lucy's. She tried to think if the girls had ever been out to lunch. They kept turning to her and asking if they could order this or that, and he kept saying, Order whatever you'd like. Orange soda? they asked. Sure. Grilled cheese? Sure. A chocolate chip cookie? Of course, whatever you'd like. Soup? Absolutely. The bill came to something like sixty dollars, and she reached into her purse, but he was ready with his credit card and paid for everything.

You didn't have to do that.

I wanted to.

Well.

This is fun for me. I don't—

What?

I don't think I've ever had an occasion to be with kids before.

Never? she asked, as she felt a sad pang in her heart.

He shook his head. No, never.

Come on, I think the girls have found a table.

They ate contentedly and in near silence save for the sound of the girls' legs beneath the table, swinging in errant circles and nudging the table, which she recognized as a telltale sign of their happiness.

After they walked home, he turned to her. Is there anything I can help you with? he asked. Or your daughter? Anything around the house? I'm retired now and truth be told, I think I need projects. Something to keep me busy.

Am I one of your projects?

His face grew suddenly red, and his shoulders slumped. No, no, no. Then, very seriously, as if there had been some crucial misunderstanding, Not at all.

Her arms were folded across her chest against the cold, but she walked towards him and kissed him on the lips, and then, walked backwards to the front door. Goodbye.

Will I see you again?

You'll see me next Saturday, won't you?

But before then?

Boy, she said, sucking in her breath and pretending as if his question really merited her thought. I don't know. We'll have to see.

Seeing his face momentarily slide into some confusion verging on despair, she unfolded her arms, walked towards him, and reached up, taking his face in her cold hands, and kissed him deeply. She was interrupted only by the banging of small fists on the glass of the front door where her two granddaughters were singsonging, Boooyyy-fffrrriiieeennnddd, boooyyy-fffrrriiieeennnddd, boooyyy-fffrrriiieeennnddd.

I have to go.

Okay.

Thanks for fixing the car.

It was nothing.

I'll call you.

He just stood there, waving his hand gently, watching her go.

She turned and said, Shoo, then.

7

He found it difficult to admit, but it was true: he was both alone and lonely. Two similar sounding words, though their definitions were unique and separate. A person could be alone, but not lonely. Or lonely, but not alone. He was both. And worst of all was the truth that he was not comfortable in his loneliness.

Charlie had friends who were natural-born loners, friends who were married but perhaps shouldn't be, and friends who were so quiet and gentle that even if they were married or involved, they may as well be alone, because they spoke very little, demanded less, and had no opinions.

But now that he had no work and no coworkers, his life felt like an isolation chamber, and he didn't like it. There was almost no one to confide in, to talk to, to break the monotony. He couldn't ask any more of Vivian than he had already; he knew he was pushing the boundaries of appearing needy, even desperate. He was afraid to admit it, but he probably *was d*esperate. So he texted the one person who always gave it to him straight. His second ex-wife, Mona, who, perhaps paradoxically, had over time become one of his best friends.

Now a good time for a talk? he typed, before setting the phone down on the kitchen counter and exhaling.

Within ten minutes she called him; they both preferred talking to texting.

You did what? she exclaimed, after he brought her up to speed.

I told you, I asked her out on a date, and it was fabulous. We kissed. I told her I'd moved back here to see if we could start over again. And I think it's going well.

Oh, Charlie, she said, her voice falling with equal degrees knowing and disappointment. Why didn't you call me before you went and did all that?

Why? So that you would have told me I was crazy? I was moving too fast? Well, I guess I don't care that I'm moving too fast. I want to move too fast.

Yes, Mona said firmly. Yes, yes, yes, yes, yes. You are crazy. You are moving too fast. Way too fast.

Okay, tell me why moving fast is so wrong. Tell me why I made a mistake.

Charlie, Mona said, taking a deep breath, I'll make it simple for you. You're a baseball guy, right?

Yeah.

If you were a pitcher, you'd be oh-and-three. Zero wins against three losses. You're just not a good husband. I'm not saying you're a bad man. But I am saying what you already know, deep down.

You're selfish. You're a good husband in those moments when it suits you. When it's convenient. When you're lonely and you need someone. Then, you're incredibly giving, and considerate, and romantic. But, Charlie?

I'm still here, he said, a bit crestfallen that Mona was not immediately enthusiastic about the new developments in his life.

Marriage really isn't about romance. Especially at our age. Marriage is about the day-to-day. Marriage is about steadiness. Marriage is a partnership. Marriage is hundreds, thousands of days without passion. Just groceries and bills and sickness and heartache and oil changes and snow that needs to be shoveled and bunions and missing reading glasses and appointments with the cardiologist, or maybe the endocrinologist, or the podiatrist. Am I getting through to you?

He and Mona had been married for less than half a year. A decision that happened with the finality and planning of a tornado. They both knew they'd made a mistake the morning after. There was no acrimony, only the bittersweet realization that their lives were incongruent, and that was okay. The whole thing would have been humorous if marriage wasn't an institution taken seriously by the family, friends, and work acquaintances who traveled to Puerto Rico for their ceremony only to learn five months later that the whole production was a fiasco.

And many people had seen it coming, in the way a person glancing down from the twentieth story of a skyscraper might anticipate a car crash happening. Both of their grim-faced parents knew and had vocalized as much. In fact, both mothers were crying during the vows. Most of their siblings were drunk for the ceremony. As were the bride and groom and their witnesses for that matter. Piña coladas.

Mona was twelve years older than Charlie, and they had met when he briefly decided to head back to school, to college, an experiment that lasted only a few months longer than their marriage. She was his literature professor, and what they'd had, while they had it, was intense. But unsustainable. He was the student in her class who was years older than his classmates, his hands thick and rough with blue-collar labor. He made intense eye contact with her during class, so intense that he didn't seem to care about the twenty-odd other students seated around him. And he made a point of not breaking eye contact.

She knew the moment he stepped into her classroom in broken-down blue jeans, work boots, and a short-sleeved collared shirt that exposed his suntanned arms and chest that she should have asked him to find another class, another professor, another campus. He was a man amongst boys, and completely unlike any of her colleagues in the English department. His literary tastes seemed curated by the shelves of a Boy Scout summer camp, or perhaps an uncle's hunting shack—Jack London, Robert Service, Louis L'Amour. But at least he read. Or had read. And there were times he surprised her, by reciting a few lines of Robert Frost, or even Anne Sexton and Elizabeth Bishop; the latter two, he would later admit, was an assignment he gave himself, a way of impressing her.

But it didn't take long for Mona to tire of his drinking and his general immaturity. She wanted to publish papers, teach, and maybe move on to a more prestigious university, which she later did, retiring as the department chair at Luther College, in Decorah, Iowa, where she and her husband, a physics professor, Nathaniel, lived in a grand old Victorian, so full of books that they had had to install steel beams beneath the sagging first floor to keep the whole house from collapsing under the weight of so many novels, poems, and criticism.

I've changed, he said, feeling a boyishness in his voice he was somewhat embarrassed by, especially since he knew she would immediately detect it. I know I've changed. I can do better. I want to do better.

I'll be honest with you, Charlie, Mona sighed. I don't think what you're doing is fair to her. From what you've told me, this poor woman has endured a great deal of disappointment, and much of it stems from you. To leap back into her life in this way, with this kind of passion... Her voice trailed off. I hope you know what you're doing.

I just feel like... I don't have that much time left, Mona, he said, immediately wanting those words back, aware of course that she was twelve years his senior, and that the love of her life, Nathaniel, had been diagnosed with prostate cancer only nine months before. I want to make the most of what I have left.

Charlie, she said, it's always been about you. What about this poor woman? What about her feelings? What about her life? What about the time she has left? Do you think it's fair to saunter into someone's life promising them the moon? How does she recover from that heartbreak, Charlie, if you don't? If you don't hand her the moon?

He cleared his throat, the import of Mona's wisdom striking him like a stone to the forehead. He struggled for something to say. And how is Nathaniel? he asked.

Oh, he's fine. I can see him now, old fool. He's out collecting acorns from the neighbor's yard. Thinks he's going to mill them up and make flour, I guess. I can't keep up with all his harebrained projects.

And his health? Sounds like he's doing okay?

No, Charlie, he has cancer. He's not exactly okay. But he's living. He's positive. He stays busy. He walks four miles every day, no matter the weather.

Huh, Charlie said, good for him.

Have you thought about that, Charlie? What are you doing with yourself these days? Since you retired? Do you have a hobby?

Oh, Mona, you know what my hobby has always been, he sighed, glancing at the empty bottle of Ridge Estate cabernet sauvignon that he had finished last night. He stood and dropped the bottle into the recycling bin and out of sight.

Charlie, she said, her voice now even and cool, like a beautiful prismatic icicle, dripping words that he waited to count, waited to catch in the palm of his hand. Charlie, she said again, I believe in you. You are, at your core, a wonderful man full of passion and verve. Sometimes—her voice trailed off, and he could hear her, adjusting the phone receiver, possibly glancing out the window again at Nathaniel—I even miss that sort of passion in my life.

But, Charlie, she can't fix you. She can't make you happy. You have to make yourself happy. You have to change. And sweetie, you have to stop drinking. You can't say that you care about the time you have left and then go and squander it inside a bottle. Find help. I'll even help you if you'd like. But please, don't break this woman's heart twice. It isn't fair.

It isn't nice, he said, finishing that old Sinatra line.

Take care of yourself, Charlie.

Hey? Mona?

Yes, dear.

Thank you. Thanks for your call. I needed it.

Anytime, Charlie. Now, if you'll excuse me. I need to fetch my husband and his four grocery bags of acorns. Poor guy looks like he has dementia, not cancer. Bye, Charlie.

And then, there he sat. In the cold kitchen. Outside, more leaves were falling from the maple trees, and an evening storm front was darkening the western horizon, obscuring the last of the sunset.

8

After the girls had fallen asleep, Vivian sat at the kitchen table playing solitaire. She liked this ritual. And it wasn't the same on her phone or a computer. There was something about holding a deck in her hands, something about touching the cards, about fanning out a lone column of cards, and seeing that rhythm of black-red-black-red-black... About moving cards, stacking cards, counting cards. She liked this little table. A cup of tea with honey and a slice of lemon nearby. How quiet this ritual was. Some nights she only played for twenty minutes. Other nights, it might be hours.

Melissa emerged from the bathroom in a thick, soft robe, a towel wound around her hair, and sat down beside her mother.

Feel better? Vivian asked.

Long day, Melissa admitted.

Do you want to talk about it?

Not really, Melissa smiled bravely. Same old, same old.

Vivian wanted to say that she was sorry, but there was no

use in dwelling overly long on a bad day; rather, she decided to invent a distraction.

Why don't you try to get away one of these weekends? A girls' getaway or something? It wouldn't have to be glamorous. The Dells, maybe. There are probably plenty of fall deals at hotels down there. Or Milwaukee. Madison. I worry about you. You're always working, sweetheart.

You're too nice, Melissa said. Oh, Mom. I don't know. It just feels like…sometimes, I can't believe this is my life, you know? I don't understand what happened. Where I messed up.

Melissa. You have two beautiful daughters, who love you. And you've got me.

I know, I know. But—is it wrong that sometimes that doesn't feel like enough? Am I horrible for saying that? For thinking that?

No, Melissa. Of course not. We all feel like that, sometimes, I think. I do. I know I do.

But things are going well for you right now, aren't they? Melissa smiled as she stood up, and pulled a bottle of Baileys from the refrigerator. Poured two fingers over a glass of ice cubes and sat back down.

Yeah, things are going well, she admitted. But maybe that's just it, hon. You can't plan these things. The idea that Charlie Fallon would somehow drop back into my life, and in this way… to be honest with you, it never dawned on me.

But you must have still felt something for him, right? I mean, deep down. You must have still loved him?

Vivian sighed, surveyed the cards arrayed before her.

No, she said at last. I didn't. I think I gave up on him a long time ago. I really did. He broke my heart, and he kept breaking my heart, and I would stick around, and hope that he'd change. This is awful, and not smart, but—I think for a while I hoped we'd get pregnant, and that he'd snap out of it. Start saving money. Stop drinking. Maybe find a job in town. I used to think about that a lot. I used to think about us as young parents. As a young family. I used to dream about that. I used to lie in our bed and hold my stomach and ask god for a baby. But towards the end, I just couldn't trust him. I couldn't trust him around a little baby. I didn't know how he'd behave, night to night. I didn't know when he'd come home. It was like—how do I explain it? I realized that it was like being married to a child. There was no accountability. No stability. Everything was dictated by alcohol. I guess the good news was, it all just didn't last too long. I couldn't point to any one night, any one act; it was just a sad blur. And then he was gone. And he never, until now, made any kind of contact with me, at all. So all of this was just—a total surprise.

Melissa took a long sip of the Baileys and offered it to Vivian, who only shook her head.

So why are you giving him another chance? You don't owe it to him.

Vivian counted out three cards and glanced at the third. Counted out three more and sighed.

Well, what if I didn't?

What do you mean? Melissa asked, a trace of sad laughter in her voice.

I mean, Vivian said, what then? What if he had changed, and I didn't give him a chance? I guess I had a feeling. I don't know, Melissa. I had a feeling about him.

A feeling?

Yes, just a feeling. But I don't know, sweetheart. No one is perfect. I've made mistakes in my life. What if no one had helped me? What if they hadn't given me a second chance? What if they'd already counted me out? He doesn't have anyone. Oh, he's got a dog, I suppose. But that's not what I have. With you. With my granddaughters. With…Jessie. He's alone. Imagine how that must feel. To be all alone with your mistakes.

She counted another three cards and added a four of hearts below a five of clubs.

I'll tell you something else, Vivian said, reaching for the glass of Baileys and taking the smallest of sips. I guess I don't have that much to lose. But it's all over if I ever get the feeling that I can't trust him. And I'm not just talking about me. I'm talking about you all. If he hasn't changed, I just can't have him around. I won't.

She shrugged her shoulders.

But so far so good. Most of the time, I'm just nervous. Which is so strange, because I know this man. But maybe it's just because I'm out of practice. Anyway, I mean, I want to have fun, and I like where this is going, but the nice thing is, I'm not worried about impressing him. That's his responsibility. He's the one who has to convince, me, you know? It's nice. I feel like, when we were married, most of the time I was just a passenger, you know? Just along for the ride. But now…it feels like I'm in control.

The red two, Melissa said, pointing. You can move that up. And then that three.

Good eyes. Thank you.

Melissa finished her drink with one last swig, and then stood.

I'm going to bed.

Good night, sweetheart.

Good night, Mom.

9

He surprised himself, or his body surprised him, his heart. But maybe, for the first time with a woman, he was not focused on sex. His body had changed. Slowed. It was less reliable in ways that made the idea of sex something that filled him with as much anxiety as excitement. He worried that his body might not come through in the clutch. Might not respond. Or respond confidently. He didn't want to hurt her feelings. Didn't want his feelings hurt either.

There had been a time in his life when a woman smiling at him was enough to fire all the cylinders, to make him light-headed with desire. But things were moving so smoothly with Vivian, and he was content for now—no, delighted—just to steal kisses. Hold her hand. He hadn't seen her now for a few days, but the other night they had driven to Eau Claire to walk the city's downtown and bridges, and they'd held hands for miles. Just talking. And the feel of her bare skin, her soft palm, her fingers. It felt better than he remembered sex ever being. Steadier. When she squeezed his hand, he knew it was her. Her doing that. It was like they were communicating just through their hands; he had no memory of sex being like that. Touching her in these small ways felt like the most important thing in the world. Like they were nurturing something together.

They texted every day. First thing in the morning, he would all but rush to his phone to see if any messages awaited him. At night, they talked on the phone for hours. Like teenagers. Almost without exception, she tired first, and he could hear her breathing slow and slow, as her words came fewer and fewer, until he knew she was asleep. And that was okay. He imagined the phone on her pillow, and he saw her hair arrayed around her head, or swept behind an ear. That red hair that had always undone him. Red now with traces of white. She reminded him of Bonnie Raitt.

Darling, he would whisper.

Darling, he would say, lightly.

Darling, he would say, louder yet, a hint of laughter now.

I'm sorry, she would say suddenly. I must have fallen asleep.

Good night, he would say.

Good night, she would say.

Days drifted by, like the dry autumnal leaves on a breeze. He puttered around the house. Various projects. Tuck-pointing the old fieldstone walls of the basement before applying a white-wash. Sanding the floors. Mowing the expansive lawn one last time before winter truly set in. Chopping and stacking firewood, surely one of his favorite things. That rhythmic work culminating at day's end with a stack of wood all neatly organized and the satisfying exhaustion that settled over his body. The old barn was an endless series of repairs, but he moved slowly from one task to the next: wiring, the construction of new stalls, insulation. But in the evenings, when the work was complete, or his body exhausted by the labor, the old farmhouse, as beautiful as it was, provided little comfort. Comfort was often a bottle of wine, and a fire in the woodstove. One glass followed by another, and then another, until the bottle was empty, and he faded, unintentionally. Until he passed out in a leather chair, startling himself awake and disturbing Blueberry, who, in such moments, stood suddenly, then surveyed him, before moving into another room, abandoning him.

It was late afternoon, the magic hour, when he arrived at her house on Halloween, the fading light platinum and gold. It was the first time he had been properly invited into her home. Most of the time, she met him on the stoop or sidewalk, and he'd become curious. Somewhat suspicious even. But now he thought he understood. It maybe wasn't about him. Maybe she was embarrassed of her house. There was a smell in the air. A smell that reminded him of poverty. Fried hamburger. Old dog. Kitty litter left out in the rain. He saw no pets—except the goldfish, of course—but could smell the memories of animals that had lived in the house. Other sad smells too. Very old cigarette smoke in the stained paint; ash ground into the tragic carpeting. Mice. The little house exuded those smells.

He hadn't noticed it before, but the neighborhood was broken. On the decline. The sidewalks were wonky. The driveways splattered with oil and gasoline. The houses all seemed to sink into the earth, as if the planet were slowly swallowing them. Porches sagged. Roof shingles cupped. Saplings grew in the gutters. Cloudy windows dripped with condensation. It wasn't every house on the street, but it was most of them. The sort of neglect that begins to infect a neighborhood when there is never enough time or money.

He didn't like it. It offended him in ways he knew weren't fair. It wasn't because he hated poor people, which he didn't, of course. There had been many years of his life when he did not have two nickels to rub together. But he hated poverty. Hated the way it exhausted people and stole their light. What troubled him was he wanted more for her, for them. They deserved more, this family, and he actually had the means to help them.

Dressed as the Cowardly Lion, he stood inside the claustrophobic entry, shoes and hats and gloves cluttering the floor, jackets piled here and there. His dog, Blueberry, stood beside him wearing what looked like Dorothy's blue gingham dress. There was a flask of whisky beneath his costume and two beers in his stomach. He was warm and happy. He shouldn't have had any alcohol and he knew it. But he hadn't had a drink in days, and he wanted to be relaxed for the granddaughters, for Ainsley and Addison.

The girls came to the door. Dressed like comic book or movie characters. Thor and—

Who are you supposed to be? he asked the one dressed like a princess or a queen.

I'm a princess, she replied proudly.

Princess who? he asked.

Princess Me. Princess Addison.

He nodded appreciatively. Makes sense, he said.

Vivian came to the door now. She wore a wig, the hair jet black on one side, shockingly white on the other, an unlit cigarette dangling from her fingers at the end of a long filter. She wore a black cocktail dress and black pumps with a fake fur wrapped around her exposed shoulders. He rummaged through the foggy corners of his vocabulary and then remembered: stole. She wore a stole.

Cruella, he sighed.

Well now, what do we have here? she asked evilly.

He kissed her on the lips, aware of the metallic taste in his own mouth, the whisky, the alcohol on his breath. He had chewed a mint in the truck on the way over, and hoped it would do its work.

Well, he said, is your daughter coming too?

No. She's going to a bar tonight. I told her we'd take the girls.

In the month since they had begun seeing each other, he had never so much as seen her daughter. He was beginning to wonder if Vivian was embarrassed of him in some way. Or if Melissa already had her mind made up that he was an unredeemable loser, the man who had broken her mother's heart. What stories might Vivian have told Melissa about him?

But wasn't Melissa at least curious to meet him? He and Vivian had been married once, before her birth, sure, but they had been married. No matter how this went, he was a chapter in her life, or her mother's life anyway.

———

They walked from house to house holding hands. Cruella de Vil and the Cowardly Lion. With Dorothy trotting beside and behind. Normally, he avoided Halloween. Avoided the rookies at the bars and taverns. Avoided the roads with drunk drivers. Normally, he thought costumes childish and unbecoming of adults. But she had asked him to join them on Halloween, and he knew it would not do to be a stick-in-the-mud. Knew that it was far better to show some honest enthusiasm. Maybe the alcohol helped, he thought. So, as she was talking to a neighbor, he stole two quick sips before popping another mint.

Dusk descended and the moon was up. A big orange harvest moon. Many evenings and early mornings while he was working on the railroad, the moon had been his friend. He liked the sensation of turning his back to it to go about his work, but knowing that it was there, looming, unseen behind and above him, glowing on. Some nights, alone in his bed, unable to sleep because of the pain in his joints, he would talk to the moon, or even sing quietly, mournfully. He wondered what she would think about that, if they ever again shared a bed. Shared a moonrise. A sunrise. He wasn't sure he wanted to stop talking to the moon. It was no less odd than talking to the dog. Or talking to himself. What do you sing to the moon? You sing Hank Williams. You sing Patsy Cline. You sing the Cowboy Junkies. Maybe you sing a little Louis Armstrong, a little Billie Holiday.

The girls tired quickly, and night settled over the city, cold and sharp. The smell of bonfires in the air. Burning leaves. They returned to the house and now the smell, that smell bothered him. He couldn't let it go. Felt trapped by it. Trapped by the smells caught in the old carpeting, the yellowy walls, the flooring, the drapes, the wood of the cabinets... He could tell, he just knew, that there were mice in the house. He had lived in enough shabby apartments to know that smell. The smell of animal hair and feces. He wanted very badly to open a window, or light a candle, but that would have been rude. So he excused himself to the bathroom, and there, sitting on the toilet seat, drank the remainder of the flask. Then he washed his face off in the sink, rubbing the bar of soap close to his nose, hoping the smell would linger on his skin and whiskers. He opened the bathroom window and gulped down fresh air.

After the girls had gone to sleep, they watched a movie. When Harry Met Sally. Blueberry the dog asleep on the floor.

We've never watched this together, she said.

Meaning, they were already divorced when the film was released.

No, he admitted, but we're watching it now. The first movie we've watched in forty years. He wrapped an arm around her shoulder. The movie was just beginning. Harry and Sally were in Chicago, and they were young.

I've never been to Chicago, she admitted. Is that sad?

His first thought was, Yes, kind of. But he didn't say that. He said instead, I do love this movie.

What was the last one? she asked. The last movie we watched together?

He racked his memory but came up empty. In those days he never considered what she might have wanted to watch. It had never dawned on him. That embarrassed him now; he felt regret.

I'm sorry, he said. I wasn't a very good husband to you, Viv. I could make excuses, I guess. I was young.

You were drunk a lot of the time.

Yes, that's true. I don't drink as much as I used to.

You were drinking tonight, she pointed out. Did you think I didn't notice? That I couldn't tell?

I was drinking, he admitted. A little.

Why were you hiding it? Are you ashamed, Charlie? Do you have some kind of drinking problem?

He didn't know how to answer her question. The movie was playing. All that smart dialogue, but he wasn't even listening. Now his ears burned. Don't screw this up, he thought, don't screw this up.

But also, quietly, he thought, Why does it matter? And also, Lay off, I haven't done anything wrong. Also, darkly, You're not my wife. You couldn't tell me what to do back then, and you can't now. Because I'm not doing anything wrong. I'm not doing anything that half this city isn't doing. That your own daughter isn't doing.

He took a deep breath. He'd worked on this. On his anger. His emotions. His honesty. You couldn't do better, couldn't become a better human, if you didn't try, if you didn't admit you were fallible. That you regularly made mistakes. That you were, in fact, human.

He had worked very hard on this notion of sloughing off his old self and becoming new. The kind of human who was curious about other people. And gentle. He didn't need to be so strong, to act so strong. He could be softer, and that was okay. Strong things broke, and when they broke, they were difficult or impossible to mend. He didn't want that.

She shrugged away from his arm and stood, ran the faucet, and drank a glass of water.

Now the smell of the house assaulted him again. It was the furnace. The furnace kicking on, stirring those smells. Mice. He imagined them in the drawers, running over their mismatched cutlery. Hopping in and out of chipped porcelain coffee mugs. Cheap mugs. The sort of free mugs an insurance agent gives you. The sort of mugs that are door prizes, too ugly or plain to pay for. He imagined the mice again. Chewing at cardboard boxes and plastic bags filled with food. Marauding their bread and fruit. Little mice, everywhere. He didn't know why he was so fixated.

He closed his eyes and concentrated. He said something he did not expect to say and had never said to another soul. I think, he started, then paused. No, I know—well. I do have a drinking problem.

She turned to look at him. One of her hands on the counter, as if for balance. She was surprised, he could see.

I think I've almost always had a drinking problem. Since I was twelve or thirteen. Since the first beer I drank. You know, the first beer I ever had was with my uncle Wally. You remember him? He was wonderful. I was twelve. We were in his garage, where he drank in the summertime. It was hot and we were watching the fireflies on his lawn. And I liked being included by him. Listening to baseball on the radio with him. What can I say? I like the way it makes me feel—the alcohol. The happiness I feel. The—lightness. I like the way the world laughs, the way the world shines, the way it sings when I'm drinking. I like almost everything better when I'm drinking, and I know that's wrong. I know there's another way. But…I'm afraid to quit. I'm afraid it won't be the same.

She sat down beside him. She touched his face. The movie was still playing, and they were just about to dine at Katz's Deli, that famous scene when Sally pretends to have an orgasm. It was a terrible moment to waste in this way. He felt remorse. That he had ruined this, their first movie together in forty years. Ruined it with his drinking. With that stupid flask.

She paused the movie, but there they were, frozen on the television, Billy Crystal and beautiful Meg Ryan, sitting at a cramped table in a bustling deli. These characters had barely begun living their lives.

Then Vivian shut the television off. She stood and reached for his hand.

He knew something was going to happen. Something. Something very important. Something possibly very lovely. He stood and followed her into her little bedroom. She closed the door behind them. His heart was beating faster than it had in a long time; he could not say how long. He felt as if he were running. He could feel his pulse in his forehead, in his ears.

She turned off the light.

The room smelled different from the rest of the house somehow. He breathed her. Breathed her clothing. The lotions he had just seen on her bedside table. He breathed the scent of her bedding and knew she must wash her sheets frequently. Now she was standing very close to him. He could feel her breasts brushing against his chest through her shirt.

He took a chance and touched her, held her breasts in his hands. It was almost too much. The weight of her breasts and the size of her breasts and the feel of her breath against his neck.

They were still wearing all their clothing, and he didn't know what he wanted. Did he want to shuck off all his clothing and risk her laughing at him, at his old-man body? But wouldn't that feel exquisite? To stand there, naked and vulnerable, to feel her breasts against his chest. Her nipples against his chest, or between his fingers. His head felt light, delirious. They were kissing in the dark. Passionately. He slid his hands between the blue jeans she had changed into and her underwear. The light fabric of her underwear. He felt the soft skin of her butt. Oh my, he thought, oh my.

I want to see you, he whispered. His hands held her very lightly, just above her hips.

He felt his body responding in the way he feared it might not, and there was a moment of splendid gratitude.

No, she said, not tonight.

But the way she said it was beguiling, alluring. Not tonight sounded to him like, Soon. Maybe even, Maybe. He could hang his hat on maybe. It was something.

Not tonight? he repeated, the way he imagined he might have, back when he was a teenager.

No lights tonight, please, she said.

Should I stop? he asked, moving his fingers back and away from her skin, almost imperceptibly.

No, she said, keep going. Don't stop. I just… No lights tonight.

So, he went that way. They kissed for a long time, very slowly. And then he dropped to his knees. It was painful. His knees on the unforgiving wood floor, but he was so thankful to be alive, to be in this darkened room with this beautiful woman, that he ignored the discomfort. He unbuttoned her jeans and pressed the fabric down. Not a forbidden amount. But the amount a teenage boy might, a teenage boy exploring new boundaries. He rolled the denim down an inch. Maybe two. He kissed her hips and her belly button. He ran his hands all over her thighs and her breasts and her stomach, and he appreciated everything that was her.

Can I, may I undress you? he whispered.

Yes, you may, she replied.

He gently slid her jeans off, helping her to step out of the fabric. Then she hooked her fingers around the hem of her underwear and tugged gently down, and she stepped out of the underwear and moved to the bed, leaving him kneeling there and nearly breathless. He held her underwear in his hands and felt the soft cotton. He touched the cotton like a blind man feeling a paper map for some mysterious geography. He pressed the underwear to his face and inhaled her like a blessing, like forgiveness, like the wind that pushed a spring thunderstorm.

He undressed, clumsily. Now he too was thankful for the darkness. That she would not see how pale his skin was. Or the hair on his shoulders and back. Or the hundred moles that dotted his skin. Or the way his hair had grown white everywhere, even some of his pubic hair. No, he was thankful for the darkness, as he slid into bed on top of her, feeling her calves rest against his. Feeling his penis between her legs. Against her thigh. Kissing her again and again until their bodies were joined.

They moved very slowly. The sound of a car driving by. The dance of headlights in the curtains. He heard her breathing heavily, heard her coming, and it was the most beautiful sound he could remember. That sound of her pleasure, her infinite happiness, it might have been the most exquisite present anyone had ever given him. For many years into the future, he would return to that sound. Roll the sound around in his memory. The sexiest thing he could remember. Her voice, quiet in the darkness, quiet for fear of anyone else hearing, her voice, I'm coming, oh my god, I'm coming.

They stood in the yellow glow of the porch light, and she kissed him goodnight. When he slung into the cab of the truck and started the engine, she was still standing there, in an old robe, arms crossed over her chest, her face looking, he thought, young. Younger than she was. She looked tired at this hour, sure, but the way a person felt tired on a Sunday morning. Just waking up. Just after making love. Relaxed.

He rolled down the window and said, I love you. He had not planned that either. The words had just fallen out, like stars.

I love you too, she said. Drive home safe.

10

Her father believed in hobbies; her mother believed in a dogged work ethic chased with fiscal austerity. She had always fallen in line behind her father. His philosophy was just more fun.

As a farmer, he collected everything. Anything and everything that came to rest on their farm was a treasure. Or a potential treasure. He housed it all in various outbuildings. License plates, rusty bicycles, chainsaws, tools, gramophones, fishing equipment…

Once a month, in the morning, he would whisk her out of the house while her mother was out feeding the chickens, they'd pile into his truck as if it were a getaway car, and they'd go to some auction. Or a string of garage sales. They paraded from driveway to driveway, garage to garage, searching for deals, surprises, lost masterpieces. He'd place a quarter in the palm of her hand, where it seemed to burn with promise. She was allowed to buy whatever she liked so long as it did not exceed twenty-five cents. The quarter felt so hot in her hand, he might have held it over a candle's flame. She couldn't wait to exchange the coin for some new artifact, some new prize.

She paid the closest attention to clothing. To the sort of clothing actresses wore in the pages of the magazines she saw on her aunt's coffee table. The sort of clothing the rich women wore at church. Many days, she did not spend the quarter. Sometimes this was easy, and sometimes it was almost impossibly hard. If they were attending a farm auction, clothing was unlikely to be a featured draw. But if they were hopping from one garage sale to the next, sometimes she kept her father tapping his toe and staring at his watch while she filed through all the garments. Sometimes she worked her own brand of childhood charm; other times, she understood that she needed to haggle, play hardball. It all depended on the seller, on the circumstances. She learned to read people.

You found a good deal there, huh? her father might ask.

This skirt's got a little tear, she'd say. But I think I can mend it. Plus, I talked that lady down to a nickel.

Her father nodded approvingly.

Rummaging for clothes was a mainstay of her life. The way she clothed her family. The way she relaxed. The way she gave presents. She never thought of it as giving something cheap or used. She only bought finely crafted garments after all. Beautiful colors. And she put love into any necessary repairs, into sprucing up those castoffs. When she gave something, it was an occasion. It was also a distraction. Something to do. A way to escape their house. To travel just a little. To take a drive. An excuse to stop for an ice-cream cone. An excuse to be surprised.

If Melissa had time off on weekends, April through October, they went to rummage sales. Having her daughter and grand-daughters in tow was a benefit. They worked as a team. Even Ainsley and Addison had eyes for quality, or at least the more interesting fabrics.

So, Melissa said to her mother on one of these outings, what do you think of this guy? Is he a keeper?

Vivian moved rapidly past tables of folded clothing, prices marked on pieces of masking tape, numbers written in black Sharpie. I don't know. What's that old saying? Fool me once, shame on you. Fool me twice, shame on me.

I won't get fooled again, Melissa winked.

He's certainly trying hard, Vivian said, blushing lightly.

Yeah? You seem happy, Melissa offered.

Well, he's grown up a lot. In so many ways, he doesn't even seem like the same person.

Melissa examined a one-piece jean dress, then thought better of it. Returned it to a table covered in garments.

You should meet him, Vivian said. Don't you want to meet him?

I do, Melissa said. Absolutely. Of course, I do.

He wants to meet you. He probably thinks it's a little strange he hasn't met you yet.

Well. Great. I can't wait.

Wonderful, Vivian said. Then it's settled. He invited us over for Thanksgiving.

Mom!

What?

The other shoppers stopped to hazard glances their way. Arguments are rarely aired out in public in the Midwest, but rather bottled up and later uncorked behind closed doors, and optimally in hushed tones, even whispers, if at all. Arguments are often won by silence, or even, oddly, apparent capitulation. Vivian had seen her father win any number of arguments by simply shrugging and walking away. Not a surrender so much as a refusal to engage.

Thanksgiving is our holiday, Melissa said. My favorite holiday. I mean, really? Now I have to go to your boyfriend's house? What if I hate the guy?

You said you wanted to meet him.

Well...yeah. You were married to him once upon a time. Of course, I want to meet him. What about Jessie? We normally see her on Thanksgiving. Mom, at some point, I think you're going to have to tell her. Or tell him.

Oh, we'll still see her.

You're not really listening to me.

I'm listening. I'm just not responding how you'd like.

But she isn't invited to Thanksgiving?

I didn't say that, Vivian said forcefully. I just think we'll do separate Thanksgivings. Two Thanksgivings. Think of it that way, Melissa. We're doubling your favorite holiday.

Whatever, Melissa replied, but I'm registering my mild disapproval. For the record.

Noted, Vivian said. We'll see Jessie in the morning, okay? We can spend the whole morning with her. Is that better?

Fine.

Look, this is all moving pretty quickly, Vivian said, and I'm not sure I want to introduce her to someone who might not stick around. Anyway, that's between me and Jessie.

Grandma? Ainsley said, completely unaware of the conversation transpiring between her grandmother and mother. Is... She paused. I can't pronounce this.

Spell it, sweetie.

Y-V-E-S.

Yves Saint Laurent. Go on.

Is that a good brand?

Yes. A very good brand. What did you see?

Some sweaters.

Wonderful. Excellent find, sweetheart. Let me have a look.

Mom?

Yes, Melissa.

Can we continue this conversation? Another time?

Another time then, Vivian said, aware of this bridge they would inevitably have to cross. The secrets that would need to be unfurled.

11

It was Thanksgiving Day. A few minutes after one thirty in the afternoon. He had not slept the night before. Too much to worry about, too much to do. Cleaning, cooking, setting the table. The whole house. And it was not a small house either. He knew that. Knew that the house was too much for just him. Him and Blueberry.

Part of the reason he was so excited, so damn excited for them, was this event, the whole day: the meal, the decorations, the music, the togetherness. That was part of his lack of sleep. He was excited. He could not remember putting so much effort into anything. It was not just all the necessary steps of preparing each dish. It was the dusting and vacuuming. Cleaning each bathroom. Washing the linens for the guest rooms. Hell, the day before he had even ventured out to the margins of his land and selected a balsam fir as his Christmas tree. The walk to the tree through the knee-deep snow had been challenging enough. He even stopped twice to catch his breath. But the trek back, dragging that tree in, had exhausted him. And then all the work of getting the tree into its stand. No easy feat for a person working alone.

But now, the house was everything he wanted it to be. Candles glowed here and there, the small flames wavering with the old house's drafts. A fire popped in the woodstove; the air outside smelled of woodsmoke. A cast-iron pot on top of the woodstove boiled, and the resultant steam filled the house with the scent of cinnamon, cardamom, cloves, and orange peels. The kitchen was rich with the aroma of turkey, mashed potatoes, two varieties of casseroles, cranberry sauce, and fresh rolls. On a counter waited three varieties of pie. And a fresh green salad. Blueberry lay on the newly washed wood floors, chewing a bone. There was a natty green and gold handkerchief tied around his neck. The Packers were playing later that afternoon.

A plan was slowly forming in his mind. Ever since Halloween, he'd wanted to suggest, to ask if Vivian and Melissa and the girls would consider, just consider, moving in with him. He knew it was a dramatic suggestion. Moving to a new community forty-five minutes away. Moving in with a man who was a new and at least partly unknown commodity in their lives. It was such a dramatic suggestion it bordered on an insane idea. So he endeavored to move slowly. Very slowly.

He still hadn't met Melissa, which left him more confused than ever. But to have this meal together, to share this day, and to show them how he lived—he felt like it was a good and expansive gesture. To make them feel at home. He had gone so far as to repaint two of the guest rooms in a palette he felt might be more welcoming to her granddaughters. Variations of yellow. He wouldn't ask anything of them tonight. Maybe not for a few months yet. Better to let the idea come to them organically. That this was a possibility. A logical choice. He would invite them over again, before Christmas. That much he knew, even now.

The twelve bottles of wine he kept stowed in the kitchen along with all his bottles of whisky stored up high in the liquor cabinet, and each bottle of beer kept cold in his refrigerator, he carried it all down into the basement, to the small room he'd made his wine cellar. That way, if he felt the urge to have a drink, it wouldn't be quite so easy. He hoped the urge would not arise. He cracked a can of root beer, poured it over a glass of ice, and took a sip. There was something good about the carbonation and sweetness, but it was not the same. Did not take him to the same place. A root beer or a Coca-Cola might hit the spot, but it didn't make the world fuzz with happiness and promise.

He lowered himself into a leather chair aimed at the woodstove and gently rubbed Blueberry's head. Only he was so excited he could dance, so excited he could sing. He stood up and walked to the bank of windows facing his long driveway, the road beyond obscured by a line of cedars. And then there they were, as he saw Melissa's minivan turn and slowly make its way up the drive to his house. Now he wanted a drink. To celebrate, to relax, to slow things down. There was time, he reckoned, time for a quick belt of whisky. But she would know. She would know from his breath, from his lips, from his body language. He took another long drink of root beer, closed his eyes, and took five deep breaths. Do not mess this up, he told himself. Relax.

He greeted her at the door. Kissed her on the lips, proud he had nothing to hide, that he had controlled himself. He almost thought he could see that pride reflected at him in her eyes. She was happy, he could tell. And she smelled lovely. Oh, he thought, all the years I wasted, like a goddamn fool.

Your place, Charlie, she said with a hint of incredulity, is really, really nice.

Well, thank you, he said. I mean, I should have invited you out here sooner. Your family too. This is long overdue. Anyway, I inherited the place. So sinking money into it to fix it up wasn't so difficult. It just needed a little work, some updating. May I take your coat?

You've been holding out on me, she said, shrugging out of the cold jacket. I never realized.

He shrugged his shoulders, casually. I mean, it's not a mansion.

Charlie, she said, it's beautiful. Look at all the old woodwork. The trim and moldings. She glanced out the window. Charlie, you even have a barn.

I guess, he said. Then, with a trace of mischief in his voice, Maybe you all could spend the night here? If you'd like, that is. I have a few spare rooms. The beds are all made up. No pressure, of course. I just wondered if it would make things easier...

She rested a hand on his chest and whispered, Charlie, are you trying to get lucky? She kissed him again.

Maybe I am, he confessed.

Melissa, Ainsley, and Addison came up the walk just then, and in his nervousness, Charlie found he couldn't stop smiling; his face was so tense it ached. The girls hugged him around the waist and then poured into the house, and behind him he could hear them playing with Blueberry, who was an older dog, and only wanted his head scratched and his white belly rubbed. The girls, seeming to have intuited this, were all sprawled on a rug, saying sweet things to the dog, who now issued groans of contentment.

Hi, he said to Melissa, I'm Charlie. Charlie Fallon. Really happy to meet you. Your mother talks about you all the time.

Melissa, she said kindly enough, shaking his hand and passing him a bottle of cheap red wine. Thanks for having us over.

There wasn't much warmth there, Charlie thought. As if the young woman didn't expect this to last. As if she thought this day, these festivities, were all a bit hasty. That this was not part of some new tradition, but just an outlier. A day they would later remember only for its strangeness. That was okay, he allowed. She didn't know him. All she knew for sure was that a long time ago he had divorced her mother.

I've enjoyed getting to know your daughters, Charlie said to Melissa, but her back was turned as she hung her jacket on a hook. Then she picked up the girls' jackets, just then lying on the floor, and hung them up as well. Sweet kids, he said.

Oh, she said, sighing, yeah, they're a handful.

You must feel very fortunate to have your mom around, he said.

They were just standing there, in the entryway, having this balky conversation, skating on the surface of new ice, while below, there was so much more he wanted to say. So much more, he assumed that she might have wanted to say too. But for now, they would just skate a polite distance away from each other, moving lightly over this cool white plane, while bubbles rose from below only to stop at that thick translucent surface, unable to pop.

I think it works out for all of us, she said, crossing her arms.

Well, he said, glancing quickly at the wine's label. Can I get you something to drink?

I could use it, she said.

And so, he showed her the way to the kitchen, walking past Vivian and the girls playing with Blueberry, who seemed to be in his tired old glory. He unscrewed the cap of the bottle and reached for a wineglass, poured. Handed her the glass.

We should say a cheers, Melissa said. Then again—wait. Where's your drink?

He found the nearly empty glass of root beer and said, Cheers, to a happy Thanksgiving. I'm sincerely so happy to meet you. So happy you're here. He realized, with a start, that an aspect of adulthood, or parenthood, that he had never had to engage was this optimism he was now displaying. This impossible facade of positivity, generosity, and kindness. Melissa couldn't care less about him, he saw. But he couldn't mirror those feelings, couldn't reciprocate in kind. He needed to represent hope, radiate implacability.

They touched glasses, and she never took her eyes off him.

I thought you liked to drink, she said. I thought my mom

told me that. Yeah, that you knew your way around a bottle. Or a lot of bottles.

He nodded his head. It was the truth. I do like to drink, he admitted. Then looked at her, meaningfully. Maybe I like to drink too much.

She nodded her head and smiled at him in a not especially kind way. This would probably be way easier, she said, if we were all drinking, don't you think? She swallowed a little wine and winced. You seem like the kind of guy who might have some nice bottles kicking around.

He bit his lip and stared at the kitchen tiling. For him, Thanksgiving had always been about wine. Every bit as much as it was about food, or fellowship. He may have never had a family of his own, but through the years, he had visited his parents, his aunts and uncles, cousins, and later, friends, always bringing a case of stellar wines that he had selected over the past year. He did not claim to be an expert in many areas or even when it came to wine. But he knew more than most people. Years of living alone had provided the space and means to become as obsessive as he chose to be. And for years, there had been no one to spend his money on. So much of his income was immediately funneled into investments, or his hobby—wine.

You're really going to do this to me? he asked, glancing at her. Not angrily. Just—resignedly.

Do what? she said with a smile.

You know what, he countered, staring at the kitchen island. We're going to drink? Aren't we?

I just like to be real.

Fine, he said, let's drink. Come with me. Like you said, I might have a few nice bottles kicking around.

He led her into the basement, to the last place he knew he should be going. But all that alcohol had a gravity. A dark pull. Those bottles down there held more than wine. They held laughter and great music and more laughter still. They held love and intimacy and honesty. Raw honesty. Bravery. Courage. Poetry. They held lingering sunsets and star-pierced nights. They held raucous dining rooms in far-flung restaurants. Basement bars hidden away from the eyes of the city. They held flirtations and liaisons. He turned on the lights as they went through the perfectly organized space, aware that his basement alone was larger than the house the four of them occupied in Chippewa Falls.

He knew that to any serious wine collector, his cellar was nothing. Two or three hundred bottles at any given time. A few truly exceptional bottles in here he had squirreled away over time. From trips to California, Oregon, and Washington vineyards. From friends in the hospitality industry. But world-class wine was so much harder to come by in the Midwest. Certainly here in the middle of nowhere, in the hinterland. The cellar was just a fifteen-by-fifteen corner of this basement. But he had taken some pride in its construction. The walls were the original sandstone block, newly restored. The shelves and storage all beefy dimensional lumber from a nearby barn that had blown down. Wood well over a century old. White pine and cedar and tamarack. The ghosts of this landscape.

She ran her fingers over the bottles, touched each label like she was reading braille. She blew the dust off the dark green glass as if blowing out a tiny candle.

So, she said, you know your wines.

He shrugged and smiled. I know a little bit. I worked in California for a stretch, he explained. When I had time off, I'd go up to the wine country. Healdsburg, mostly. This was before everything took off. You could buy a case of wine for just under fifty bucks, easy. Wines that might now cost, I don't know, hundreds more. I learned a few things. Made friends with folks just starting those first great vineyards. We stay in touch. So, I get access to stuff that, uh, most people probably can't. But, he coughed, I am trying to quit, Melissa.

It's hard to be sober in Wisconsin, she said. Alcohol is like air here.

She continued looking at his collection. Occasionally picked up a bottle and spun it slowly in her hands.

I was a sales rep for a wine company for a while, she said. Over in Minneapolis. So, yeah. I made friends too. Chefs, sommeliers, vintners, restaurateurs. I probably would have moved out to California and worked out there but then, uh...

Then what? he asked.

Well, she sighed, as she tapped a fingernail on the label of a 1995 Château Mouton Rothschild and arched her eyebrows. I got pregnant with Ainsley, she said, pointing upstairs. And I knew I'd need help. It just seemed like the smartest thing to do. To come home.

He nodded.

Where do you work now?

Oh, she sighed again, I don't want to think about it right now. She emitted a sad little sound. Sorry. No. That's rude. During the day, she said with a quick, deliberate smile, I work for a company that sells natural gas. And propane. I'm an accounts manager, which means, mostly I answer phone calls and bill people. Nights, she continued, I waitress a little here and there. Or bartend. She nodded. So that's me. Super exciting. What about you?

She continued circling the room, examining bottles.

I'm retired, he said. Thirty-plus years working for Union Pacific.

Yeah, she said, smiling at him, but…that doesn't exactly explain it. All this. Right? I mean, your cellar might be worth, what, fifty thousand dollars? That's not normal. Definitely not around here. And this house? You've got a lot of money tied up here. You drive a new truck. Buy your clothes from, where, Orvis and Patagonia? So, like, there's something else… Not family money. Mom would know about that. She pressed a bottle into his chest and said, This one for sure.

A 1996 Château Margaux. Worth about $1,600. Why not? he thought. The regret of draining the bottle might be outweighed by the joyous experience of drinking it. He did not need to be lying on his deathbed thinking about the dozens and dozens of bottles of beautiful wine he never actually drank.

I, uh… Well, back in the mideighties I was working for Union Pacific. Out in California, as I said. I did track maintenance back then. And, uh, I met this kid. I mean, he wasn't really a kid. He was a college guy. Cal Poly. And he kept telling me about this company. Apple. How they made computers. I didn't know anything about computers. I just thought that was something only governments could own. Militaries. But he kept telling me that someday, off in the future, everyone, or every family at least, would own one of these things. I couldn't even spend my money back then. I was always traveling. I didn't even keep an apartment, you know? What was the point? I wasn't married. No kids. Having stuff didn't really matter. So I invested.

In Apple? she asked, smiling now in a genuine sort of way. What year?

With Apple, eighty-six, he said, allowing a small trace of a grin. Satisfaction. A good guess gone right as rain. But, I mean, later there were some other great recommendations from that kid. Like Google. Like Cisco Systems. Microsoft. Later yet, Facebook. Amazon. He owns a hedge fund now, skis in Switzerland, surfs in Tahiti. Still takes my calls too. Good kid.

What did a share cost?

About eighty cents. Give or take.

She shook her head, rolled a bottle of Lokoya Mount Veeder cabernet sauvignon around in the palm of her hand, like a bowling pin. How many shares?

Through the years, about fifty thousand shares.

She was working the math in her mind. A big number.

I got very lucky, meeting him, he said. He taught me plenty. But I manufactured some of my own luck too. There were a few other good guesses. Feelings I had. I remember liking the commercials for this drink company? Snapple comes to mind. I used to like to drink that on the railroad. Cool bottles. Bought quite a few shares of Snapple. But I mean, I've never had any kids. I've been divorced three times. Heck, I'd have a hundred thousand shares but my third wife, not your mom, took half.

He laughed.

What? she said.

Just—that was an expensive divorce.

Oh?

Yeah, that third time around lasted longer than the others. About six years. She lives in Panama now. Owns a coffee plantation. Sleeps with the president sometimes. Or his cabinet. I don't know. I used to keep track.

And here we are outside of Spooner, Wisconsin, she laughed, just living our best lives.

She tossed him a six-thousand-dollar bottle of wine like it was a baton.

Christ, he murmured, you've got expensive taste. And a good eye. This is one of my better bottles.

Well, I know you want to impress me. Come on, she said, those will need to breathe.

————

This was it. What life was. Young children, her grandchildren, in the kitchen, sniping bites of food. Soft music playing, like a warm breeze. The scent of food cooking. A warm house. A fire crackling. Outside, more snow falling slowly, as if sifted down from above. Huge flakes. The girls wanted to go outside and make a snowman. There was still time before the meal, so Melissa offered to take them. Three bottles of wine sat waiting on the granite kitchen island.

We're drinking, I guess, Vivian said.

I guess so too, he said, sidling close to her. There was patient rhythm in his mind, now, like that Willie Nelson song, Christmas Blues, that just made him want to bob his head real gently and sway his hips. In such a fashion that he might not be dancing. But he might be. He kissed her and then slowly wrapped his arms around her waist, resting his hands in the small of her back. She was dancing now too. The same secret rhythm. She rested her head on his chest and exhaled.

I want to take care of you, he said.

Hmmm, she purred. That sounds nice.

What do you want? he asked.

More times like this, she said.

I can't believe it, he said, my luck. That this is happening. Does it feel right to you?

It does, she said quietly. It almost scares me.

Scares me too, he admitted. I don't want to screw anything up.

But we're not the same people, she said. Not the same people that we were. So young.

Yeah, he said, who wants to be young?

He worried though, that in the most important ways, he

was. The same person. He could almost feel the bottles of wine breathing behind him. Like fat men at a table, breathless for a rich meal.

He'd uncorked the bottles effortlessly, surely, if with reverent ceremony. Melissa sat on a stool, extending a hand to sniff the cork, raising her eyebrows with appreciation, nodding her head in approval. They were both that sort of monster. And the wine was a monster too. Ready to slink into their bodies like a shape-shifter and make of the night what it wanted. Magic or tragic. It was always impossible to know until he'd gone a sip too far. A thimble too much.

He moved away from her. We should eat, he said.

I'll gather everyone up, she said, moving towards her coat and snow boots.

When he was sure she was outside, he poured himself the tiniest sip and closed his eyes, hoping the night would only be magic.

It was.

Everything slowed and blurred in a gentle glow. There was the quality of sitting on a carousel, watching the faces of people you love slide past. Warm light. Rich food. The fresh forest smell of the newly cut pine tree. And with the wine, his body felt as if it were floating, as if he were weightless. In some other man's dream. Melissa kept refilling his glass, and her own, and occasionally Vivian's, and time did not exist. Or if it did, then to no great effect. There was nowhere to go and nothing to do.

After the meal, Melissa and Vivian insisted on cleaning up, and he sat back in his leather chair and closed his eyes. But the girls wanted to watch something on TV, so he tried to show them how his fancy remote worked, which they found hilarious, before they settled on How the Grinch Stole Christmas. Somehow, they had never seen the classic cartoon before and sat rapt on the thick rug, with Blueberry there beside them. His great muzzle in Addison's little lap. How perfect was Boris Karloff's voice. He closed his eyes. So warm. Safe. Full.

When he woke up, he was afraid he had slept the night away. He stood unsteadily. The fire had died down. It was very dark outside now, the snow falling more heavily. It dissolved slowly against the windows.

Hello? he called.

Blueberry trotted towards him, then yawned. Stretched before collapsing back onto the floor.

Hello?

The dining room was clean. As it was before. No trace of the holiday. No trace of his guests. The kitchen, too, was immaculate. He opened the refrigerator, where all the leftovers had been packed neatly into Tupperware containers and marked with tape: stuffing, turkey, cranberries... He closed the refrigerator door. Leaned his head against the refrigerator. He had gotten good and drunk and passed out. Passed out, like a lush. A stupid lush.

Stupid, stupid, stupid, he said, banging his head not softly on the refrigerator door. Stupid, stupid, stupid.

Hey. It was Vivian. Standing there in the doorway. Her socks were off, toenails painted red. She scratched her calf with one foot. She looked tired. Concerned. What are you doing?

You're still here?

Melissa took the girls home. She has the day off tomorrow.

She was okay? To drive?

Yeah. We sat for a long time, drinking coffee. Eating pie. Trust me, she was fine. She is fine.

I'm sorry, he said. I didn't sleep last night. Guess I was just...I was so excited, I couldn't.

He turned and rested his back against the refrigerator.

I wanted everything to be perfect, he continued. I guess by the time it all came together I was just exhausted.

He closed his eyes but heard her moving slowly towards him.

Come on, she said. Show me where you sleep.

She took his hand and, walking towards the staircase, asked, This way?

They took the stairs slowly, regularly. He liked looking at the arches of her feet. At her soles. He had always liked her feet.

She led him into the bedroom and undressed him. The room was cold. She pulled the blankets back and slid into bed. Then pulled the covers back over her. He did likewise, and she held him. She was almost naked, her breasts pressing against his back. Her mouth against his neck. She rubbed the tops of her feet against the soles of his feet. It felt exquisite. To warm those blankets up together. To look out the window and see nothing but snow expiring against the glass. No stray headlights. No moon. No radio towers blinking red. Nothing. Thanksgiving night.

I'm sorry I fell asleep, he said groggily.

Hey, she said quietly, sternly.

What? he asked apologetically.

Stop saying you're sorry, she whispered into his ear. Just—
thank you for tonight. That was...one of the nicest evenings I've
had in a long time.

Me too, he said. Me too.

12

One night, later that week, she woke from a dream, unsure what was real and what wasn't.

In the dream, the past many weeks had been part of an elaborate reality television show. Charlie, the Charlie she'd fallen back in love with, was actually an actor. But the real Charlie's story was purchased by producers to create a plausible backdrop for a new romance. They paid real people for their memories, their insights into former lovers. Then, actors were cast. As for the real Charlie, he was still a drunk, still down in New Mexico. He drank at a tavern near the railroad tracks where the sounds of freight cars groaning, clanking, and laboring were a steady soundtrack.

She woke, suddenly, aware now of the cameras that had been watching them the whole time, just out of sight, microphones hidden. She was surrounded by actors, she saw now, everyone playing their parts, facilitating this fresh new storyline. She couldn't see the audience, but she could practically hear all the snickers and jeers. How foolish of her to think any of this was real.

There was no way to fall back asleep now. She tossed and turned all morning until it was time to get up and make breakfast. At seven o'clock, she called his house. She knew it was stupid, but she had to.

I need to ask you a question, she said. And you're going to think I'm crazy, but...I have to.

Can I have a sip of coffee first? he asked.

What kind of wedding cake did we have?

Uh. Coconut.

She thought for a moment.

Anything else? he asked after a moment.

We buried something in our yard. That place we rented. What did we bury?

You mean my mom's parakeet? he laughed. You know she actually died thinking he escaped his cage. Speaking of graves. She used to talk about that. Wondered if he'd ever fly back home. I used to say to her, Oh, sure, Mom. Yeah, I bet he just migrated back to Costa Rica or Belize or whatever. He's with his family now. But I'm sure he'll be back.

Okay. One last thing then.

Look, I have no idea what the last four digits of your social security number are. Okay? Sorry. I never knew. I barely remember my own.

I'm allergic to one thing. What is it?

Viv?

Yes.

Are you okay? It's, uh, a little early for trivia.

I know. But, just—humor me, please. What am I allergic to?

Mangos. Which never bothered me because until we were married, I didn't even know what a mango was.

Okay, she sighed, I guess it's okay then. You're real enough.

Real?

You can go back to bed.

Vivian?

I'm sorry. Never mind.

I still blame you for that parakeet, she heard him saying, even as she hung up the phone, and leaned against the counter, shaking her head at herself.

13

He happened into Melissa one night, after leaving Vivian's house. All evening he'd helped Vivian with the girls. Now he understood her exhaustion. It wasn't even all the chasing after them, or hula-hooping. Bouncing down a frozen hill on a blue plastic sled. Far more sapping was the sheer concentration, the focus. The effort of doing everything, and from every angle.

Pulling away from that busy little house, he was ready for a beer or two. Ready to relax. To sit at a bar. To ignore some unimportant game on the television. It wasn't even like he needed the drink. Or drinks. But beer was nothing. Beer was water. One or two or maybe three beers. A handful of pistachios or peanuts. Then home. Getting drunk was no longer on his radar. Besides, he needed to be sober enough to drive. He was tiring a little bit of all the driving, actually. It was worth it, to see her, of course. But he'd put hundreds and hundreds, maybe thousands, of miles on his truck just driving between Spooner and Chippewa Falls. He didn't know how long he could keep this up. It seemed ultimately a little unsustainable. This long-distance relationship between two sixtysomethings.

Melissa worked at a sad old bar near the river. The kind of place where no one would ever find you, even if they were looking. A dead-end place where souls went to be forgotten. There was no romance about the place, not even, he suspected, dirty love. The men and women who came here were bankrupt in every sense, their bankrupt vehicles parked outside over a sad expanse of broken asphalt and cigarette butts, discarded lighters, wet matchbooks, crushed beer cans, and disappointing lottery tickets. Leaving his truck, he thought more than once about turning right around. But sometimes these places could be gems too. Hidden gems. You never knew until it was too late. Until the door closed shut behind you and everyone sitting at the bar turned to look.

He took a seat at a corner of the bar, low-key in the gloom. Unobtrusive as an empty bottle, or maybe a hat rack. Just another sad man in the shadows. He drummed his fingers against the bar and peered around. At the dusty, ancient taxidermy. The glowing televisions. The less-than-classic jukebox. He was surprised to see her and tried to wave a hello, but she didn't see him.

She might have been buzzed, or a little stoned; her eyes betrayed a sad sort of dazed tranquility. Standing in the threshold between bar and kitchen, she wore a lopsided smile, as a man, slightly older than her, touched her waist lightly. The way you'd touch the strings of an upright bass. They were flirting; it was easy to see.

Her shift must have been done. Or maybe it was just that kind of place, where the line between on duty and off duty was blurry at best. But she was drinking a glass of beer. She used the glass, with its amber liquid, like a useful prop. She knew she looked good. He could see that, and it made him sad. This woman knew she could attract just about any man. It wasn't just that she was Vivian's daughter, and beautiful for it. It was more than that. She was so smart she could be whatever kind of woman a man desired or needed. She could be an art professor on sabbatical, taking care of her elderly mom. Or she could be a single mom who danced for men when her kids went to sleep. She could be a jaded housewife who sold cosmetics out of her garage, or a seemingly devout Baptist wife with a gleam in her eye, flirting with the devil himself.

He watched them for a half hour or more. During that time, something had turned. It might have been that one moment, when her boss leaned heavily against her body and whispered something in her ear. Something crude, maybe. Something hard, or nasty. Too nasty. He saw her face darken, and there was something like fear there, on her forehead, in her eyes. As if she were trapped. But, then, how do you walk out on your job? How do you walk out on your job with two little children at home? How would you cry foul in a place like this?

He stood from the bar, walked beside its battered mahogany curve. Hey, Melissa, he called. Hey. It's Charlie.

At first, she seemed afraid of him too. Or perhaps just startled. Then simply a look of resignation that she could hardly ignore him. Setting the empty beer glass down behind a wall, she touched the man's shoulder and walked slowly towards Charlie.

What are you doing here? she asked without any particular drama. Like this was an inevitable coincidence. Fated in a place this small.

He shrugged his shoulders, shot the man a look. You know. Just out here living my best life, right? he said. Good old Chippewa Falls, Wisconsin.

Yeah? How long have you been here?

Long enough to see that some asshole may be bothering you.

She leaned closer to him, whispered, He also happens to be the owner.

Doesn't matter, he said, in a low voice. You don't need this place. C'mon, Melissa. Let me take you home.

It does matter, actually, she whispered. He pays, very, very well.

I don't care how much he pays you. You don't have to take that.

Yeah, well, I think I do, she said. She leaned closer. That's part of what he pays for.

She pushed back from the bar and crossed her arms, shot him a look. A look that begged confidentiality. A look that said, Please, don't make me say anything more. Just forget this place. Erase it. And don't ever come back here.

Are you sure? he asked. Are you safe?

I'm fine, she said. Go away, okay? Please. This is really not a big deal.

She walked away and then, as if tied to the bar by an invisible cord, she turned and came back.

But listen, thanks. For checking on me, I mean. She rapped a knuckle against the bar. Honestly, I'm fine.

Okay, he said. Nuff said.

He drove home feeling heavy. Not at all feeling lighter, or more relaxed. Each mile its own tedium, and he felt guiltier and guiltier the farther away he drove.

14

One night he invited Vivian over to his house for dinner. Lasagna. He was so proud of himself. Even though she'd made lasagna from scratch perhaps hundreds of times in her life, he walked her through the recipe—just as a man who never cooks would—all the various ingredients, all the frenzied shopping, the manic chopping, all the sautéing, all the layering. She nodded her head approvingly while sipping a glass of very nice red wine; already she felt the faintest bit tipsy. Not drunk, no. Just one of those days when she hadn't eaten enough, hadn't drunk enough water. The wine was moving through her bloodstream, slowing everything down. She couldn't wait to crawl into his bed and simply fall deeply, deeply into sleep.

I'll just make some garlic bread real quick, he said, and then we'll be ready to eat. Give me twenty minutes, tops. Hey, make yourself at home. Look around. Maybe you can help me decorate this place.

He poured another inch of wine into her glass and went about his preparations and cooking. She had to hand it to him. The kitchen was clean. No pile of dirty dishes. No untidy surfaces. Even his clothing was immaculate. Forty years of living alone had in fact informed his housekeeping. She shook her head for a moment in disbelief, in stunned wonder.

She moved from room to room, like the first guest at a party, before any of the other attendees had arrived. The house was fairly stark. Some tastefully framed prints she recognized as Ansel Adams. But mostly, the walls and surfaces were bare. She realized, in a swell of sadness, that after all these decades, he still had no family. No children. No spouse. What photographs could he hang on his walls but those taken by other people?

He wasn't a bad decorator; she had to admit, though, for her tastes, the house felt a bit antiseptic, like an executive rental. The rooms were well appointed in a way. Thick rugs. Elegant lamps offering indirect warm lighting. Bold dark paint. The furniture looked to be Ethan Allen or some equivalent, and all so new, she wondered if some of the chairs had ever been sat in. At Thanksgiving, she'd been too busy with her granddaughters, or washing dishes to take too much stock of the house, but she found herself scrutinizing everything tonight, while he whistled in the kitchen.

Ten more minutes, she heard him call from the kitchen.

In the small room he called his study, where there was a desk, some bookshelves, and a wide computer screen, she peered out the window at the barn, looming in the dark. She took a sip of wine and then examined the shelves. An autographed baseball resting on a display case, the signature tidy enough that she recognized the name—Nolan Ryan. A few dozen books. Not titles she had read. Mostly histories. A few novels. But near those books were two framed photographs that stood out in this house, precisely because they were personal. She set her glass of wine down on his desk and reached for the first photograph.

The picture was old, it seemed. Definitely from the eighties, judging by the young woman's voluminous black blow-dried hair, and the bold rainbow colors of her top. She was beautiful, like Cher. Slender suntanned arms, gold bangles stacked on her wrists, gleamingly white teeth. She was leaning against an ancient tree. A tree so wide it nearly obscured all of the photo's background. But if she might have guessed, Vivian would have said the photo was taken in a park, or a college campus. There was a path winding behind the tree, and a few figures walking, out of focus. She set the photograph back, took up the next frame.

The woman was in this photo as well, but so was Charlie. She was unprepared for the hurt, the jealousy, the feeling of being punched right in her belly, but they were holding hands on a beach, a sunset melting behind them. There was a flower in the woman's hair, and though her right hand was intertwined in his, her left hand rested on her thigh, and Vivian could see a ring there, set off by the white of her dress, and the darkness of her skin, the darkness of her hair. They had the shine of new love. The shine of promise.

Dinner's ready, she heard him call.

She walked back to the kitchen, dazed.

Hey, he said, quietly, you forgot your wineglass.

She didn't want the photo to bother her, but it did. This empty house. No evidence of his life at all. Not a single photograph of her that she had noticed. And yet. Two photographs of a woman he had never mentioned, not once. The jealousy and confusion coursed through her body, like cold venom. She couldn't stop herself.

Who is this? she said, holding the photograph in her hand.

Oh, that's my friend, he replied. Yeah. That's Mona.

Your friend? This looks like a wedding photo.

Well, yeah. It is. Yeah. That's our wedding photo. Um. After you—sorry. After we were, after you and I were divorced, I got married to Mona. It was a mistake. Getting married. But... Should we sit down for dinner? I'm not dodging your question; it's just that, maybe we could sit down and talk about it.

Vivian really could not respond, but she moved into the dining room, the photograph almost dangling from her hand. She sat down, stunned, while he brought their plates to the table, while he poured her a glass of ice water. Steam rose off the lasagna into the room.

It's probably too hot to eat right away, he said, but there's salad. Do you want some salad?

Charlie, she said abruptly, two photographs in your whole house. And both are your ex-wife. A woman you've never talked about. She felt something breaking in her chest, something falling, her heart, her happiness. A palisade, collapsing into a gorge. You don't have any photos of me, she said, though her voice was trembling.

He reached for her hand. I'm so sorry, Viv, he said. That's— look, this is my fault, and I can explain. I should have explained. He took a deep breath, paused, examined the ceiling, as if the words he sought to retrieve were projected there.

Mona is my friend, he said at last, which really did nothing to soothe her. The photograph was still in her hand, and now it felt toxic, felt like something she wanted to throw or tear into pieces. She found herself handing him the picture and standing up. She was suddenly exhausted. Exhausted by the long drive to his house, exhausted by the day's routine, exhausted by the glass of wine and the ever-darkening days. She just wanted to go home.

Stop, he said. Please.

Mona and I were married for a matter of months, he said. Two years after our divorce, sorry. About four years after she and I divorced, she married a friend of mine. I didn't know him back then, but he's become my friend. They've been married ever since. Mona is twelve years older than me, and he's, god, he's almost twenty years older than me. They live down in Iowa. She was my professor, which, I know, is...I don't know how to say it. Fucked up. But it was what it was. They've been like my mentors, okay? They've been my steadiest friends. I hope that maybe someday we can drive down there and visit them.

She could only look down at her feet. The jealousy undissipated. The sense of being wounded still acute.

I don't have any photographs of you and me, he said at last.

I wish I did. But I—when we separated, I just left. I didn't take anything. And I regret that. All these years, don't you think I wanted something of ours? Some reminders? Of course, I did, Viv. Look, I understand. And I can put those photos of her away, I can. I get it.

I'm so tired, Vivian said. I'm tired, and I'm sad.

Please, why don't you, look—sleep in my bed, okay? I'll sleep in the guest room. Or, whatever. You can have the guest room. But don't drive back tonight, okay? Please. Let's just get some rest, and we can talk about this tomorrow morning.

I don't know about all this, she said, slumping in her chair, staring out the window into the night. What we're doing. It's like we've lived all these different lives, and I don't know how I'll ever understand, how I'll ever be sure that you're giving it to me straight. That you're telling me the full truth. I mean, how do I know you're not still in love with her? How do I know that some old spark in you isn't going to flare up again, and then what? What was all this?

I don't know, he said, glancing at the table, at the meal he knew would now go uneaten. But I'm telling you the truth, Viv.

I'm being stupid, she said, taking a deep sip of the wine, and laughing darkly. I mean, what do I have to be jealous about? That you remarried?

And like I said, he began again, it didn't last. It was a mistake.

I'll tell you why it bothers me, she said, feeling the wine take hold, even as her tongue loosened. It's because you went off and you lived in all these different places. And you met all these fancy people. You went to college. You're smiling in those photos. You know how many photos of me I have where I'm smiling? How many photos of me there are on vacation somewhere?

He hung his head in defeat while Blueberry entered the room and stood beside him, resting his head on the table and staring at the lasagna.

Do you ever think of what you left me with? The mess you left me with? Isn't that just like a man though? No, no, no—you go on. Go on and have your adventures. And I'll stay back here, picking up the pieces. God, she sighed.

What?

I acted like your wife even when you were gone. Even after the divorce.

What do you mean? he asked. I don't understand.

They left the table, all of that food still steaming. She took the stairs like a somnambulist and barely felt part of her body, but rather a ghost inhabiting a shell. Her feet moved up the staircase, and on the second-floor landing, she turned into a guest room, shut the door, and collapsed onto the bed.

Sometime before dawn, she woke, and sat up on the bed. Outside the window, the northern lights were flickering in pale greens and faint pinks. The night felt like a hallucination.

She was startled when she opened the guest room door and Blueberry was standing right there, wagging his tail, pressing his head against her thigh. But then her heartbeat slowed, and she ran her fingers through his coat, closed her eyes, breathed deeply. In the bathroom, she splashed icy water on her face, cupped her hands and drank. She did not want to see her reflection in the mirror.

She arrived home just as dawn surged over her neighborhood. The house was still quiet, and she slipped into her bed, and pleaded for sleep to find her, if only for a handful of minutes before life resumed, undaunted.

15

In the morning, she was gone, but that evening, he sent her a text, and she responded, a bit coolly, a bit politely. Time seeped in, hours and then days, and time seemed to smooth away whatever she had felt, that shock. She never again asked him about Mona, and though he wasn't ashamed of the photographs or his friendship with his second ex-wife, he stowed them in a desk drawer beneath some paperwork. He was ashamed that he hadn't considered the photographs from Viv's perspective. That he hadn't considered the relative fragility of their renewed relationship, how tenuous everything was. How they were still relearning one another. Still healing old wounds. He made a note to take a photo of her on one of their walks. Or maybe a few photos, and have them tastefully framed. It wasn't a capitulation or concession. He wanted a photo of her, photos of her. He wanted to begin filling this house with artifacts of their relationship. Reminders of her.

Something changed in their interactions, but he didn't experience the change as bad, only—a lessening, a slowing. He told himself it was natural, even needed. They still held hands, still laughed, and kissed and made love, but the intensity seemed just slightly muted, like a DJ gently, imperceptibly, turning the volume down at a party. This was better, he told himself. How they had restarted was unsustainable, like a teenage romance bound to burn out. No, this was safer, wiser, calmer.

But he did miss that sparkle.

16

She pushed a shopping cart down the toy-aisle at Walmart, holding the girls' Christmas lists in her hands. Lists marked out in crayon and marker, all oversized misspelled writing. She was pleased to recognize a few of the things they wanted, mostly from the TV they watched. Nickelodeon. Dolls that did not look like the dolls of her youth. These dolls, they looked...demented. Whatever.

Well, easier to think whatever if it hadn't all been so expensive. What money she had was through social security. And that wasn't much. Sometimes she sold things online. When it became clear that she couldn't afford a storefront, she'd moved Violet Vintage to the internet. eBay and Etsy. She knew clothing; as a mother she knew quality, brand names, fashions. Even if culture arrived in Wisconsin months after some new thing had already become trendy on the coasts, she had always paid attention to what was cool. A lifetime of never having what she wanted manifesting as an educated longing, a sharp set of eyes.

So expensive, she said under her breath as she turned a shiny package in her hands.

What was that? Charlie asked.

I don't know, she said, throwing her hands into the air. It's all just plastic. And so expensive. And I know what they'll do with it. I mean, they'll be ecstatic at first. A week, maybe. Two, tops. And then...nothing. I'll find this toy out in the backyard covered in snow. I guess you buy that week. A whole week of joy. That's something, isn't it? I'd pay twenty dollars for a week of happiness. I'd pay a lot more than twenty dollars.

She liked Walmart. For one thing, it was comparatively cheap. Even as everything was getting more expensive, everywhere, and seemingly by the day... But most importantly, she never felt judged here. On any given day, almost all of the shoppers were clearly some kind of desperate. Or close to it. The garments they wore. Tired sweatpants. Shoes worn down to the thinnest of soles. Hand-me-down jackets. Everything they bought at Walmart moved right into their lives to be used immediately and used hard.

Let me help you, Charlie said. Won't you let me help you?

She looked at him as if he were crazy. No, sir, you may not, she said. I saved up. I love this time of year. I want to pay.

She did not say how much the gifts delighted her too. That Christmas morning was still exciting to her. These two little girls who still listened for the hooves of reindeer on their roof, though they had never grown up with a fireplace or chimney; Santa Claus came in through a kitchen window they left open an inch.

Or the unlocked back door, if he so chose. How she delighted in staying up late on Christmas Eve. Sneaking into the living room and displaying the stuffed stockings and piles of presents. Then falling into bed, exhausted. There were only so many years when a child believed in magic, and that was something. Something precious, really. To still believe in magic.

I wish you'd let me help you, he said again. She could hear something rising in his voice or wanting to rise. Something he had to tamp down. She chose to ignore it. To seek out the toys the girls wanted and cross them off her list.

Melissa at least was easy. She just liked gift certificates. Nail salons and massage therapists. There wasn't enough room in the house to collect much. Even a thick hardcover book seemed conspicuous.

The total came to close to three hundred dollars, which stunned her for an instant. Charlie stood right there, of course, making a production of his hand on his wallet. As if she wouldn't have enough money. As if he'd need to swoop in and save the day. She paid, cash, quickly, and snatched all the plastic bags before he could. Before he could feel the actual weight of all her efforts.

Back in the cab of his truck, he was quiet. The first tense quiet that had descended upon them. The kind of quiet that portends a real disagreement. The sky just before a storm, clouds suddenly massing up, like soldiers before a battle.

She had nothing to be angry at. The day had gone just as she planned. Her errands were done. But then, neither did Charlie now. Maybe he was just hungry. He'd always been that way.

Confusing anger for hunger. Maybe if she suggested they have lunch, maybe then he'd relax. He could eat. He could pay for it all. Feel useful, the way he liked to. Feel that he had contributed.

But at an Olive Garden near the mall, they ate mostly in silence.

He sighed at length, petulant. She didn't remember this side of him. Nor had he shown it to her since they started back up. She wanted to say, Just take me home. She didn't need this. She loved him. Or maybe she did. She could love him. But her life had not been broken before. A little emptier. Colder. But not broken. Were it all to go away now, she would just continue on. Wouldn't she? Not that she wanted that. She just wanted him: excited, kind, passionate, patient. A wonderful companion. Was this what it was like? Being with someone all the time? That inevitably, the mask would slip, and you would see another side? A much less attractive side?

Suddenly he said, I don't understand why you're so stubborn.

I'm so stubborn, she said slowly. Well, I don't understand why you don't understand. I'm not a little girl, okay? I would like to pay for my own gifts.

Come on, Viv. Don't be like this. I could help.

I actually don't want your help, Charlie. Then they wouldn't be my gifts, would they? They'd be your gifts.

But, he began. His voice trailed off, but she could pretty well follow the arc of his thought.

But I don't have as much money as you do? she offered helpfully. But this is a lot of money for me? But what? She began to feel angry. But we live in a small shitty house? But my car is a rust bucket? I see you—she thought about the right word—crinkling your nose in our house. Taking stock of everything. Like, if we were gone for a weekend, you'd probably rush off to rent a dumpster and throw it all out. All of our things.

That's not...he began. But his face was red. She had seen right through him. Marked every stupidly transparent facial expression. Every note of distaste. Now, c'mon. That's not fair.

We, are, happy, she said slowly, firmly, in a lower voice now. Lower and a whole lot less civil. She could hear the growled warning in her own voice. My grandchildren are happy, Charlie. They are surrounded by love. We do not want for anything. There is plenty of food. So we don't have a room full of fancy stupid wines, thank you very much. But then again, Charlie, maybe you shouldn't either.

He cocked his head as if to indicate he had taken enough slaps and jabs, that last comment a sucker punch that had hit its mark. She immediately wanted it back.

I'm trying, he said. Look, we're at lunch, we're fighting, and I haven't had a drop. I mean, would I like a drink right about now? Hell yeah, I would. But I didn't. Not until just now. Until you said something. And I have to say, I don't like to be reminded I'm an alcoholic. I know I'm an alcoholic, all right? I'm trying.

You know, she said, I'm actually not very hungry. I think I'd like to go home now. I have work to do.

But the meal hasn't even arrived, he said.

Please just take me home, she said again. I'm happy to pay for the food.

No, he said. Come on, Viv, you're not going to do that.

Look, if you don't want to bring me home, I can call Melissa. I can call my daughter.

No, no, no, he said. He threw some cash on the table. More than enough. And then they were standing, and she was walking well ahead of him and right out of the restaurant.

He tried to rush ahead, to open the door for her, but she wouldn't have it. She took the other one, made her way to his truck. Climbed into the passenger's side and stared out the window. The mall was busy, and they would suffer an interminable amount of time trying to leave this parking lot. Trying to merge into traffic. Driving north on 53 back to Chippewa Falls.

I remember when this was all farmland, Charlie spat. Oakwood Mall. I don't see an oak tree anywhere.

She shook her head. I don't need your money, Charlie, she said. When did you even get this way? When we were married, we had nothing. I know your family. You came from nothing. You used to tell me about eating sandwiches made of Cheez Whiz and potato chips. Your dad drove a semi. And I never once looked down on you. It never dawned on me. All I cared about was you. And we were happy enough when we were married. I mean, it was fine. We never even knew the difference. We were happy. Being poor, that wasn't what ruined everything.

Oh, he said, nodding his head in mock approval. Yeah, that was my fault, wasn't it? All my fault.

Well, she said, it was.

He pounded the steering wheel in frustration. Vivian,

goddamn it. I've apologized, he said loudly. I've apologized how many times? I...was...a...look—I was a kid. I acted stupidly. I drank too much. I'm an alcoholic. You think I don't know that? I'm trying. Sometimes I make mistakes. Just now, I made a mistake. I'm so sorry.

He was shouting. They were still parked outside the restaurant, and he was shouting and pounding at the steering wheel, and when she looked out, she could see diners pointing at them. Looks of real concern on their faces. One table was talking to their server, who seemed very troubled.

Please, she said wearily, let's just go. I want to go home. She wasn't scared. Just disappointed. Just sad.

He shook his head and put the truck into reverse. Fine, he said, I fucking hate the mall anyway. They pulled into traffic aggressively though, and for the first time since he'd reentered her life, she felt afraid.

Had she given any thought, forty years ago, at the time of their divorce, to what he might end up as, this might have been her guess. Angry, red-faced, gunning the V8 of a big pickup truck. That old man in a pickup truck driving angrily, with no regard for other motorists. The other human beings all around them, walking across the parking lot. The parents holding their young children's hands. The teenagers, clearly out on a date. And all the people they couldn't see. Not the children in their car seats. Not the group of laughing teenage friends, their whole lives ahead of them and yet undiscovered. Not the man just released from jail after twenty years, twenty years for possessing a little pot.

Not the woman in blessed remission from cancer, who wanted only another sunrise on the beach, or a hug from her grandchild. He wasn't thinking of any of those people. Just himself. This aggrieved man. Aggrieved over the stupidest reason: that she was proud and would not accept his money. For the briefest of moments, she thought, Like a whore should.

What if she put it that way? That taking his money made her feel like a whore. Would that clarify things? Or maybe he liked that. Maybe that made her his. His possession. No, no, she told herself. That's too much. Charlie isn't like that.

She felt sick. She felt lovesick. The promise of what they might have been. Those first kisses. After forty years. All that loneliness. Traveling through time without a partner. She thought she'd found it again. Love. But so much of her life had been a disappointment. And maybe this was no different.

Not her grandchildren though. Those two girls were what she was living for now. She felt immediate resolve. They needed her. And her daughter needed her. That need was priceless. Because it was family. Her family, their love, their home. It was all they had.

When they crossed the bridge over the Chippewa River, the dam off to their left, she said, Just let me out here.

They were still at least a half mile from her home. Maybe a mile away. She didn't care. It was cold, very cold. But she'd manage. She couldn't stand another second in his truck.

That's crazy, he said. It's freezing out, Vivian. At least let me get you home.

131

Stop this truck right now, she said, pulling out her phone, or I'll call the cops. Her voice was as even as the frozen river, and just as cold.

He pulled the truck onto a side street, and before he could even put it into park, she was out the door. But she'd left the presents behind.

She was thirty steps away when she heard him. You forgot the presents, Viv, he shouted out of the cab.

He might have said it in a meaner way. Might have said nothing at all. But it sounded, his voice sounded, about as sad as she felt. She stopped right where she stood. Started crying. Not what she wanted to do. Not at all. It was terribly cold, for one thing. And embarrassing. It was awful. This whole day had been awful. She just wanted to take a hot bath. To put a hot washcloth over her face and lie in that warm place between disconnection, relaxation, and sleep. Nothing. No one to watch over or feed or clean up after or take care of or suffer or explain to or heal or worship or even love. Just warm, soapy water lapping at her skin. A few candles. Some old country album playing on her phone.

She heard the truck idling but did not want to turn back. That was the last thing she wanted. To let him see her tears. God, she did not want that. Now she heard the truck in reverse, as it inched back towards her. The sound of the exhaust pipe juddering. The engine's low rumble. Snow and ice crunching beneath those new black tires. She stood still and wanted to just disappear. Just become vapor and blow on away.

Please get in the truck, he said, as kindly as a man might.

She pinched her eyes shut, and then opened them against the harsh white world. She walked to the passenger side of the truck, where he had already reached over to open the door for her. She crawled inside.

He drove her the rest of the way home without saying a word, then waited while she unloaded her presents, and when she could not close the door because her arms were so full, he leaned across the seats. I guess that the only thing I want you to know, he said, is that I love you. And I'm sorry about the ways I let you down. I didn't know better then. I do now. I am trying.

He glanced down. She thought, He must be collecting his words. She could see it on his brow. He was looking at each word, holding it in his mind, like a precious stone, before he showed her anything. What was in his heart.

It was cold outside. The snow in the sky looked tired, like it was losing a slow-moving chess game.

I want you to… I want to earn back your respect, he said. And then, with nothing left at all, he just said, I love you.

He closed the truck door and drove away slowly, his brake lights two sad valentines in retreat.

17

But everything felt so much lonelier without her. Without so much as her voice over the telephone. Without her text messages lighting up his cell phone. Without her hand in his. Without her breath on his neck. They still hadn't even had that many dates—they'd only reconnected, what, less than three months ago—but he found himself sustained by the promise of their next meeting, and now, that promise seemed in jeopardy.

He drank more than he ought to have. Drank almost by himself, though he thought of Blueberry as a friend, so there was that comfort. And the comfort of stepping out into the night on his back porch and lighting a joint and inhaling deeply. He didn't smoke marijuana often, thought of it as something of an especially decadent dessert. Now each star winked at him hello. The coyotes off in the night, carousing, calling to him.

One night he played the sound of an injured rabbit on his cell phone, played it out into the night, just to see what predator might visit him. And within less than five seconds, an owl swooped out of the complete darkness and came so close to his hands he could count each yellow talon, so close he might have reached out to steal a feather. He felt very alive just then, his body trembling. The owl might have landed in his arms, or on top of his head. Might just as well have flown off with his phone glowing bright as it winged up into the low-lying clouds heavy with snow.

He returned to the warmth of his house. The dog asleep on the wood floor. He knelt slowly and then lay down on the floor beside Blueberry. Swept his fingers through the animal's fur. Rubbed at his skull, scratched behind the ears. Itched below his expectant jaw. Then just petted that sleek black coat. They stayed that way some nights for hours, until he fell asleep, and the dog relocated. Leaving him there on the floor, half-drunk and a little stoned. The house was too big, didn't he know. Too much for one old man getting only older. An empty room wanted a soul like a shelf wants a book. And this house of his was mostly empty.

One morning, after he made a pot of coffee and well before he could even consider a drop of alcohol, he wrote her a letter. He had to start over many times, throwing each misbegotten and defeated draft into the woodstove to blossom into flame. He was self-conscious of his words. His spelling. His handwriting. Lord, it looked just like a boy's.

How was he supposed to write down all that he felt? Where does a person even begin? All the way back to their first dates, over forty years ago. To their very first date. A county fair. Kissing beneath fireworks. Kisses that tasted of ice cream, dissolving away against his tongue, against his teeth, like the fluff of cotton candy. Holding hands after wiping the sweat off his palms on his blue jeans. Her head on his shoulder. Her hip pressed into his on the Ferris wheel. Or later? Their honeymoon? Making love during that lightning storm. Trying to make a baby. The excitement of that. Where would he start?

Or how he felt now? Like the luckiest man in the world. Like he held the winning lottery ticket. All he had to do was not go and lose it. Not burn it. Not drop it and watch it blow away, into the river. I haven't done enough to earn your trust, he wrote. I know that I only have so much time, and I don't want to waste any of what is left. I want us to be together, Vivian.

Only somehow the letter never assembled itself together right. The words did not cohere. Did not equal either what he thought and certainly not what he felt.

Most days, just around noon, he did begin drinking. Drinking slow. Down to the cellar, touching those beautiful bottles. Carrying one or two upstairs. Building a fire in the woodstove. Little breaks to walk down the driveway to his mailbox. Nothing ever there but bills and coupons for things he had no need for. He pitied the mailperson who had to deliver such useless paper. No love letters or draft notices. No postcards from Venice or birthday cards from a great-aunt, a Hallmark card and a two-dollar bill. Just days of worthless flyers and sales pitches. He could have filled a whole room in his house with all those mailers. Neat stacks of insultingly glossy paper.

He wasn't hungry much, but sometimes the loneliness drove

him into town just the same, and inevitably, into the arms of a tavern. There was a reassurance in that, certain promises and expectations between tavern and patron. There would be music and alcohol. Someone to talk to, if only politely; he wouldn't be alone there. There would be televisions glowing, and usually neon lights, which is not nothing. Better than sitting alone in the dark. There might be food. Certainly, there were ways to gamble. Clever games by which to part a patron from their money. Dice. Scratch-off tickets. Electronic machines. One night, at his lowest, he lost a thousand dollars in a bar he could now never return to, for shame. Driving home that night, he actually considered aiming the truck off the side of a bridge, right down through the ice of a frozen lake. If it were a cold-enough night, and the ice re-formed, no one would even notice he was gone. Not for many months anyway. Not until spring.

The dog helped. Blueberry needed him, after all, for food and water, and seemed to relieve himself only on proper walks. Walks with him. Which was at once an inconvenience and a blessing. Four or five times a day, he had to leave the house and trail behind the dog like its shadow. Other tasks, too, kept him from quitting. Feeding the birds. Standing under a white pine, with birdseed in his hands, waiting for a chickadee to land on his fingers. It happened one day. A chickadee alighted on his palm. It was the lightest thing he had ever held. He began crying. It was Christmas Eve.

He drove out into the country beneath a clear December sky more decorous and fragile than any crystal chandelier. He drove without any direction, Blueberry sitting in the passenger seat staring at the road ahead. At a crossroads with three empty corners, he pulled into the parking lot of a small old Lutheran church. In the cemetery beyond the church, the gravestones shone under the moonlight. Under the starlight. The snow was unbroken for as far as he could see. He thought of the souls lying there, under this purity, in that repose to which there was no end.

He walked into the church and sat in the back, the Christmas service already underway. One young girl turned to take in his entrance, and she smiled in a sad sort of way that broke his old heart. He winked at her, and she quickly turned back to face the pastor.

Charlie did not believe in god, but that night he prayed. He prayed to be a better man. Prayed for strength. And when the other parishioners stood to sing the Christmas hymns, or to join together in prayer, he stood too. When the brass offering plate passed his way, all lined with burgundy velvet, he dropped two thousand dollars' cash and felt good about it, like he had evened some scales, however preposterous that thought might be. Later, driving home, he felt lighter. He could imagine certain challenges now, but could also see their solutions, could imagine trying harder.

After he crawled into bed he reached for his phone and typed: Merry Christmas, Viv. Hope you're having a wonderful holiday. I miss you.

When he set the phone on the bedside table, he exhaled, turned on his side, and felt the starlight on his face. The moon was already high in the pellucid sky, and he waited for it to say good night or Merry Christmas. Waited, too, for the impossible chime of his doorbell to ring and for her to walk into his arms. Or the telephone to ring. A text to ding, like a happy little bell. He waited until two o'clock in the morning, heart pounding. Sure that something would happen. Some sign of her. Of her longing. But nothing did. Nothing happened. And so, he closed his eyes and fell asleep.

18

You're really not going to call him? Melissa asked.

No, Vivian replied, stirring cream into her coffee. Or—I don't know. Do you think I should? Even after the way he acted?

Mom, she said. I didn't say marry him and, you know, take his last name. I didn't say move right into his house and adopt a kid from Malawi. I didn't say you should bake him a cheesecake. But he's alone, isn't he?

She knew he was, but she said, I think he still has some people here.

Mom, Melissa said again, call him. At least say Merry Christmas.

I don't want to think about him right now, Vivian said. This is our holiday. Our nice day. And I'm looking forward to seeing Jessie today, and I don't want to think about him.

Okay, Melissa said, but I think you're kind of being a bitch. Sorry not sorry. And at some point, Mom, you're going to have to tell him about her, aren't you? It isn't really fair to either of them, is it?

Melissa, Vivian said, honestly.

Christmas Day held a special rhythm for Vivian. Slow and sweet. Presents. Soft clothing. Little surprises. Her grand-daughters and their hugs, their kisses. Her two daughters—Melissa and Jessie. Coffee and a dash of rum. Carols on the radio. Her slippers. A candle burning on the kitchen table. A ham in the oven. Hot chocolate mustaches over the girls' lips. Melissa hugging her, saying, I love you, Mom. Jessica saying, Thank you, thank you, thank you, for all the inconsequential gifts mounded in her lap, beneath a smile wide as the Mississippi River. All of these blessings. She turned the thermostat up, two whole degrees.

I mean, Melissa said, do you like this guy?

Vivian knew, as she thought about it, that she not only liked this guy. She loved him.

Well, of course, she allowed. But...it's okay to take a break. I just think we were moving too fast. I didn't care for the way he was... She couldn't quite express what she wanted to say. Actually, she realized, he had not done anything really wrong, except in the truck maybe—that reckless macho speeding. She didn't care for that at all. But then, maybe she had antagonized him. Maybe he was afraid. She knew that a man who was afraid often did dumb things. Dangerous things, even.

I think he really likes you, Mom, Melissa said. Like, really likes you. Like love.

Okay, she said, I'll call him. If you stop harassing me, she said lightly, I'll do it. I'll call him.

I don't really care either way, Melissa said, nonchalantly. You do you.

Vivian took her cell phone into her room. Like a teenager, she thought to herself. All these years in this house, with her daughter and granddaughters, there had never been a single reason she needed to isolate herself, to conduct any sort of conversation behind closed doors. Nor did any part of her find this an affront. She thought instead, But maybe now I have a life of my own. Maybe now I have something outside of this little house, and that is okay. It suddenly felt very good, very welcome to dial Charlie's phone number.

He answered almost immediately and began talking before she could say a thing. Merry Christmas, he blurted, and then he was off. How was your morning? Did the girls like their toys? I bought you all some presents. Hey, would you consider, would you maybe like to get together? How are you?

All like that. All just—so sweet. Like a beloved dog meeting you at the door. Like you were the grandest prize in the universe. She began laughing. It broke in her. That happiness she had known when they first reconnected.

I'm okay, she said. I'm good, actually. How are you? How was last night? Did you have any place to go?

Uh, no, I—no, he stammered, but that's okay. I mean, I went to church last night. Which felt really good. A little church in the middle of nowhere.

You don't even know where you were? What church you went to? Were you... Her voice trailed off sadly.

No, he said assuredly. No, not at all. It wasn't like that. Not a drop in fact. It wasn't like I was drinking. I just...wanted to drive, I guess. Wanted to get out of the house.

Now she realized that she had made a mistake. In not forgiving him. In not moving past a moment. She could not imagine herself in that house all alone, with no one to be with on Christmas Eve or Christmas Day. Could not imagine it at all. The cramped chaos of their little home was such a comfort in so many ways. The voices passing through the thin walls. The toilet flushing. Water spilling into the sink, splashing off hands. The inescapable drone of the TV. All of it meant she was not alone. And more than that, the people she loved, who shared this roof, they all turned to her for stability and knowledge. They turned to her almost every hour for help, for kindness, for love, for counsel. What if there was no one to do that, to lend her the reassurance of needing to reassure? What if she had love to give, and no one to accept it?

Why don't you come over? she said. Not now; we have to clean up the house a bit. She thought of Jessie, wasn't ready yet for their meeting, for the explanations she would need to offer. She continued, Have dinner with us. Nothing fancy. Just ham and some potatoes au gratin. A salad. The girls love that meal.

She could hear the thankfulness in his voice when he said, See you soon. Would five give you enough time? Is five o'clock okay?

Five is perfect, she said. Goodbye, Charlie. Merry Christmas.

Charlie must have done his own shopping and some time ago. He was well prepared. For the girls: a miniature motorized Jeep Cherokee, pretty in pink. Ran on a battery. A two-seater. They have to share, he said with a tremendous grin. Somehow, he managed to unload it from his truck and park it out on the street, wrapped up in a white bow. The girls did not even consider shrugging into their coats. They barely managed to slip their boots on. Ripped the bow off. Circled the Jeep and, for a moment, a scrum near the driver's side door before Addison, the younger sister, conceded and jumped into the passenger's side. They buckled themselves in. Then, joy. A toy that was mostly unthinkable in their neighborhood.

It was dusk, but they toured the sidewalks nonetheless. Stopped at a corner, looked both ways responsibly, and then cruised across the street at about a mile per hour. Maybe two. Neighbors stepped outside onto front stoops, eggnog in hand, to give the new drivers a big wave. When they were safely parked in the driveway, a full-size Jeep Wrangler drove by slowly and honked in tribal acknowledgment, positively thrilling the girls.

Oh my god, Melissa said. I'm worried they'll pee themselves.

Vivian and Melissa stood beaming beside Charlie. And when Vivian went into the house to check on the ham, she kissed him chastely on the cheek and said, Merry Christmas.

19

Before dinner, he said to Melissa, I have something for you too.

He left the living room and drifted back outside. Retrieved something from the truck, a tall rectangular gift all wrapped in paper, and nudged his way back inside the house with it. If it was a box, it was not light.

Here, he said, setting it on the flimsy coffee table. Then, as if reassessing the table's integrity, he lifted the gift and set it on the carpeting between Melissa's feet.

But, Charlie, I didn't you get you anything, Melissa said.

Not yet, he replied, grinning.

She pulled the paper off the box. Slowly, carefully. Like he had given her a bomb. Or a bowling ball. Something she couldn't possibly use. But when the paper was crumpled on the floor, she opened the box itself to find twelve bottles of wine. She pulled each one out, marveling at the bottle she held, then stared at him. Incredulous.

This is—she said, eyes wide—like, nuts. This is bananas. I

can't... She hesitated. Charlie, I can't accept this. I know, she said, waving her hand over the box, how much all this is worth. I could buy a car with this box.

He nodded his head slowly. If you wanted to, he said. Or you can drink them. You're about the only person I know who would appreciate these bottles. And look, I had some time to think about it. If something happened to me, I have no idea what would happen to that cellar. Maybe—maybe—one of my cousins would know that they were worth something? But I could also see someone donating them to some church. Here, they'd say, carting in box after box of wine. Guess you should be all set on communion juice for a while. Anyway, it's up to you now. I'd actually like to give you another case or two. If that's all right.

He sat down in a folding chair Vivian had set up just for him, crossed his legs, and rested his hands on his stomach.

She looked at him, stunned. Okay. But, I mean, what am I supposed to get you? A grandfather clock or something? A fancy fucking shotgun? She let out a little snort. Jesus, she said, my mouth is watering, thinking about these wines.

Here, come with me, he said. Let's talk out in the garage.

What's happening? Vivian asked.

Oh, Charlie said over his shoulder, as he shrugged into his coat and held the door for Melissa, we'll be back in a minute.

They stood in the garage, breath steaming out before them. There was no ceiling light, but Melissa turned on an aged yellow trouble light, and they stood there, on the cracked concrete, the cramped garage barely wide enough to fit a Volkswagen Beetle inside if it was utterly empty. Which it surely was not, between the dilapidated lawn mower, a wheelbarrow, toys, balls, bicycles, a broken washing machine, and their garbage cans.

I don't know if I like this, Melissa said. I don't know if I like where this is going...

I need a favor, he said quietly.

She looked at him evenly, arms crossed over her chest.

I want to take your mom on a trip, he explained. Just for a weekend. But that means she won't be around to help with the girls. We used to take little trips back when we were married. Did she tell you about that?

She told me how poor you guys were. And that you had some kind of crappy camper or something?

He nodded and smiled in the wan light. That's right, he said. One of my uncles gave me that old camper. It leaked any time we got rain, and smelled like mildew and rot, but we couldn't always afford to stay in many motels. Anyway, I want to take your mom away for a weekend. A surprise.

Melissa offered a sweet small smile now. The kind of smile that suggested she knew Vivian could use a vacation, a break.

I think that's a great idea, she said. Where are you going?

Just down to Iowa, he said. I want her—I need her to meet a friend of mine. A couple friends.

Well, Melissa sighed, how romantic. No shortage of corn anyway.

I happen to think Iowa is beautiful, he countered. And I

doubt anyone from Iowa really cares what other people think about their state.

Fine, Melissa sighed. Iowa is a stunner. God, it's cold out here. Can we, uh, put a pin in this discussion? Look, yeah. Yes, I can spare her. Christ, you don't need my permission anyway, not really. But I appreciate it. I do. This way I can plan things out. Hopefully take some time off work. Or get a babysitter. So—yeah. Thanks. And thanks also for the wine. That was completely over-the-top. But beautiful. Okay, can we please go back inside now?

She switched off the light, and they returned to the warmth of that little home.

After dinner he helped Vivian clean the dishes. Since he didn't know where anything was stored, it was decided he should wash and rinse, and she would dry. They stood close together at the sink. They didn't speak but that was okay. There was a pleasant quiet in the house. The girls were exhausted. Out in the living room, the television droned on. Maybe they'd fallen asleep out there, in the blue wash of the flashing screen.

Thank you, he said, for inviting me over.

She kissed him on the lips, held his face below the jaw, rubbed his earlobes between her fingers. He wanted to return her touch, but his hands were sudsy and wet.

Will you come home with me? he asked. I think everyone's asleep here.

She returned to drying dishes without answering him.

It's all I want for Christmas, he said softly, slyly.

I got you something anyway, she said.

You didn't have to do that. Honestly, Vivian.

I wanted to, she said. Anyway, I hope…

You hope what?

Nothing, she said, glancing down. Anyway, let me get it. Your present.

She left the kitchen. He turned on the sink and filled a glass with cold water. Drank the water down. It was warm in the house. Warmer than he ever kept his own home. That smell was there too, though he didn't want to think about it, coming up through the vents. He propped the window over the sink open just a bit, enough to let in a little stream of cold air.

Here, she said, a thick present in her hands, all wrapped up in handsome red paper and tied with a neat green bow.

It looks big, he said, whatever it is.

She perched on a chair while he shook the box, chewing at her fingertips, like she was nervous.

Should I sit down too?

No, she said, you stand. You'll want to stand.

He opened the package to discover in his hands a beautiful camel jacket. He held it to his nose, and the jacket did not smell like the house, but only her. Only her soaps and shampoo and whatever lotion it was she wore. He allowed the length of the jacket to relax and fall, and though he knew it was somewhat gauche, he looked at the label near the collar.

Burberry, she said, helpfully.

Well, even I know that brand, he said, raising his eyebrows. But, Viv—how did you…? His voice trailed off.

I found it, she explained, clearly pleased with herself. At a resale store. They must not have known what they had. And here she allowed herself the softest of laughs. I was so, so thrilled. Come on, you have to try it on.

He slid his arms gently into the sleeves, preparing himself for the fact that the jacket, by all rights, should not fit. But it did. It fit perfectly. He'd always wanted a camel jacket.

It smells like you, he said.

She stood, kissed him again on the lips. Yeah? she whispered in his ear. Well, I slept with it last night.

This, he decided, was the sexiest thing a woman had ever said to him. Ever done for him.

He whispered back in her ear, Please?

She withdrew, gently, and studied him, his face.

Please, what? she asked, smiling.

Please, he said again. Please come home with me. There is something I'd like you to see.

He reached for her hands, and they stood that way for a moment. Then she nodded, and said, Let me get some things. Go warm up your truck.

Before he left the house, he peered into the living room. Melissa was asleep on the couch, both girls snuggled beneath her arms. The television was still on. He stole into the room, in his new jacket, reached for the remote control, and shut the screen off, then blew a kiss at the girls and their mother.

———

They drove to his house in companionable silence, holding hands. The headlights caught snowflakes in their projections. Big slow-falling snowflakes. He parked the truck outside of his house, and when she began walking to the door, he smiled.

Hey now, he said. There's something I want to show you. Over here. Come on.

They walked to the barn beneath a festival of swirling snowflakes. Inside, he flicked on a long bank of lights. The old building smelled of hay and of horses. She looked at him. At his face. Just like a girl on Christmas morning surprised by some gift she had thought entirely unreachable, unobtainable, if not almost unimaginable. Much of her life, in fact, she had imagined just this. Just this barn, just the sound of a horse greeting her, those low nickering and huffing sounds.

Come on, he said, this way.

At the horse's stall she reached her hand beneath its muzzle and nuzzled her head against the animal's thick neck. She ran her hands from poll to withers, and he stood back, leaning against the old cedar post of the next stall, which was empty.

Where'd she come from? Vivian asked.

Montana, he said quietly. I have a friend out there putting his ranch up for sale. Wanted to sell his favorite horses to a few good homes. He wasn't so sure about selling her to me, I should add, but then I mentioned you, and he came around. Said he had a special mare that might be okay with a big trip east.

What's her name?

Shelby. On account of that's where his wife was born. Shelby, Montana.

Vivian rested her head against this sweet animal's neck again.

The wife died then? she asked.

No, he said quietly. But she's got Alzheimer's. I guess she knew for a little while but didn't say anything. Knew they'd have to sell the ranch. Move into the city. She was a country girl, through and through. Lorna is her name.

You knew her? Sorry, you know her.

Yeah, Garth and I worked together on the railroad. She ran the ranch while he was gone. Brilliant woman. And tough as nails to boot. We used to like to shoot clay pigeons when I visited. I never bested her. Not once.

I'm sorry, she said. Sorry to hear about your friend.

She'd be happy to know that Shelby was here. That you'll take care of her.

She turned to face him, said, You're such a different man, Charlie, than you ever were.

I was a boy then. He shrugged. I wish I could do it all over again. Wish there were a way to go back and make different decisions. You and Lorna, you would have been friends. Maybe we would have traveled together like some couples I know. Taken trips to Europe, or Alaska. Stayed out at their ranch.

She ran her hands along the horse's muzzle one last time and then took his hand, and they walked into the cold, quiet house, slowly summiting the stairs to his bedroom, and on this night, they fell asleep quickly, exhaustion overtaking them at once.

20

She awoke before dawn. The eastern horizon painted in pale pink and peach. She'd left her change of clothes and her toiletries in the truck before he showed her the horse the night before, so she dressed in the same clothes and quietly made her way through the house. The old dog followed her outside, relieving himself in the snow and then pressing against her hip as they walked together to the barn.

Good morning, sweet man, she said to Blueberry, happy for the dog's company, scratching behind his ears. He stretched and yawned in satisfaction.

In the barn she found Shelby standing, waiting for her. She rubbed the creature's muzzle for a long time, breathed in her scent, whispered sweet nothings to her. She refilled her water, fed her some oats, and then walked back out into the cold.

For a man who seemingly knew next to nothing about horses, Charlie had done his due diligence. There was a ten-acre pasture all properly fenced with a feeder and a cattle trough, both of which looked to be brand-new. The water of the trough gave off a ghostly cloud of steam, and as she approached it, she saw that he kept the water free of ice with two electric heaters, their long orange extension cords running through the snow.

Morning, he said from behind her. You're up early.

He gave her a big hug from behind, held her close. The sun was rising now. The dog peered up at their faces.

What do you know about horses? she asked him.

Not much, he admitted. But there's a neighbor girl who does. She comes over every day after school. Brushes her out. Mucks out her stall. The deal is that if she helps me for three months, she can stable her own horse out here. I'm told they're social creatures.

She rested her head against his chest. The morning air felt sharp in her nose, in her lungs. I've got to get back, she said.

Do you?

I do.

But it's so far. Couldn't you stay? Just another day?

I know, I know. You must be tired of all this driving. But I do have to get back, I do. We'll plan it better next time. Maybe a whole weekend.

Or a week? he suggested.

He drove her back to Chippewa Falls, idled the truck at the curb outside her house, and she waved to him before ducking into the house. Immediately she felt too warm. Checked the thermostat: seventy-five degrees. She sighed, irritably, she might have admitted, and turned the dial back to sixty-two.

In the living room, Melissa was watching cartoons with the girls.

Vivian poured herself a mug of coffee and sat at the kitchen table, staring out the window above the sink into the backyard at a bird feeder perennially empty of seed. By and by her daughter joined her. Took her hands in hers, broke her melancholy reverie.

You all right, Mom?

Oh, I'm fine. I'm fine.

You must be all right, Melissa said with a smile. You spent the night. Her comment had the quiet curiosity of a question. She ran her fingers over her mother's hand gently, massaged the palms.

Hmm, that feels nice, she admitted.

So it was all right?

He bought me a horse.

Get out.

She shook her head slowly. I really couldn't believe it either. Beautiful horse.

Well, where are you going to keep it? How are you going to feed it?

Oh, she sighed, I think he's going to handle all that.

Mom, she said excitedly, really? But that's great, isn't it?

She nodded, stared into her coffee mug. I think he wants me to move out there. She looked up at Melissa. She was surprised to see that her daughter wasn't offended or surprised.

Well, she asked, is that what you want?

I don't know. This all just feels like it's moving very fast. There's a lot to consider. Jessie for one. I don't know how I feel about living somewhere else. Feels like I'd be leaving her.

Mom, you wouldn't be leaving her. You'd still visit her. I know you would. And she's a woman. She has her own life. If you missed her that much, you could move back. Or ask her to move up there with you.

I don't know. I haven't even told Charlie about her yet.

Well, yeah, Mom. That's overdue. Don't you think?

Vivian didn't respond. Took a nervous sip of her coffee.

Mom, I don't get it. Are you happy?

Yes.

And you like him? You trust him?

She felt herself smiling, felt herself blushing.

Then…what do you want? Something different? Something worse? I wish I had someone in my life that was so nice to me.

But what about you and the girls?

Melissa pushed away from the table just a bit, glanced in the direction of the living room. I mean, we'd definitely miss you, she said, but—look, in a year, Ainsley will be in school full-time. Both girls are going to need us a lot less. I can find something for Addison. The truth is, we've been spoiled, having you. All your help. And it's not like you'd be moving to Hawaii. You could come over whenever you want. Listen to me; I can't expect you to make all your decisions based around us. That isn't fair. If I'm being honest, I can't believe you've helped this much.

Vivian swallowed, focused her eyes on the table, held the mug as if it were a wooden fence post, something solid. Now that the notion of leaving this house and her daughter had been established as a possibility, she was not even sure she could. Or wanted to. Because then what? Just Charlie. And his big house. How much of her life would be directed by his manic romantic energy, his money? What if all this blew out just the way it had somehow rekindled? Was she prepared for that disappointment? To move her things into his house only to move them back out again? And even if it did work, would his house ever feel like her house? Her place?

She stood somewhat abruptly from the table and walked to the sink. Held the edges of the stainless-steel sink and gazed at that sad little wintry backyard. A frayed wind sock swaying with the wind.

Mom? Melissa asked. Mom, you okay?

Yes, she replied, because she knew she should. That was the word she was supposed to say. But all she could think about was time. How much time had passed. In her life. And what time was ahead of her? How much easier was it not to change at all, to simply dwell in the comfortable little eddy time had carved away for her in this old river town? Or was there something to letting go? Letting go and drifting into the current, down and away from that eddy and into gliding waters she could not predict.

21

Two weeks after Christmas, Melissa called him. He was surprised at first, then tickled. Until he heard the jagged edge in her voice. She was not all right. Something was wrong.

Can I drive up to your house? she asked. I just need your help, Charlie, and I don't have anyone else to ask. Please.

Well, I mean, he stammered, you've got your mom, don't you? You've always got your mom, Melissa. It's an hour's drive up here. At least forty-five minutes. You know—

No, she said forcefully. Just you. I can explain more when I'm there. Okay, I'm coming over.

Before he could say anything, even bye, the line was dead and his brain buzzed with curiosity, with dread. So this must be what it was like, being a parent.

The house was always some semblance of immaculate; still he set about tidying up. He polished the granite surface of the kitchen island until it shone like a mirror. He cleaned the first-floor toilet and sink. Gave the entryway and living room a good vacuuming. Then there was nothing more to do but pace the house, occasionally walking to the front windows to stare down the length of his driveway. The day was overcast, and out in the field, snow was collecting on the horse's back, like the crest of an old ridgeline.

She arrived in less than an hour, and the moment he opened the front door, she fell into his arms. He was not sure what he had expected, but this was not something he had even considered. He was slow to return her hug, but then he did, rubbing her right shoulder blade gently. The young woman was sobbing. Really sobbing. He could feel his shirt growing damp beneath her face.

Hey now, he said gently, come on. Let's sit down. Tell me what's happening.

I'm sorry. I've been holding it all in. I didn't know who to tell.

His back was turned to her as he led them towards the kitchen.

I'm pregnant, she said.

He could hear that she had stopped following him. Was standing still in the hallway. He turned back to her. He didn't know what to say, so he remained quiet.

How far? he finally asked.

Two months.

But this isn't a good thing?

She shook her head no. Such a guy thing to say, she muttered.

I'm sorry, Melissa. I, uh—tell me how I can help you. Anything.

I just need your help for a weekend, Charlie. Drive with me over to Minneapolis. Then—I don't know. I guess I could check into a hotel for a few nights. Just until I can go back to work. Until I can be there for my girls. Look my mom in the face.

You're not going to tell her?

No.

What about the father?

She shook her head no.

Do you know who it is?

She bit her lip and looked at him.

Melissa, if you're hurt, or you didn't ask for this, you need to talk to the police. I can't. I mean, you have to—

It was stupid. I'm stupid, okay? I should—I should have known better. I shouldn't have... God, I just thought—I wasn't thinking. I just want to move forward. Because this is an impossibility. I need to stop this and move forward. Start over.

Do you have enough...? I mean, can I help out? Do you have enough money for everything?

I have enough. For the procedure anyway. Or the medication. The doctor. Whatever.

Fine. But then, if it's just the same to you, I'll bring you back here. You can recuperate here.

But my mom can't know, all right? She can't. I know that you two are...in love or whatever, and look, I think that's great. But if she knew that I did this, she'd never forgive me. She loves my kids more than she loves me, I think. And she especially loves babies. This would crush her.

Oh, come on now. I've never heard your mom say even the slightest negative thing about you. She adores you. This happens all the time, Melissa. Are you sure you don't want to tell her?

But you can see it from my vantage, can't you? I have two kids, neither of whose dads are around. I should be doing more. Working a better job. I have a college degree. I've had good jobs, good opportunities. Had a nice place in Minneapolis. Drove a nice car. I ticked off all the boxes. But I blew it. I always blow it.

She hung her head, hair falling over her face.

You're an alcoholic, he said quietly, like me.

She looked up at him but said nothing.

That was the wrong job for you, Melissa. You were way too close to the fire. That would be like me working for a brewery. A winery, or hell, a distillery.

I haven't drunk any of that wine you gave me. Not yet. It's— too fine. You gave me this amazing present, but it's almost too much. You're the only person I know—other than me—who'd even appreciate what they were drinking. So I'm holding out. Or maybe I will sell it. I don't know.

I shouldn't have done that. Shouldn't have given you that wine. It was like an O. Henry story, you know? I wanted you to be able to change your life, but I also wanted it to be a tough decision. It's not a virtue, but you get to be my age, and, well, sometimes a person forgets that a gift should be a gift. Not a lesson with a thousand strings attached.

Beautiful wines though.

He grimaced. Come on, let me make you some tea.

I think I want to quit drinking, she said. I can't keep doing this.

He looked at his feet, the floorboards. Maybe we can help each other, he said.

She looked at him. How? How are you gonna help me? I told you. I know booze. I know beer and wine. I know drinkers. And you, you're well beyond a normal drinker. Charlie, you know this, but most people don't have wine cellars.

He sat down beside her. Putting a little distance between them. Not so close that she might have been his daughter, but not so far away that they were strangers either. Their hands might easily have touched but didn't.

I love drinking, he said. I've always loved drinking. But it might be time for me too. I, uh. Well, I love your mother. And our first time around, the reason we broke up, it was my fault. My drinking. And I do not want that to happen again. But at the same time, I'm afraid it could.

Maybe, if we hadn't broken up, he thought, you would be my daughter. And it dawned on him. Maybe if I can hold this together, you will be my daughter. Maybe I could actually be your dad.

She loves you too, Melissa said now. But I think she's afraid.

Afraid of what?

She shook her head. I think she's afraid you'll come between her and me. Actually, between her and the girls is maybe more the thing. I think she feels responsible for us all. I don't think she trusts me. And I guess she's right not to.

Maybe you'll think I'm being hokey, Melissa, but I'm going to say it anyway. I'm not a religious guy, but...I think we all travel at different speeds. Like, back in high school, there were always those kids that were peaking right then.

Glory days.

Yeah. That was their peak. Can you imagine? Looking down from the top of the mountain, at the rest of your life, all the decades ahead, and knowing that none of it, not a day or night or moment, was ever going to be better than your prom? Some stupid football game? You and me—

And here he gently patted the side of her knee, dearly hoping that she would understand the touch just the way he intended: that he liked her, that he understood her, that he did not feel comfortable stretching his arm around her, or kissing the top of her head, as he would if she were his daughter, but that for now, this would have to do, this faintest of gestures.

I don't think we've peaked. Not by a long shot. I think our best days are ahead of us.

———

Two weeks later he walked her inside a clinic. A strange feeling. He was not her father, and yet there he was, parking the truck on an asphalt lot and escorting her towards the doors of the clinic. On the other side of a fence separating the clinic from a neighboring house was a tall yellow cross, right in the backyard, and a sign too. God loves you and your unborn child, the sign read.

163

He felt his blood pressure rise, and he placed his body between Melissa and that sign, Melissa and that cross.

He thought he understood Vivian's daughter well enough, or hoped he did. She was essentially alone. Two children already, yes. But she had no partner, not even an ex, to pick up some of the slack. To take the girls on weekends. Or help with groceries and gas, utilities and clothing. If there were child support payments coming in, they didn't amount to very much. There didn't seem to be such a man, but there must have been one once. And if he wasn't around now, Charlie assumed it was because the guy was in jail, or worse. He thought about her job. If he was reading between the lines properly, her work was no prize, and no guarantee either. There was drinking too. That much he didn't have to guess about.

For all those reasons, this was the right thing to do. Another reason too: it didn't matter what he thought. He held the door open for her.

Do you want me to come in?

No. It won't take long.

You sure? I don't mind.

I'm sure. I'll text if something changes.

———

They drove back east in silence. He was worried. Worried that she would weep. That however composed she was before or during the procedure, he would be ill-equipped to help her afterwards. That he wouldn't know what to say. He didn't know if there would be blood, so while she was inside, he laid the softest fleece blanket on her seat. A blanket of dark blue. He hoped that was okay. Dark blue was not pink, or baby blue. It did not suggest a gender or the color of some unpainted nursery wall. If there was blood, it would not show. He had offered her a pillow, but she said, No, thank you. Just tilted her eyes towards the fogging window.

He turned on the radio but was frozen by the sound of James Taylor's voice. Fire and rain. He didn't know how she would receive it just then, his music, which, at the lowest points in his own life, had always comforted him more than any holy psalm or verse. He reached to turn the radio off, but without saying anything, she caught his hand and turned the volume up, as if to fill all the space between them. Then, when the song ended, she reached back out, shut the radio off, and turned back to the window.

I don't know why I do these things, she said. I wish I didn't. I wish I was a better person. A better mom. She shoved her hands between her tightly clenched thighs and brought her feet up to tuck them beneath her bottom. Her entire body seemed coiled into its smallest possible form.

He turned towards her and touched her shoulder. We're almost there, sweetheart. We're almost home. He decided at that moment that he would think of her as his daughter. Even if he never told her. Never told anyone. He liked this private revelation. That he could love someone who did not even know they were loved by him. That this philosophy could extend to the limits of his life if he so chose. But with Melissa, he would simply safekeep that love within his chest.

When they arrived at his house, he showed her to a guest room looking out on the pond. He understood her need for this time. This was a break in her life, a fissure between past and future. He imagined the way in which lightning brands the wood of a tree. This was that moment, and he was to be her caretaker through it. He accepted this role with seriousness. She had come to him needing a place to heal, and that meant something. Meant she trusted him more than any friend she had never mentioned. More than her coworkers. In this one way at least, more than her mother. She must genuinely trust him, he thought. She must need him.

He shut the guest room door and then stood in the silence of the hallway. A few moments later, he could hear her. Her voice, feigning happiness, lightness. She was on the phone with her girls, pretending this horror she had endured wouldn't always be an invisible scar. And what could be worse than a scar no one would ever see? At least a person could grow proud of their scar. At least the scar was a story that might be shared. Some of the worst scars we inflict upon one another, he realized, were the invisible ones.

She was laughing now, but it must have been about the saddest laugh he had ever heard. Laughter that dissolved into crying so jagged she had to cover her mouth. Crying so pained that after a few moments, even her daughters detected that their mother was in pain. He imagined her being forced to collect herself, because he heard her sniffle, and then say, No, no, no. Mommy's okay. I just really miss you two. I love you. Okay, please say hello to grandma for me. And please be good for her. Okay then—bye, my babies.

He walked downstairs before he had to hear her collapse again.

He wasn't hungry, but he could imagine a drink. Could almost taste it. He closed his eyes. Pressed the lids down hard, like he was sealing off some nightmare reality. He could almost feel the basement steps beneath his feet, the light switch his right hand would flip, the air cooler down there, his hands on dusty green bottles, blowing on the old glass, reading labels slightly peeled away from their bottles, until he came to the bottle he knew would emcee, deejay, and cosign the whole evening. All the days of sobriety felt good, but he imagined them washed aside in the instant the wine touched his tongue, winding down his throat, coating his teeth, and hitting his body like a blush of purple heat.

She came down the stairs, mustering an exhausted smile.

He leaned against the kitchen island and tried to focus on her, the feelings she'd been contending with. He braved a smile.

I was thinking, she said. Well, like I told you, I want to stop drinking.

He nodded. But?

But not today.

Not today?

Not today. I think I want a glass of wine, if that's okay. Or two. I want to make a fire in that woodstove. And I want to be quiet and just look at the flames. And maybe that's wrong, but…that's what I want right now. That's what would help me get through this night.

Okay, he said. Well, I can't very well let you drink alone.

I'll be out there. In the living room.

You bet. I'll take care of everything. The couch is comfortable. Just relax.

She turned back to him suddenly. Should I feel guilty, Charlie? I don't want to feel guilty. I wish I could get drunk. But you won't let me, will you? You'll watch me. You understand what I want. Just—I just want the edge off. I want it all softened. Isn't that okay?

He sighed. I think it's okay. One bottle, between us.

Promise?

Promise. One bottle.

They sat in the velveteen darkness, on deep, firm new furniture, and let the fire's orange-red light wash over their faces. Blueberry lay on the floor, dreaming, his legs running him nowhere. From a turntable in the dining room, they listened to Dave Brubeck, then Miles Davis, then Bill Evans, then John Coltrane, the volume very low. They said not a word. And they fell asleep that way, their glasses empty, rimmed in the tiniest purple crystals.

Sometime after midnight he touched her shoulder, and she went to bed. When her bedroom door closed, he collected the glasses and carried them to the sink. He squeezed soap onto a sponge and began cleaning the glasses in the warm water issuing from the faucet. He closed his eyes and felt regret for opening the bottle. They didn't need the wine. And he was older. He could have suggested anything else. A walk. A cup of coffee or a sugary soda. Ice cream. A joint. Maybe even a cigarette. He needed to be stronger. She was leaning on him. Looking to him for guidance.

He lost his grip and the glass shattered against the porcelain of the sink, breaking in his hands, and then there was blood, swirling with the splashing water and twisting like a pinwheel down the drain. There was some pain too, but mostly more regret. He shut the faucet off and wrapped his hand in paper towels.

In the bathroom upstairs, he bandaged the hand and then stared at himself in the mirror. It was past midnight, and the entire day seemed at once a breakthrough and bad secret. He did not sleep well that night.

22

Something was off. Something didn't feel right. She couldn't say what exactly. But she didn't believe Melissa. Didn't believe that this was a girl's weekend, or time with her old friends in Minneapolis. Melissa would have talked about it a good deal more, and a good deal earlier. She would have worried about her clothing and shoes, about whether she had enough money. She would have picked up extra shifts at the bar, or even asked to borrow some cash. She most certainly would have gotten her hair done. But she hadn't done any of those things. When she hurried out of the house, it was like she was going to miss an appointment, not as if she were racing towards a cold glass of champagne and a hot Jacuzzi full of her laughing friends.

For their part, the girls did not notice. If anything, they were more relaxed without their mother. Perhaps because they knew their grandmother wouldn't ask them to clean their rooms or read a book, or the other maternal directives Melissa was keen on leveling at the girls. With the Saturn back at the mechanic's and

Melissa driving the minivan, they were somewhat stranded at home. Which suited Vivian just fine. They could all sleep in and enjoy a couple days hunkered down in the living room, popping corn, and watching movies. She was knitting a nice blanket for Charlie, and the completely unscheduled weekend would give her the time she needed to finish it.

She liked the quiet of knitting. The near mindless repetition of stitches. The rhythm of the needles. The fluidity of her fingers. Her warm place on a couch, a blanket pulled across her lap and one or both girls tucked beside her. She wondered if Charlie could ever imagine this intimacy. The way her grandchildren were always there with her. Their scents on her clothing. Their warm breaths in the morning. The things they said and asked. The ways in which they depended on her. All of it, so different than the responsibility of being a mother. The weight of being a mother.

Her role, thank god, was not to correct every bad behavior, to punish, or to monitor their educations. Her role did not even carry the burden of always being there, the way the parent should and must. No one demanded anything of her. She could give what she had when she had it. Though she didn't think of herself as old, there was recognition, especially in the past few years, that time was a growing shadow in every room. And she didn't need to think of this fact as a negative thing, or a threat, but as a reminder that these were sweet days, sweet moments, and she could stretch them out if she so chose. She could watch the girls as they slept. She could brush their hair and braid their hair and feel their backbones pressed against her chest and stomach. She sensed that there would be no more grandchildren, and in some ways, she hoped that was true, because what few resources they had were already tested. But sometimes she wished there might be. A new baby that she could cuddle with and bottle-feed. A new baby to hold in her arms. A new baby yawning and blinking up at her.

Charlie was not in town that weekend, he had explained. Something about visiting a great-aunt in Milwaukee. Still, she couldn't help herself. Texted him a few times. His replies were briefer than normal, but that was understandable. He and some other family members were cleaning out the aunt's house before she was admitted to a nursing-home facility. On Saturday night she called him.

Am I catching you at a good time?

Oh, sure, he replied. I, uh, I just got back to my hotel room actually.

Is it nice, the hotel?

Well, he said, somewhat clumsily, you know. Nothing fancy. I'm not staying downtown or anything. Just a place off the highway. My cousins are here too. With their families. There's an indoor pool. A continental breakfast. That kind of place. Anyway, how are you?

Oh, nothing exciting. The girls just went to bed. I was going to read a book.

A silence opened between them, and he cleared his throat, then yawned.

When will I see you again?

How about Wednesday night? he suggested. I could take you out for dinner. I've been hungry for Mexican.

She sighed, as if uncertain how to say what she wanted, then sighed again.

Or we could have Chinese. Pizza, he offered. Whatever you want. Afterwards maybe we could go back to my place.

No, Mexican is fine.

Viv, are you all right?

It's just—I'm probably crazy but, well, you wouldn't understand maybe, because you never had kids, but as a parent, you have this sense. She felt a twinge of regret just then, for holding her parenting over her knowledge of his lack of experience. She continued, This sixth sense. You just sort of know when your child is lying. Or withholding something. And, I don't know, but I think Melissa is lying to me about something. I can't remember the last time she's done that. I wouldn't even say anything to you, but I don't have anyone else to tell—

No, it's okay. I'm glad you're telling me.

I hate to say it, but she drinks too much. Always has. She hasn't done this in a long while, but when Ainsley was about one, she just left for a weekend. Didn't even tell me where she was going. Some guy just pulled up in front of the house one Friday night, and she jumped into his car, and I didn't see her again until Monday morning. We had this huge fight. About responsibility and being a good mom and how I was prepared to help her, but also how if I ever thought she was putting herself ahead of my grandchildren, or endangered those girls, or brought someone dangerous into our home, that I wouldn't tolerate it. And we haven't had a single problem since then. But—

I'm sure it's nothing, Viv. She works hard. Probably just needed a break, you know? Everyone does sometimes.

I hope you're right. But you don't know her the way I do. I love her so much, but...you never stop worrying about your kids, Charlie. No matter how old they are.

I'm sure you're right. Hey.

Yes?

I love you.

She chuckled. I love you too.

So, anyway, I'm going to bed now.

Okay.

Good night then.

Good night.

The phone call had done nothing to tamp down her suspicions. If anything, it felt like Charlie was just half listening when he wasn't dispensing pleasantries, or polite excuses. She shut off the remaining lights and moved into her bedroom, where she exchanged her clothing for a flannel nightgown as soft as a child's stuffed animal, and then slipped between her cold sheets, holding her phone to her chest.

She typed a message to Melissa, the screen glowing against the darkness in the room: Hope you're having a great weekend. Send pictures. Be safe. The message shot through the distance separating them, and she continued staring at the phone. Many minutes drifted past until there was a reply: All good, Mom. Thanks for your help. See you tomorrow night.

She did not sleep well. A worry scratched at her, a worry that came and went and then came right back again. The worry that her daughter's life might somehow become sidetracked, or even hijacked, that her drinking would grow out of hand, that the wrong man might derail everything, and it was no longer a matter of just Melissa's life, but her granddaughters'. Children needed continuity and comfort. Routine and reinforcement.

For the longest time, she lay absolutely still, listening to the faintest noises in the house and the neighborhood beyond it. The rare car driving past. The furnace kicking on in the basement and the subsequent breath of warm air. When no sounds found her ear, she focused on her hands resting above her heart. The steady rhythm there. Her pulse in the tender flesh of her ear against the cool of the pillow. Finally, sleep did come. But not as a relief, rather a surrendering.

23

In the morning, he came down the stairs to the kitchen to find Melissa drinking a glass of water. Look, it shouldn't be any of my business, he said as he fixed a pot of coffee, but you brought me into this, so I'm going to say it: your mom knows that something is up. Now, I can absolutely understand why you don't want to tell her anything, I really do. But have you considered it? You two seem like you've got a strong relationship. A good friendship even.

She was silent for a moment, standing there with the morning light slanting in. Blueberry nuzzled against her thigh, and she scratched him beneath his jaws.

I don't think she'll take it well.

Why? he asked. You and the girls are everything to her.

It's just that—she kept her eyes focused on the dog, kept her hands busy with the work of massaging the animal—it'll be confirmation that I'm a screwup. That I'm still making these mistakes and I'm past thirty years old. At some point, I'm afraid she's going to lose patience, you know? I guess I just haven't disappointed her enough yet. She laughed darkly. Then she shook her head. I mean, it's bound to happen someday, but so far, she hasn't left us. When that day comes, my reality is going to change quickly. But I'd rather just have her leave because she wants to, you know? I don't want it to seem like a breakup. Honestly, what I want is for her to move in with you. My mom and I are close, but there are still times she gets up in my business, and frankly, there are times I wish we had some space. A little distance between us.

All right then, I'm just saying: you'd better be prepared.

I know.

Because she's going to quiz you tonight. You know that, don't you? And she'll probably quiz me too.

She nodded. Yeah, she was already texting me, looking for pics. It's like, geez, c'mon, Mom.

Oof, he murmured. And what exactly were you supposed to be doing? A ladies' weekend?

Yeah. Look, I don't want to think about it. I don't want to think about her. Any of it. People lie all the time.

He studied her. How do you feel?

Not bad. A little sore maybe? A little nauseous. I can't tell if I should eat or not.

You're welcome to stay here as long as you need to. Just know your mom is going to send out the search parties if it's much past dusk.

I know, I know. I just…I want to regroup, or something. I wish I had more time. To come up with a plan.

Well, he sighed, can I give you a little advice?

Sure.

He inhaled deeply and considered where to begin. He had never told anyone what he was about to share with her now. But he suddenly felt very good, very light. He thought for a moment about what he was going to say, and then he said it.

Six years ago, I was working in Albuquerque. New Mexico. I loved it down there. Loved everything about it. The food. The climate. The people. It was the end of my career, and if I could have chosen anywhere to end things, I could not have chosen a better spot than New Mexico. Big clear blue skies. Mountains. I'd burn piñon pine in my woodstove every morning. There is only one reason I moved back here, but I'll get to that here shortly.

Anyway, it was my birthday. My fifth-eighth to be exact. All the guys I was working with took me out to this fine Mexican restaurant, and we were having a hoot. Sitting outside, in a court-yard all strung with white Christmas lights. The air was perfect, you know. A late spring evening, the sun going down later and later, and the smell of flowers everywhere.

Well, we got to taking shots of tequila. Not good tequila or cheap tequila but, I'm telling you, the great stuff. Shot after shot after shot. The truth is, teenagers count their shots. Real drinkers don't even want to know. And we had no idea. We're eating good food, there's a tres leches cake and singing, and everyone's having a great time, and the end of the night comes around, and we all get up and go to our cars, and the next thing I know, I'm sitting on the side of the road with police lights flashing everywhere.

Turns out, I crashed into a parked car. Must've passed out.

The airbag was all blown up. Broke my nose. Face all scratched up with the cracked windshield, bits of glass everywhere. I get hauled off to the county jail, and I spent the night there. And in the morning, I called my attorney, and I was out.

I was embarrassed. I began remembering things I'd said at dinner. Crass things. Dumb things. Felt kind of tortured by wondering what else I might have done wrong. Work didn't think it was funny, even if my lawyer could get most of it wiped away.

But the thing was, I realized that none of those guys loved me. They'd never love me. They might like me, as a coworker or as a boss, or maybe even, you know, as a guy. But they'd watched me get into the car at the end of the night. And they had most definitely tried to get me drunk. The more I thought about it, the worse I felt. I could have killed myself, yes, but worse than that, I could have killed someone else. I could have killed someone's mom. Could have hurt a kid.

That's terrible, Melissa said. They could have just, I don't know, called you an Uber or a taxi or something.

Yeah. That was the least they could've done. Now, I know I'm not their father or uncle or brother or close friend, but I was a person, and these folks just watched me get into my car. I mean, I was so drunk I fell over in the parking lot. They joked about it later when I came back to work. You were so drunk, man, you fucking tackled a cactus. I realized then that they thought the whole thing was funny. And it scared me. That this was what my life was. Those guys, they were my people. My family. And they didn't love me. And here I'm almost sixty years old, right? I don't have anyone. I'm a ghost before I'm even gone.

So I did this thing, this thing that a teacher of mine from back in high school once told us to do. Some iteration of it anyway. I thought about it, and I thought, You're fifty-eight years old, man. Who loves you? The top five people. And I thought about it, and I thought about it, and I realized that my parents are dead. Two of my brothers are dead. My aunts and uncles are gone. I don't even know where all my best friends from high school might have disappeared to... I thought about my whole life, Melissa, like I was rifling through my days as if they were files in a cabinet, and I'm looking for faces. For friends. And I could only think of two people, and one of those people was your mom. The other person was my friend Mona, but that's another story. I thought I could easily come up with five names, but in the end, I could only write down a few names.

And I knew, at that moment, that I had to find Viv. I had to find your mom. And I had to try to make things right. And I didn't even care if it wasn't quite meant to be. I was even prepared for the fact that she might be married again. That I'd find her, but I'd have to go out for coffee with her and her husband. I mentally prepared to like the guy, even if I wanted to hate him. I was prepared, or thought I was prepared anyway, if she didn't completely fall head over heels for me. Because I believed more than anything that I could be a good friend to her, a best friend even. If I didn't screw it up.

She sighed deeply, and then swept her arms wide and went to him, and then squeezed him, and he hugged her back.

So what do I do? she asked. Make a list. Top Five People Who Love Me? That's easy.

No. I think your list needs to be titled, Top Five Things I Want for My Life.

He poured them both mugs of coffee, and they sipped, quietly.

She looked at him, arms crossed. Not defiantly. Or angrily. But at that cusp, that brink of decision-making just before acceptance. That battlefield of doubt. She was there, and then, he could see the idea took, and she grasped it.

Top Five Things I Want for My Life?

I think so. I think you should go up to your bedroom and write them down. The Top Five Things I Want for My Life.

Oh my god, you sound like such a dad.

What he thought was, Thank you, my dear—sometimes I wish I were. What he said was, I'm serious.

Yeah, I know.

But you should do it. This is your opportunity. This, this is your low moment. You didn't want to do what you had to do, but you did it. And now you're here. And your mom is going to be expecting something from you. But you don't have to give her what she thinks is coming. You can give her something else. Something surprising and good. You can go back home and say, You know, after this weekend, I've decided I want to go into nursing. Or you can say, You know what, Mom? One of my girlfriends thinks I can get my old job back. My old job in Minneapolis. Or, Hey, Mom, it's not fair that you have to spend so much time babysitting my kids. I'm going to figure out childcare.

Okay, that's enough, Charlie. Enough dad lecture. I get it.

He held up his hands.

I guess coffee is your truth serum.

I'm sorry.

Don't be. I think I needed to hear that. Anyway, I'm the one who dragged you into this. I asked for your help. I really can't thank you enough.

It's just. I see so much of myself in you. So much so that, if I'm being honest, Melissa, I have to remind myself that there's no way you are my daughter. Because there are so many moments when I want that. When I'd like to be that person for you. A parent, a father. And I want to show you my mistakes so you can stop making yours. And I'm sorry your real dad isn't around.

Me too.

What happened to him anyway? Your father?

Oh, it's a long story. A long sad story. I don't like to think about it. She glanced down at her feet, at the floor. To be honest, the first few weeks you were back in town? You were probably wondering why you hadn't met me? Mom had never told me she was married before my dad, that she'd been divorced. She never said anything about you. Ever. So you just show up in town, and everything is so hot and heavy and natural between you, and then she just comes out with it one night, that you two were married, and it was like—a mind fuck. No, no, no. Not like that. I don't like that word—fuck—you know, commingling with my thoughts of you two. I mean, sweet, sure, definitely. Good for you both, but mostly, I mean, it was, like, a complete surprise. I mean, now that I know you, I wish you were my dad. Because my real dad was nothing like you. He was—she blew out a breath the way people do when they don't want to begin crying. He was really tragic. I don't know what else to say.

I'm sorry.

No. Not your fault. But like you said, here we are, and I'm telling you what's what.

Fair enough.

All right. So go up to my room and make my list?

Yeah.

She refilled her own mug and then was walking down the hallway towards the stairs when she turned quickly, like a teenager, on the pirouette toe of her foot, and said, Thank you.

You bet. No problem.

No. Everything. This whole weekend. Nobody other than my mom has ever done anything like this for me. And I truly appreciate it. I didn't know where else I was going to go. Who else I could have asked for help. I'll never forget it.

All right. Well, you're welcome. You're most welcome.

She turned and walked up the stairs, and all at once the big house felt not at all too big but, simply, filled with love. And in that moment, a memory came to him unbidden: A morning, many years before. Early morning, before dawn. Back in New Mexico. He was standing in the desert with a group of people from work watching a hot-air balloon inflate. He was just standing there in the cold, holding a paper cup of steaming coffee, watching a flame burn against the darkness, the colorful fabric of the balloon slowly inflating. That was how his heart felt now. That was how this house felt.

———

Just before dusk she came down the stairs with her single small piece of luggage. She'd done up her makeup and taken some time with her hair. He knew there must be a well of sadness within her, however well camouflaged for the moment, but she looked beautiful. And she was acting perfectly for that matter. Acting like this weekend had been just the trick. A rare reprieve with old friends in the big city. She gave him a hug, and when they separated, she handed him a piece of paper, folded three times.

Don't read it now. But later, okay?

I look forward to it. And hey, maybe there'll be some way that I can help you. Because I would if I could, and I still have some friends out there. Not many. And maybe not all in the right places. But—you never know.

That's right. You never do. Thanks again, Charlie.

Go on now.

Hey. Can I tell you something about my mom, please?

Sure.

She's like me. She doesn't think she deserves nice things. She's never had nice things. Never. So she's suspicious of them. Her whole life, I think, has just been dedicated to helping other people. Does that make sense?

Yes, it does. Thank you.

They hugged one last time, and he kissed her lightly on the cheek.

Good luck, he said.

She closed the door and walked out into the fading light of dusk towards the old minivan. He watched her sitting in the vehicle as it warmed up. Her eyes were closed but her lips were moving. He imagined she was trying to get her story exactly right.

———

Later that night, he unfolded the piece of paper and read her list:

TOP FIVE THINGS I WANT FOR MY LIFE

1. *I want to quit drinking.*
2. *I want to move to a big city. Minneapolis or Saint Paul. But maybe Milwaukee or Duluth or even Chicago.*
3. *I want to earn my MBA.*
4. *I want a job with benefits. I want two weeks of vacation, every year. I want to get my eyes checked and my teeth cleaned.*
5. *I want to see a glacier before they're all gone.*

24

She was too old to be swept off her feet, but these past few months, it felt like that was Charlie's goal. Only something began to trouble her. Or maybe trouble was too strong a word. She just felt constantly…overpowered? If they went out on a date, he always paid for dinner or their movie. He sent flowers once a week, like clockwork. They arrived on Monday mornings with the certainty of a newspaper subscription. When the delivery driver arrived at her house the first time, he had the look of a man arriving at the wrong address. And now, now he knew her name. Charlie was always coming over to their house to fix a loose doorknob or to shovel their sidewalks free of snow. She felt not just desired, which was lovely, but also, somehow, smothered. And yet, when she wasn't with him, her own life, their house, her daughter and grandchildren, all of that could feel suffocating too, in a completely different way. A smaller tighter way.

One night they were seated in a fancy restaurant in downtown Eau Claire. Everything was expensive. Pork chops for forty dollars. A steak for fifty. The prices confounded her. Where did all this money come from? She glanced around the dining room, and there were couples in their twenties and thirties sprinkled here and there, laughing casually in their chic clothing. Checking their phones. No one was gawking at the menu prices or excusing themselves to go someplace cheaper.

She shook her head, took a long sip of the twelve-dollar glass of wine she had ordered, and laughed softly.

What is it? he asked, leaning back in his chair.

I don't know, Charlie. Sometimes, I just don't understand.

Don't understand what?

I don't understand, well, where all the money comes from. I mean, where are all the jobs paying all this money? And why couldn't I ever find a job like that? What did I do wrong? Did I miss something? Some announcements in high school, you know, pointing me in the direction of a six-figure salary?

Now he took a sip of his ginger ale, glanced out the window, and laughed darkly.

What?

Is that really what you want to talk about?

She crossed her arms. Maybe.

You don't think it's always been this way?

Eau Claire? Chippewa Falls? Wisconsin? Where?

The world.

The world? How would I know?

Do me a favor. Take another sip of your wine.

She uncrossed her arms and brought the wineglass to her

lips. Took a sip. Set the glass down on the white tablecloth and considered the light of the tea candle between them. The dining room smelled wonderful, and she felt warm. Outside a light snow was falling, and couples walked down the sidewalks with their arms intertwined.

Okay, and now one more favor. This is very important. Take another sip of your wine.

Not that I'm complaining, but you're not even drinking, Charlie.

It was true. Lately, he found that a club soda on the rocks with a slice of lime somehow did the trick. Or almost did the trick. Even a ginger ale.

I know, he said. It's not easy for me, to be honest. But I'm trying. And hey, don't forget about my favor.

She couldn't help herself and smiled. Took another sip of wine. Below the table, she eased one foot out of her shoe and rubbed it against his calf.

You know what I think? Charlie asked.

That I should relax?

That you look incredible. I can't believe how lucky I am to be here with you tonight. That after all the years that went by and all the stupid decisions I made, that somehow, this is possible. You're the most beautiful woman in this restaurant.

Come on, she laughed, that's not true.

Yes. It is, he insisted.

You're not even looking. I could easily point to ten women who are most definitely prettier than me. She scanned the room. Okay, five or six anyway.

You're exactly right. I'm not looking. I don't need to look.

He reached for her hands.

Hey? he said.

What?

Don't worry about money, okay Viv? Don't worry about prices. Just—be here with me.

She withdrew her hands and worried the hem of the table-cloth. It's just that—I want to do something special for you.

Okay. You could kiss me.

She smiled. That's not what I meant.

He laughed. It is what I meant.

No, listen to me. You're always doing nice things for me. For my daughter. For the girls. Around the house. I want to do something for you. A surprise.

He took a deep breath, wiped his mouth on the cloth napkin, and said, I think I understand.

She had expected him to say something dumb. To make a joke. Something about sex. Or to run this conversation in a circle. To say that this, their renewed relationship, this date, all of it, was the surprise he was looking for.

You think you understand?

He nodded. If I was in your position, I might feel...a little bit...overwhelmed. Is that fair?

Well. Yes. It is.

And maybe you feel like the way things are going isn't fair? Like I'm somehow always in control?

She felt her face flush. The wine. This man. She turned to

189

the kitchen, a controlled chaos of hurried waitstaff and cooks, smoke, flames, plates held aloft, voices calling out orders...

She leaned across the table and took his face in her hands and kissed him. Kissed him like they were in some foreign city, in another country entirely, where there were no tethers tying them to these small Wisconsin cities, to winter and snow, to their houses, to the routines that acted like rails, directing their lives. It was all she could think of doing. His tongue tasted like sugary ginger. She sat back down.

Now he was blushing.

She reached across the table and held his face below the jawline. She thought about their first date, so many decades ago. He was so beautiful. So handsome. So trim. Such narrow hips beneath those wide shoulders. She thought about sitting on her bed in an old apartment after the date and releasing his belt, folding his blue jeans away from the zipper and pulling his pants down. She was embarrassed now, that what she remembered of their date wasn't the date at all, but how badly she had wanted to make love to him that night.

It was spring, she remembered that. Her bedroom window was open, and it had started raining just before they entered the old house where she rented a room. His skin was wet, but hot. She remembered how he rolled on top of her, pinning her arms to the bed, and kissing her throat until she thought she'd pass out, and then, still held in place, he teased her nipples, and kissed her ribs, and then began licking her pussy, and just before she closed her eyes, she looked out the window, and there was rain falling so hard it passed through the window screen and beaded on the white paint of the sill. And her hands, and her forearms. Cool rain. And she ran her hands down the hot skin of his back and tried to cool him off, but she could not. Then he pulled the blankets over them, and the air smelled of lightning, and damp soil, and lilacs.

Did you ever think about me? he asked.

She was still back in that bedroom, back in that vivid earlier time, but his voice called her up, moved her through time and back towards the present, into the dining room. She looked at him. She did not mean to, but she bit her lip.

He had asked a well-meaning question, but it was the sort of question a person asks who doesn't remember their transgressions, their shortfalls. It was an innocent question, a selfish question. And instead of thinking of their first date, and those moments of promise, when everything that lay ahead of them was unknown, or better yet, brightly imagined, it reminded her of the opposite. Of all the years that separated their first date, the first year of their marriage, and now. Those forty years of disappointment and hurt.

You broke my heart, she said at last. What we had—especially at first—it was the best I ever had. You were my husband. I worshipped you.

He looked down at his lap.

I know we were young, Charlie, but everyone was. And other couples, they made it. Some of our friends from back in those days, they made it. I see their pictures on Facebook. Their grandkids. The vacations to Florida. Their lake cabins. We could have done it too. There didn't need to be a forty year break.

Those last two years of our marriage...you were awful, Charlie. Awful to me. Every night I went to bed, and I prayed for you. I prayed for us. I was still religious back then, you know. I used to make you go to church sometimes. God, you hated that. Near the end, you made a show of being hungover in church. Can you imagine that? How that made me feel? Sitting beside my drunk husband in church while he snored?

He closed his eyes and ran his hands through his hair.

After our divorce, I stopped believing. You know, I took our vows seriously. I thought that god would protect us, protect our marriage. I asked him for help so many times, Charlie. When you didn't come home at night. When some bar would call me to come pick you up. When you'd come home, but you'd bring two other guys. Guys I didn't know. Drunk guys, Charlie. Sometimes, I didn't feel safe. Strangers. In our house. I used to go into our bedroom and lock the door and pray that no one would try the knob, because I didn't know if it would be them or you.

He sighed, glanced out the window, across the street.

Sometimes, I don't know what to feel, she said.

What do you mean?

I mean, I'm sixty-four years old. What am I doing? What are we doing? What are we supposed to do? Get married again? Move in together? I mean—

Their waiter seemed to have swooped beside the table without any warning and now stood between them, a plate balanced in either hand, an ill-timed and unknowing smile animating his very young face. Here is the gnocchi for the lady, he said. And for the gentleman, the porterhouse, medium rare. Anything else I can do for you at this time?

They sat quietly, looking at their plates as if they had never ordered the food in the first place. As if this food was an uninvited intrusion.

No, thank you, she said. Everything looks just lovely.

The waiter nodded and disappeared. The volume of the dining room rose. Neither of them reached for their utensils, but by and by she did manage to reach shakily for her wineglass and bring it awkwardly to her lips.

Charlie sighed before clearing his throat. He stood, and set his napkin in the seat, and she assumed that he was retreating. That he was marching to the bathroom to reassess all of this, what they had been working to rebuild these past many months. Part of her wanted that. For him to go away, and for things to return to how they had been. Peaceful. No surprises. No great heights from which to fall.

But then he was standing next to her and lowering himself to his knees.

What are you doing? she asked.

He was looking up at her, and he was not exactly crying, but his eyes were moist, and they were scared too. She could not remember the last time she had seen a man look that way. Like he was on the verge of losing something, something incredibly dear. Like he was on the verge of losing everything. Like he was afraid.

Vivian, he said, I am sorry. I am sorry for anything and everything I did to disappoint you, and to hurt you. I am sorry that I was an alcoholic. That I am an alcoholic. I am just so sorry that I did not realize that I could lose you. I am so sorry for everything. And I don't know how to convince you that I'm not still that man I was. But I'm not.

The dining room, which only a moment before had been loud with laughter and the music of cutlery on porcelain, ice cubes against glass, all of those sounds dimmed down, and she was aware that people were watching them, watching him.

I love you so much, he said. I love you so much, Viv, and I hope you love me too. I hope that, however it looks, we are together for as much time as we've got left. And if you don't love me, I won't like it, but...I'll understand. And I'll still be a good friend to you if you want. I'll still come running, any time you ask.

All the ways I treated you back then? All the ways I hurt your feelings? I'm here now to do the opposite. I'm here to try to make you happy. I'm here to try to make your life easier, not harder. Sometimes I just wish you'd let me. I wish you'd just relax and trust me. Mostly, though, I just want to say to you that I'm here to try my best and love you the way you deserve.

She did not want to, but she began crying. She realized that he had taken her hands in his and was now looking at her face with the hopefulness of a boy. She leaned down and kissed him.

The dining room, which had been frozen in confusion and curiosity, returned to a normal volume level, normal activity, but a few tables were pointing at them and smiling, giving them the thumbs-up sign.

They think I just proposed, don't they?

She could only nod her head and laugh.

In which case, I can kiss you, right?

She nodded again, laughed again, and he kissed her in a way she felt deeply, a way that conveyed to her that he meant everything he had just said. The kiss was soft enough to be exploratory and timid. Soft enough that it might just be from a friend experimenting with the boundaries of friendship. But long enough, and desperate enough, that she knew it could only mean love. That this man was very much in love with her and meant every word he had just said.

The young waiter showed up again, beaming, holding a slice of cake with a sparkler garishly glowing golden. Compliments of the kitchen, he said. Congratulations.

They looked at each other and smiled. Thank you, they blurted out, laughing.

25

One morning there was a knock on his back door. Blueberry rose lazily from his spot on the kitchen floor and pretended the part of a guard dog as he trotted to the back of the house, barking lackadaisically a few times before stopping to stretch, yawn, and then collapse on a new patch of cool wood flooring.

So fearsome, Charlie said, scratching the dog's head as he made his way to the door.

It was Vivian, holding what appeared to be a picnic basket.

He gave her a kiss and held the door open. She rubbed at Blueberry's head and then moved into the kitchen and set the basket down.

I can't believe you drove all the way up here. To what do I owe this surprise?

I just thought that, with the nice spring temperatures today, maybe we could go for a little drive. It's what old people are supposed to do, isn't it? Scenic drives?

First, we're not old, he said going to her and wrapping his

arms around her waist. I've never used a senior-citizen discount in my life. Secondly, I'm occupied for the moment. Unless you want to go upstairs? he suggested, raising an eyebrow.

Yeah, well, no. Come on. No funny business. I don't want to dillydally. I've got a plan for us.

Fine. But I'm going to drink my coffee. And do Wordle.

I already finished. Took me two.

I saw that. You must have cheated. Or gotten help from Melissa. Who do I have to help me here? Blueberry? Sweet dog, but useless when it comes to Wordle.

Oh, you're not useless, are you? she said, rubbing the dog's head and scratching below his muzzle.

So they sat that way, for a half hour or so. Charlie at the kitchen island, sipping his coffee, staring at his phone, intermittently reading a newspaper article, or flipping to a Sudoku puzzle. Outside, the morning brightened and brightened some more.

You're a very...deliberate Wordle player, she said.

Well, I mean, I've got twenty-four hours. Why not use it?

It wasn't really that hard a word.

I'm so close, he said pensively.

Since you are otherwise occupied, I think I'll go visit Shelby, she said. I feel bad I can't see her every day, but...come out to the barn when you finish. She gathered up her light jacket and then stood in the doorway. It's so strange, she said, quietly.

What?

Just that, when we were married—you know, forever ago—I

could have never pictured you this way. Sitting. Working puzzles. Not saying a word. You were always talking back then. Or yelling. I think silence used to make you nervous or something.

He did not care to darken the morning, or the easy loveliness of the moment, so he only smiled, but for some reason, he internalized her words, and rolled them over and over, like worrying a river stone in his pocket, and he realized that she was of course right.

That rightness did not surprise him. But what did surprise him was the sudden depth of his memory. As if he'd just dived very deep into a cold, clear northern lake, where his oldest memories lived near the bedrock, near some ancient resting sturgeon in its safest place, and he remembered that in his childhood, when his father was very drunk, he often grew terribly quiet, and he would sit in his chair, silent, until without any warning at all, he would fly into a rage, angry at the most inconsequential things. A pot left on the stove with cold soup. A counter sticky with sugar. A cupboard door left open. Oh. The number of nights when he slammed those cupboards, a few times with Charlie's young hand in the space before the door shut... He shook his head and recentered himself in the present. Focused on Wordle.

There. Got it in five, he said with some satisfaction. Arrow. Those double letters always trip me up.

Five. That's not bad, Vivian said, smiling victoriously and bouncing her eyebrows. I mean, it's not two, but...

He rose and went towards her slowly.

Oh, now you'll pay attention to me? she said. No, I'm going to check on the horse. Be ready in twenty minutes.

They packed a green thermos of coffee, Vivian's picnic basket, and a backpack with a thick Faribault blanket.

You sure you don't want to take my truck?

I'm one hundred percent sure, she said. Then you'd be in control. Today, you're my passenger.

Will you at least tell me where we're going?

No. I won't. I want it to be a surprise. What is it you're always telling me? Relax? So great. Relax, Charlie. I've concluded this is my only choice with you. If I decide where we're going, it has to be kept a secret. Otherwise, you're liable to take control.

He did as he was told and leaned back in the old battered passenger seat of Vivian's Saturn to survey the countryside blurring past.

How's Melissa doing? he asked, after some time had passed.

Vivian turned and glanced at him briefly, then returned her eyes to the road. She's good. She was a little weird a few weeks back. I couldn't put my finger on it, exactly. I thought maybe she was lying to me about something. A new boyfriend maybe. Or drinking too much. But now I notice she's been looking at colleges. And places in Saint Paul. Minneapolis too.

Places? he asked, playing dumb.

Vivian's voice cracked with reserved sadness, but she replied, Oh, apartments, I guess. I suppose it makes sense. Better jobs there. Better money. More opportunities, I suppose.

He reached for her hand. It must be hard for you, he said. I'm sorry.

I didn't mean to—she indicated her eyes, the unbidden

tears—I didn't mean to be sad. But it's been on my mind. I don't know where I'll go, or what I'll do. I can't imagine having to drive to go visit my granddaughters. She shook her head.

Maybe you could go with them? he suggested. I mean, if I'm being honest, that wouldn't be my first choice. But I'd understand. I'd completely understand.

I don't think so. I think this is partly what I was hoping for Melissa. That she'd feel confident enough to go out and make her own way. I can't just tag along now that she wants to be free, to be on her own.

She pulled the car to the side of the road. The middle of nowhere. For early spring, the sunlight was bold and bright, and in the ditches, and down the faces of the fields, meltwater ran freely. There was no traffic. He unbuckled his seat belt and leaned towards her, allowing her head to rest on his shoulder while he offered an awkward hug. He tried his level best to say nothing, simply to be there for her. A sounding board.

He held her and wanted to say that he loved her more for a moment like this. For trusting that he was there for her now, in a way no one else was or could be. She must have trusted him to show this side of herself, this vulnerability. How strange, to feel the intensity and size of your love expand in the face of so much sadness and uncertainty.

Come on, he said, let me drive. You can relax and tell me all about it. I want to hear everything.

She sat up straight, wiped her cheeks, and gave him a mock-fiery look. Oh no, I promised myself that you wouldn't drive today. This isn't your date. It's mine. Besides, you don't know where we're going.

Fine, but I offered.

You're always offering.

Well, I'm a nice guy, Viv.

———

Less than an hour later she parked the car in an abandoned parking lot surrounded by jack pine, oak, and white pine.

Haven't been here in forever, he said with some wonderment.

Me neither, but today, I don't know. Maybe this will sound strange. But I felt like the place was calling me.

She stood beside the car, holding the picnic basket, closing her eyes against the warmth of the sun, and holding her face upward, toward the light, the way he imagined a flower might. The sadness looked to have passed, and he wanted to go to her, and kiss her, but he just stood there, looking at her, appreciating her.

Do you hear it? she asked. The waterfalls?

He closed his eyes, too, and focused on the sounds around them. Blue jays cutting from treetop to treetop, distant traffic, the wind blowing through the high boughs of trees. And then, the susurration of unseen water.

He could see the waterfalls as he had, so many decades ago, when he had come to this place, long before he met her. When he was a boy on the hottest days of summer and his aunt would pile so many cousins into the back of a station wagon and they would race down the foot-worn paths to the scramble of rocks and the crashing, surging water, there to find safe pools to frolic in, to cool down, to splash.

How he interacted with the waterfalls differently as he aged. From an innocent boy escaping heat and the tedium of summer boredom, to a teenager smoking cigarettes and drinking beer, and later, visiting with girlfriends, holding each other tightly against the pressure and flow of the water, skin slippery, skin hot, skin forbidden...

He ran a hand over his face. The last time he was here with her, he was very drunk, throwing empty bottles into the river and jumping from outcropping to outcropping, scaring her, pretending to lose his balance. She had been so upset, so afraid, she packed their things and sat in the car, fuming. He shook his head, shook away the memory. He was momentarily conflicted by the desire to be free of that memory, indeed free of that old iteration of himself, and the knowledge that he was here now with the power to be different and better because of those old mistakes. The membrane between the present and the past was thin for him today. Memories swirling like ghosts. He shook his head.

I hear it, he said quietly.

She took his hand, and they walked down the broken path, beneath sheltering tree limbs, the wind always more forceful closer to the river, and the air wet with what water was carried above the violence of the falls.

When the forest opened and he could see the river for the

first time, and the waterfalls, and the rapids, and the ancient rock, he squeezed her hand and kissed her cheek.

Thank you. I didn't know that I needed to come here. But I did.

You're welcome. Let's find a place in the sun.

They settled on a flat rectangle of water-smoothed stone, the midday sun toasting them benignly. Downriver two fishermen sat on empty white plastic buckets, smoking cigarettes. Overhead, eagles circled lazily. Now and then, the shadow of a passing stranger, or passing strangers, caused them to sit up and say hello. He lay on his back, and she rested her head on his stomach. He ran his fingers through her hair.

You haven't asked me many questions about the time after our divorce, she said. In fact, you've never asked anything about Melissa's father.

I guess I just figured when you were ready, you'd tell me. Or that maybe it wasn't the best time, and you didn't much want to talk about it. I've never heard either of you talk about him. Well, that's not entirely true. He did come up one time with Melissa. But she didn't want to talk about him. And you don't even have any pictures of him in your house. Also, back when we were married, I know I had a short fuse, but I could also get jealous. And I didn't want to bring that kind of energy or emotion to what we're trying to do, you know, now. But it doesn't mean I haven't wanted to ask. I've definitely wanted to ask.

What we're trying to do?

Yeah, he said smiling, our courtship, so to speak. This, you know, second courtship.

You've been courting me then?

Yes, I've definitely been courting you. Or is that out of style these days? Is that sexist? Because I could use another word. We've been chillin', I guess.

It's an old word, she said, looking off towards the fishermen. But I like what it implies.

What's that? Courtship? What does it imply to you?

That you respect me. That you're taking your time. That you don't feel entitled to an outcome.

Well, I'm definitely hoping for an outcome.

Hmmm, she said, leaning towards him, towards their kiss, I see good things ahead.

Their lips separated, but for a long moment he felt her eyelashes against his cheek, which was an exquisite sensation, more intimate even than a kiss, like a butterfly alighting on his face, or a hummingbird fluttering beside his ear. He closed his eyes and filed that feeling away in his memory, a bit wistfully.

It wasn't a good time, she exhaled, and we were married for a long, long time, Roy and me. Twenty-two years, actually. After you, after our divorce, I was single for a while, I guess it was maybe two or three years, and then I met Roy.

He was so different than you, and in the beginning, that was refreshing. He was steady. He was a mechanic. Owned his own shop. That's one thing I remember about him. His hands were always oily, always greasy, and there was a sink in his garage, in his house, where he used this soap, with pumice in it, and he'd scrub his fingers and hands and forearms until they were almost raw. The soap smelled like oranges. Early on, he was very conscious of that. Of how he smelled and looked. His fingernails.

I got pregnant with Melissa before we were even married. My parents pushed us to get hitched though. Our wedding day was very simple. There was a little ceremony at the courthouse in Chippewa. My parents were our witnesses. Afterwards they took us out to dinner, and when we came home that night, I don't know... It just felt immediately different. God, maybe it's awful for me to say this, but it felt like he stopped trying. Like he stopped trying the minute he could.

Charlie pulled her even closer to him. Against the sometimes cool of the wind off the river and the benevolent spray of the river water.

He wasn't like you at all. He wasn't spontaneous or fun. He wasn't, I don't know, sensual or romantic. He didn't even really talk a lot. We were just, I don't know, partners. He was never mean to me, or abusive, but over time, he just talked less and less, and then he had his accident, and everything got worse.

God, it was terrible. He was at his shop one day, and you know those hydraulic lifts they use for propping cars up, so mechanics can work underneath? Anyway, there was a malfunction or something, or maybe someone even did it on purpose, we could never find out, but basically, a car dropped, and hit his head. Cracked his skull open.

She shook her head. No tears. Just a dry, windblown, desolate memory.

He should have died. That would have been the humane

thing, the compassionate thing. For all of us. But he was taken to a hospital, and they somehow saved him.

He was never the same, Charlie put in.

No, she said, shaking her head again, glancing up at the sun. No, he wasn't.

But you didn't leave him.

No. I couldn't. I just, couldn't. He was older than me, and his family—well, they were awful. They never visited. Never thanked me for anything. I couldn't leave him alone. So I did everything. I'd wake up in the morning, get Melissa and—get her ready and off to school, make his breakfast, and then go to the shop, and even though I didn't know anything about cars, I did my best. He had a couple of employees who helped me for a long time. Good guys.

For a few years I'd take him with me to the garage, like I was taking a kid, or a dog, but he wasn't always appropriate, you know? Or polite. The accident changed his brain, and sometimes he'd shout at customers. Or laugh at their beat-up old cars. It was demoralizing. Like we were all part of this charade to try and somehow keep his life together, but there was no point. He was never returning to normal.

Eventually, the business went under. I just couldn't keep up. One of the mechanics retired, and then it just became too much. I couldn't leave him home alone, so I worked nights and weekends, and that's what kills me. Melissa had to be with him, you know? Like a babysitter. They'd watch movies together or whatever, and she'd call me at work if he was confused or wanted to leave the house.

Now Vivian began to quietly cry, and he held her very tightly.

You didn't do anything wrong, he said. you were doing your best. Doing what you thought was right.

I shouldn't have done that to her. Shouldn't have asked her to do that. She was just a kid. Watching this—this man. And it was her dad, sure, but she'd have to help him in the bathroom and, you know, help him with his clothes sometimes. I shouldn't have done that, shouldn't have done that to her.

She covered her head with her hands and began sobbing. Some kids standing on shore pointed at them, and Charlie held up a hand to let them know that everything was okay, but it didn't look okay, he was sure of that.

How could I have asked her to do that? How could I have asked her to watch him? Her own father? No kid should have to do that.

She wiped her face, but it was evident she was tormented by that time, all those years of helplessness, of trying to do the right thing without knowing precisely what that meant. Of feeling trapped. Of wanting more for her daughter.

She just kept shaking her head, like every thought she conjured, every memory that arose was painful.

When he passed away, she sighed, it was a tremendous relief. Melissa was seventeen. Someone would say, some doctor now would say that it wasn't so much relief as PTSD. Or that I had been in shock for years. Because I just wasn't there for her. I couldn't be there for her. I was just—exhausted, you know? That's the biggest regret of my life. And it's this huge long regret that

I can't even parse. I regret marrying him, yes, but then he's also the reason I had Melissa. And he wasn't a bad man. He was, well, he was my husband.

I'm sorry, he said again. But, hey. Hey, look at me now.

She turned her face towards his.

You did the best you could, Viv. You kept your family together. You didn't abandon anyone. You tried as hard as you could.

Then he held her as tightly as he could. And they stayed that way for a long time, until the midday sun dipped towards the treetops and the afternoon cooled and the fishermen packed up their buckets and rods and tackle boxes and disappeared into the shadows. They held hands as they walked back to her car.

I'm sorry, she said quietly.

For what?

For talking about sad things. This wasn't exactly like our first dates out here.

I wouldn't trade this afternoon for anything. And trust me, I wouldn't want to be back in that time, or be the person I was.

Me either, she admitted. Me either.

26

While Melissa and Charlie carried boxes and furniture upstairs to the second-floor apartment, she took the girls to the Como Zoo. It was suddenly May. Spring, in bloom. The parks, gardens, and boulevards of Saint Paul full of daffodils and tulips, the redbud and dogwood trees heavy with blossoms. The air smelled exotic with pollen, with wet soil, new grass. The city, though not as large as Minneapolis, bustled. Traffic, bicyclists, joggers, dog walkers, the light-rail commuter train, freight trains, airplanes overhead, taking off from MSP Airport, or landing. She understood why Melissa had decided to move here, how invigorating it must feel.

This zoo's so much better than back home, Grandma, one of the girls shouted over her shoulder.

This was true, though also not quite fair. There was a small zoo in Chippewa Falls, but whatever big-city ambitions it may have entertained were undercut by the realities of a small-town budget. Over the years, this had meant small enclosures and animals that simply stared out from behind bars, like prisoners. Recently, the zoo had been greatly improved, but Vivian had memories of visiting the zoo and only wanting to leave. Or better yet, to find some way to liberate those animals, black bears running for the closest forest, tigers, lions, and zebras running down the streets, confused but giddy with their newfound freedom.

She sat on a park bench between the girls while they chewed their hot dogs. If they felt any nervousness about moving here, they didn't show it. Vivian had driven them past the school where Ainsley would begin kindergarten; Addison's day care was only a block away from the new apartment. Then around the neighborhood. Playgrounds, grocery stores, restaurants. It was wonderful, really. People from seemingly every culture around the world.

When they returned to the apartment, it was late afternoon. Melissa and Charlie were seated on the front porch, drinking beer. The girls ran past them, up a steep set of stairs to their new home. There was only the sound of laughter now, laughter and footfalls tripping down that staircase all the way out to the street.

I bet that tastes good, Vivian said, from halfway up those steps. She leaned against the wood rail. You two deserve it. That was a lot of work.

She couldn't quite untangle in her own mind what it would mean to disappear alcohol completely from her life, or Charlie's. And could he be an alcoholic and do this, what they were doing now? A beer or two. That didn't seem too harmful. That seemed like restraint.

Couldn't have done it without your boyfriend here, Melissa said, giving Charlie a light slap on the back.

I avoided having kids for just this reason, he joked. You have kids, you're going to be moving them around for, what, the first five years of their adult life? Guaranteed. Dorms, apartments, the first new house. I have friends who just got exhausted and started hiring moving companies. Friends who, if they were smart, should have founded some moving companies.

I don't believe that, Vivian said, swatting at him. Shush.

No, it's true. They're invalids now. All because their kids kept moving. One of my friends, he was a tremendous athlete back in college, played a few years of pro football. Now he looks like Quasimodo, all bent over. It's because he moved his daughter to nine different apartments in six years. Nine.

Vivian glanced behind Charlie, and there was already an empty bottle of beer sitting on the porch.

Should I get us some pizza? she asked. You two must be hungry.

I can go too, Charlie said, lurching forward from his seat only to grab at the small of his back. Let me. Seriously.

Seriously, Vivian said, sit down. What are you always telling me? Relax? Well, so, relax. The pizzeria's just around the corner.

Can I at least give you some money, please? he asked, reaching awkwardly for his wallet.

No, you can't.

See, this is what happens, he told Melissa. Now I'm immobilized. She's probably going to want to drive us home too.

I absolutely will be driving us home, Charlie. You've had two beers now.

Speaking of beers, he said, shaking his empty bottle over an empty flowerpot, could you kindly grab me another, please? They're going down easy.

Are you sure? Vivian asked.

He gave her the slightest look, a look she hadn't seen from him in decades. A dismissive look, a look of condescension. Then the look disappeared nearly as quickly as it had developed. She found herself walking up the stairs and touching his shoulder gently, with her hand, as if to communicate, to ask again, Are you sure? In the kitchen she reached into the refrigerator and plucked two bottles of beer, then set them on the counter near the sink. She searched the kitchen drawers for an opener and, coming up short, just stood there a moment, taking the place in.

It was a very nice unit. The landlord, a friend of Melissa's, had bought this turn-of-the century fixer-upper and divided it into two apartments, renovating just about everything. The Doug fir flooring was newly sanded and finished. The walls painted. New appliances. The windows were old, sure, but there was a kind of charm or character in the way they allowed light to pass into this long rectangle of space.

Hearing the girls giggling in their bedroom, Vivian carried the two unopened bottles to the doorway of their little room and peered inside. They were standing at the window, which looked down into a neighbor's tiny backyard. Vivian joined the girls, and watched as an old woman was engaged in what looked to be her tai chi practice. Vivian stood with them, watching, until the woman glanced up to smile and wave. Immediately the girls dropped onto the floor, as if the woman might somehow not notice the young faces spying on her, but Vivian shifted both bottles to one hand to give a wave back. The girls were whispering on the floor. Vivian sat down on the new bunk bed Charlie had purchased and assembled.

So you two decided that even though you could each have your own room, you wanted to stick together, huh?

Well, yeah, Ainsley replied, we thought the other room could be yours, Grandma. If you ever wanted to live with us.

Would you like that? Vivian asked, emotion causing her voice to wobble.

Sure, Addison said, but Mom says that maybe you'll move in with your boyfriend.

Oh, is that what she said? Vivian was quiet for a moment. Well, would that be okay? If I moved into Charlie's house?

Do you want to? Ainsley asked, crawling back onto the bed now to peer out the window again.

Maybe, Vivian allowed.

I like Charlie, Ainsley volunteered. And he really likes you, Grandma.

You think so?

Both girls looked at each other, giggled, and Addison said, Duh, Grandma.

Vivian rubbed their heads and walked the two bottles down to Charlie and Melissa, who were laughing and nodding their heads as the sun set to the west, over Minneapolis.

I couldn't find an opener, she said, exhaling.

That's okay, Charlie said, freeing his keys from a pocket. Everyone should keep a church key on their key ring. He popped the tops off both bottles of beer and handed one to Melissa.

I'll be back, Vivian said, kissing Charlie on the cheek. She could feel his skin beneath her lips, hot with sunburn.

She ordered three large pizzas—Melissa and the girls loved cold pizza as leftovers—and perched herself at the bar to wait for their food. A server brought her a cold glass of water, which she drank gratefully. The pizzeria was filled with young couples and young families. Black families, Asian American families, Latin American families… There were gay couples, old people, artist types. This place, this simple restaurant, gave her some measure of comfort. Melissa wouldn't have to worry about fitting in here. Everyone fit in here. The neighborhood felt safe, interconnected, tight.

Before she knew it, three pizza boxes were set before her, steam escaping from the folds in the cardboard. She paid the bill and walked back to the house. Melissa and Charlie were, if not drunk, certainly feeling no pain. She called the girls down to the porch, passed everyone paper plates and paper napkins, and they ate as the new evening drooped slow and blue over the city, lights blinking on and cars cruising by.

Which friend owns the house, dear?

Oh, Christine Cooper. Remember her? From high school? She's doing amazing. Works for Target corporate. She's great.

Did you reconnect on your girls' weekend?

Melissa cocked her head to the side and continued chewing

her pizza crust. Then pointed a finger at her mom and said, brightly, Exactly—that's how I found out about this place.

But Vivian had seen something. It wasn't just Melissa's pause either. Charlie, sitting beside her, had flicked his eyes at Melissa just for a moment before aiming them down, at his feet, and keeping them there, even now.

Before her question, he'd been boisterous and loud. But now he was completely withdrawn. Even his shoulders were hunched, as if he were trying to disappear. And the way Melissa was also avoiding her eyes. And the quiet that now settled over the porch, leavened only by the girls' chitter-chatter.

Girls, Vivian said, setting her plate on the railing of the porch, would you like to watch some TV? Come on. Bring your pizza. Grandma will make you some Kool-Aid, and you can watch a movie in your new house. Your first movie. She all but whisked the girls back up the stairs. Minutes later, she stood before Melissa and Charlie, quietly fuming.

Now, I don't know what's going on. But something sure as hell is. I swear to god, it better not be between the two of you, because I don't think my heart could take it. But maybe that's what's been happening all along, huh? Maybe that's what's been going on, and I've just been too old or too stupid not to see it.

No, Mom, that's not it. Mom—

Please don't patronize me. I knew something was off. I just knew it. So come on. Come clean with me. No more lies now.

They both sat silently on the stoop, staring at the sidewalk, their pizza pushed aside, Charlie now pouring out the dregs of his beer, wiping his hands on the thighs of his pants, and sighing deeply.

Charlie? Are you in love with her? Is that it? Treat the old lady nice, right, but sleep with the one who's really got it?

Stop it, he said. Vivian, please, stop. You're going to embarrass yourself.

Well, someone's got to start telling me something.

Let's go home, Vivian.

Home? she repeated, starting to cry, starting to feel her body shudder with rage and disappointment and confusion. Home? What home? Your home?

Come on, he said, standing. I'll take you to your house in Chippewa. Or you come to my place. Look, we're all tired. Come on. He held out his hand for her.

No, Charlie, Melissa said, holding her head in her hands. This is on me.

What's going on? Vivian asked, alarmed all over again.

Mom, Melissa said, let's take a walk. I can explain everything. And let's just be clear—there's no reason to be mad at Charlie. He didn't do anything.

A small bare laugh escaped the younger woman, and she steadied her face again in seriousness. I am in no way attracted to Charlie, Mom. He's just—Charlie is just my friend. Okay? He's been nothing but good to me. Besides, I'm totally not attracted to older guys. I promise.

Vivian held her elbows in her hands, staring at Charlie as if she had no reason to believe her daughter.

Mom? Look at me. I'm telling the truth. This isn't about Charlie at all. Now, will you please come with me? Just a short walk. She reached for her mother's hand, but Vivian turned slightly, as if she were not ready for the walk, as if the evening gloom had chilled her body to the point she just wanted to get warm again.

I can clean up, Charlie offered, and keep an eye on the girls.

Thanks, C, Melissa offered, giving his arm a quick squeeze.

Then Vivian and Melissa were walking toward the stately houses on Grand Avenue, with their wide emerald lawns, their towering oak trees, windows all aglow with amber light. Parents pushing expensive high-canopied strollers passed them by. It was two blocks before Melissa said anything.

Mom, I had an abortion.

Vivian stopped. Closed her eyes. Clenched her fists. What? When?

That weekend. That weekend I lied to you about having a girls' weekend here, with my friends. I needed an excuse to be away for a couple of days.

And Charlie helped you...

Melissa nodded her head. He was the only one I could trust. And, Mom, he didn't want to help me. Definitely not at first. He was afraid of something like this happening. He didn't want to do anything to hurt you, or disappoint you, but I kept asking him. I was desperate. He was so kind, Mom.

How though? How did this even happen?

My boss. At work. We'd been fooling around a little bit

and...I don't know what to say. It was all wrong. He's married, for one thing. I should have said no. Sometimes, like early on, I wanted it, you know? I wanted to fool around. But towards the end...

Oh, sweetie. How are you? How is your body?

I'm okay, okay. I didn't want... God, I know it sounds awful. It's hard to say out loud, but I didn't want another child. I'm barely hanging on as is.

But, Melissa, why didn't you talk to me? Why didn't you ask for my help?

Because Mom—I knew you would've freaked. I knew you would've berated me, made me feel guilty. I feel guilty enough. At least with Charlie, he didn't say anything. He just, you know, got me to the clinic and then took care of me afterwards. We talked about our lives. And I'm sorry, Mom. I feel like I've been a screwup, you know? That I've made your life harder, and that isn't at all what I ever wanted or planned. It's part of the reason why I wanted to make this move. To start fresh. Charlie helped me see that—that I didn't have to keep living the same way, in the same rut. God, I'm just...sorry. I'm so, so sorry.

Melissa was crying now, standing there on that street corner, traffic moving past them like a river of light, sound, and steel.

Mom, it's done, Melissa finally said, collecting herself. It wasn't meant to be. I'm sorry. A million times over, I'm sorry. I'm trying to be better.

Vivian closed her eyes, exhaled, let all her disappointment and anger and confusion go, and then hugged her daughter, who immediately collapsed in her arms crying, repeatedly saying, I'm sorry, Mom, I'm so sorry.

It's okay, sweetheart, it's okay.

I'm sorry I lied to you.

It's okay.

I didn't mean for it to happen. I feel so stupid.

It's done now. Okay? It's done.

They were quiet for a moment. Then Vivian said, Well, maybe now's the right time to tell Charlie about Jessie. An airing of grievances. No, not grievances. An airing of secrets. She looked at Melissa. Reached out for her hands. As if to steady herself. As if to communicate years of secrecy and shame from her body to her daughter's, like osmosis.

You're not angry at me? Melissa asked.

How could I be angry at you, with what I need to share with Charlie?

———

When they arrived back at the apartment, Charlie and the girls were asleep on the couch, the TV flashing from its newly mounted perch on the wall. Charlie was in the middle, a girl under each arm, his own head back, mouth open. Some of the windows were open, and the linen curtains lifted in the evening breeze like the hem of a dress.

I hate to wake him up, Vivian whispered, even if I am a little angry with him.

Melissa reached out for mother's arm. Don't be angry at him, Mom. Please. He only wanted two things—to help me out, and not to make you angry. He loves you so much, Mom. And we can all see that he's the best thing that has happened to you in, like, forever.

Vivian felt herself chewing her bottom lip. For so many years—decades, in fact—every decision she had made, had been predicated on the priority of keeping her family together. Under one roof. Safe. So she could protect everyone. But today, today, had been a sea change. They were not all under one roof, moving forward, and it was difficult for her to see that as a triumph. That all those years of hard work and heartbreak had led to this day, this independence, these unlikely people gathered in this house in Saint Paul, Minnesota.

Well, she sighed, if you need me, for anything, sweetheart, just call, okay?

I know, Mom. I will. I will need your help.

All right, then. I guess I should wake this lug up. She placed her cold hands inside his shirt, on his shoulders, and he startled awake, looking at her, she thought, with apprehension, which she found just a little bit endearing. Come on, old man, she said. It's our time to go.

On the ride home, he was quiet in the passenger seat. He never once asked to drive, or commented on some fancy ice cream parlor or top-notch brewery he knew in Stillwater or Hudson. He just watched the lights of the suburbs as they moved back east, first out of the Twin Cities metro area, and then over the Saint Croix River, and back into Wisconsin. In the countryside east of Hudson, the levels of ambient light decreased, and she could no longer see his face as easily. Only the briefest of snapshots in the passing lights of the oncoming cars on the other side of the highway. But she knew he was awake.

I have another daughter, she said, suddenly, squeezing the steering wheel and feeling her eyes well up with tears before she'd even begun, really. She glanced across the car at him. After we separated, she said. She felt relief. A release. A pressure slowly decreasing.

He sat up and looked at her, as vulnerable as she could ever recall him looking.

I should have told you, she said, but...it wouldn't have made anything better. You weren't ready back then, and I could hardly have known what sort of man you'd become. I didn't know. I was young and—

Wait? You're saying this daughter, she's my daughter? I have a daughter?

Yes, she's your daughter, Charlie.

When? When did you—

A month or so after we separated. I didn't even know where you were at that point. I didn't have a phone number for you or anything. You signed those papers and disappeared.

He sighed. Well, where is she now? Is she okay? Does she know about me? Can I see her?

She lives in Eau Claire. In a group home.

A group home? I don't understand. Is she okay? Can I see her tonight?

It's late already. I don't think we could stop tonight. But we could see her tomorrow.

Why is she in a group home?

She has Down syndrome, Charlie.

Down syndrome?

He was silent a moment, several moments, as he took all this in. So how old is she now? he asked.

Nearly forty. Actually, she'll turn forty this summer. August first.

I can't believe it. What's her name? My daughter's name? He was crying now, happy tears running down his face, like warm rain. I have a daughter, he whispered, running his hands back and forth through his hair.

Jessica. Jessica Ann. She has my last name. Peterson. But I call her Jessie.

I don't know what to say, Charlie said. Sometimes, it feels like I could keep saying, I'm sorry, for the rest of my life, and it wouldn't be enough. Everything you've been through. He was silent for a long time. The moon was a ripe peach over the night-black treetops. I can't wait to meet her. I don't think I'll be able to sleep tonight.

Then they drove and drove through the night, but Viv noticed he had tucked himself against the door, made himself small. He was looking out the window determinedly, and not saying a word, or reaching for her hand as he sometimes did. The miles clicked by, and the minutes too. Just silence. She peered over at him, but his face was turned, and now she didn't know if he was lying or not. Maybe he was angry. Maybe he was irate. She supposed he had a right to be. This secret she had buried for so long. A daughter that might have changed his life, might have brought him back here sooner. And what then? Might he have matured faster? Quit drinking sooner? They would never know.

You're not angry at me? Vivian asked.

Well, he said, laughing a little bitterly, I wish you'd told me back in October or November. I mean, I guess maybe I wished you'd told me twenty years ago, or ten, or even five. Yeah, I've missed a lot of time. But...I guess I understand. Why would you tell me if I wasn't going to stick around? Or if I was a drunk? Or mean? No, no, no. I'm not angry. How could I be angry? He reached for her hand. I can't believe what you've just given me. This gift.

Vivian took a breath. The reason why I was so upset with Melissa, isn't that she made the wrong choice. She made the right choice, for her. And anyway, it's done with. It's just that I almost made the same choice with Jessie, with our daughter. It's actually a lot harder now. Harder than it was back then. Legally, I could have done it. And, believe me, I thought about it. You were gone and I panicked. But I had this aunt and uncle and, I don't know how they knew, how they got wind. But they offered me a place to stay. Out in Montana. North of Missoula. I'd never been out there. One weekend, they came to Chippewa Falls for a reunion or something, and I just loaded up my things and drove right back with them. You remember how it was, how things were handled back then? A girl would be pregnant one day, then she'd disappear for a year or two, and come back, like nothing had ever happened? Well, that was me.

He said nothing, only squeezed her hand.

It was a blessing, actually. They were so kind. So patient. They owned this ranch out there, and I had all the silence I needed. All the peace. To recover from you—from our divorce. I delivered Jessie right in their home. A midwife came out and helped me, held my hand. See, they knew everyone. And it worked out. But what was most important to me is that they introduced me to Jessie's parents. To the people that raised her. Because I just— couldn't. I did my best, but I couldn't. I tried. For two years, I tried. But I was too young, and I couldn't stay there forever. So, my aunt and uncle introduced me to the Stapletons. They were farmers. Wheat farmers. The gentlest people you could imagine. We made everything official. She had a wonderful childhood. They sent photographs. Letters. But I couldn't visit. I didn't have the money or the time, and soon enough, I was remarried, and then Melissa arrived.

So that's one thing that is hard. We decided, me and the Stapletons, that Jessie would only know me as her aunt. If I ever met her, or if I sent her mail or money, that's how I'd present myself, as her aunt. So maybe you can be an uncle. The Stapletons were—they're gone now, both of them—they were angels. But they definitely had a code. They said that being a mother was more than just a word. And being a mother was about more than blood bonds, too. It was a privilege. It came with responsibilities. The day-to-day. The nitty-gritty. They didn't think it was right that they do the work of parenting only to have to split the credit. That was hard for me, because of course I was still her mother. Her mom. I was the one who'd brought her into the world and named her and breastfed her and cared for her. But I couldn't argue with them. So I accepted it. And you'll have to understand it too, Charlie. I wouldn't want you to enter her life and confuse her.

I understand. God, I feel like a broken record, but I'm just so sorry, Vivian. I should have been there for you.

Well, you're here now, she said.

I always wanted a daughter, he said. Sometimes, when I'm driving around town, I'll see a woman who would be about Jessie's age, and I'll think—and I know it's stupid—but I'll think, there she is. And I'll imagine everything about her. Where she lives, who she's married to, how many grandchildren I have, her job…

Vivian chuckled. Well, Jessie probably isn't anything you might have imagined. She's different. Wonderfully different. When I gave her up to the Stapletons, all I was focused on were her needs. How much work she'd be. All the attention she'd need. All the ways I thought she wouldn't be able to function in the world. I didn't understand the first thing about Down syndrome.

Now her laughter dried up, as years of regret, love, and loss blew over this subject that for decades had been entirely secret. Also, the unexpected joys of that time, all kept hidden.

But I shouldn't have been afraid, she said at length. I never should have been afraid of my own daughter. All she needed was love. Love and patience.

Before the Stapletons both passed away, she continued, they contacted me, and we set up a plan for Jessie. She'd move back here, into a group home. She'd have a little trust. Enough money to cover all her needs, plus a little more, for security. And I would be around for her. This was only two years ago, actually.

She was shaking her head again, shaking away the past, all of her mistakes. But I should have told you earlier. Of course, I should've. I don't know why I was so afraid. But I was. I was afraid. I felt guilty. I felt terrible for abandoning my daughter. For giving up on her. Just because she was different. I mean, that made me a monster, right? Who does that? Who gives up like that? On their own flesh and blood? On their own daughter? But I have to admit that telling you now, sharing this with you... It's also a relief. A tremendous relief. I always worried what would happen to her if—when—I'm not around anymore. I know she'd always have Melissa, but now... Now she has you, too.

He reached out, across the darkness of the car, and gripped Vivian's shoulder, before moving his hand upward to gently massage her earlobe and run the backs of his fingers against her wet face.

I wish, he began, I wish that we could stop looking back. I wish that we could just start moving forward. In a new way. You're happy when you're with me? Aren't you?

Of course, Charlie. I'm so happy.

I am too. I'm as happy as I can ever remember. Even the hard times, like tonight. But it feels real to me, and important. I just found out that I have a daughter. A daughter. I'm as excited about living, about my life as I've ever been. I can't wait to meet her, can't wait for tomorrow. And I bet you feel the same way. Maybe everything has worked out.

Well, she'll love you, that much is for sure. And she's perfect, Charlie. She's exactly who she is. That's what I love most about her.

Hey, he said, I need to apologize for one more thing, and then I hope I'm done. At least for today. I'm sorry we were drinking. It was a hot day, and we'd worked and worked, and well, it's just really hard to beat a cold beer. But I need to stop. To stop drinking, altogether, I know that. I'm ready. I really am. I hope you can see that. That I make mistakes, but I'm trying.

I know it, Charlie. And I see it, I do.

They drove on, in silence, past sleeping farms, past sad little motels, brightly lit parking lots and fast-food joints, past factories and warehouses, and expanses of forests.

When you're our age, she began, there's no one left to ask for advice. We're supposed to have the answers. We're supposed to be the wise ones. And there's so much in our past, and a whole lot less up on ahead. I find myself just lost in my past, thinking about my mistakes, wishing I could redo things. I don't want to, but it's what I do. At night, in bed. I wish I had done this, or that. Do you do that to yourself?

Well, yes and no. Because where would I even start? I never thought about our wedding vows. Like, you told me, with your second marriage you felt you had no choice but to stay with your husband—'til death do us part—all that jazz. When you and

227

I were married, I was just in love. I never considered time, or sickness, or death. Vivian, I was like—a kid. I was just a stupid kid, totally in love. I thought everything would last forever.

And it's the opposite, isn't it? Everything is so fragile. And nothing lasts.

Or its lasts only as long as it can. As long as it should. I think our best days, our happiest days are still ahead of us. I keep saying that because I want you to believe it too. I want you to believe in us, in me.

She sighed, I don't want to sleep at my house. I don't know that I can take that right now. That quiet.

Sleep with me, then. Please. At my house. Or sleep with Blueberry, anyway. He likes you. Charlie raised an eyebrow in the dark, rakishly. Come on. What do you say?

He is a sweet dog, she said. Sure, I'll sleep at your house. I haven't been seeing Shelby enough either. My dream was always to have a horse, and really, I ought to be there every day. But I've been so busy.

Well? he asked again. What do you think? Spend the night?

Sure.

With me? Or Blueberry?

I'll sleep with you, she said, smiling.

———

When she woke the next morning, Charlie was no longer beside her, but Blueberry stood vigil at the foot of the bed, staring at her, wagging his tail, his breath hot and smelling of kibble and warm saliva. She sat up, stretched, then reached to massage his muzzle. There was a nice view from Charlie's bedroom, looking out over a pasture and a small pond. The sun had risen, and there was fog over the pond and near the tree line at the edge of the pasture.

She smelled coffee and scrambled eggs and bacon. Down in the kitchen, he was whistling and singing. Blueberry trotted off, downstairs she supposed, and she followed the dog. When she entered the kitchen, Charlie was seated on a stool at the granite island, looking at his phone and absent-mindedly scratching the dog's head. She laid a hand on his shoulder, and he startled a moment, took his eyeglasses off, then leaned back into her body. It was a nice thing, this familiarity, placing his weight against her softness. She kissed his neck and wrapped her arms around his chest and smelled his cologne and soap, and the coffee on his breath.

I love you, he said. And then he started to hum.

Well, I love you too, she said, and it surprised her. How easily the words came. How nice this morning was already.

How'd you sleep last night? she asked.

Not a wink. He smiled. Feels like Christmas morning. Which reminds me, I want to bring a present for her. For Jessie. What does she like? Flowers? Balloons? Does she like snacks? Some kind of treat? Cake? Ice cream?

Vivian smiled. They do a really good job at her home, Charlie, of feeding everyone nutritious meals, you know? They like to keep junk food to a minimum.

Now it was his turn to smile, Right, so, what does she like? Cookies, soda, candy?

She likes orange soda, if you must know. And popcorn with melted butter. She likes to eat peanut butter out of the jar. She'll eat a whole container if I'm not watching her. Gosh. What else is she into? Garfield. She likes anything related to Garfield. John Candy movies. She likes Korean pop. BTS is her favorite.

Wait—what? Who?

You're old, so you haven't heard of them. But everyone else on the planet has.

So, I should buy her an album? Or what? A CD?

No, she laughed. She's got her own phone. Downloads all her music straight to the phone, like everyone else living in this century. We can't text her now because she's probably not awake just yet. She likes to sleep in. But soon enough. Oh, I don't know where my phone is. Maybe in the car. Doesn't matter.

What else?

She loves dogs.

He raised his eyebrow. Does she now?

They both looked at Blueberry, who wagged his tail expectantly.

I think we eat some breakfast, then give the dog a bath, then buy some junk food, and go visit our daughter. What do you say?

I can't think of a better day, she said.

Can I get you a cup of coffee?

Yes, please, she said, sitting down on a stool.

He placed a mug in front of her and sat down too. He was humming again.

What's that? That you're humming.

Rocky Raccoon. The Beatles. Rocky Raccoon checked into his room, only to find Gideon's Bible.

I remember your mom telling me, after we got married, that when you were a kid, and you were happy, you'd always hum while you were eating breakfast. She called you the Wisconsin Humming Bear. I wish I could have seen you then.

She smiled. Say it again.

What? Rocky Raccoon?

No. The first thing.

What? Oh. I love you. And I love that you're here.

I love you too. It's nice. Being here. But...

But what?

It's so quiet, she said, and then began laughing. And then they were kissing. Their hands on each other's faces. Their fingertips electrified in that way lovers have. Their mouths tasted of coffee and sugar and cream. The kitchen was warm, and their hands were warm, too. His hands on her back and then her breasts. Her hands on the small of his back, then holding, cupping his shoulder blades.

What are we doing? she asked quietly, still kissing him. Aren't we going to see Jessie? Shouldn't we get ready?

Shhh, he said.

He took her hand, and they climbed the stairs to his bedroom, closing the door on the dog, who, for a moment, scratched and whined before simply flopping down in resignation.

The bed was still warm. They moved very slowly. They kissed slowly, their lips swollen. Memories blurred and bent into the present. In one moment, they were together in the now, making love as the morning sunlight passed through the windows and shone off the wooden floors. But in other moments, they were making love as they had. In the past. Forty years ago. They were making love in the back seats of cars, windows steamed with their efforts, rain drumming off the roof, sliding down the windshield. They were making love at a party, on a bed all piled with the winter jackets of other guests, laughter just outside the door, the thrill that someone might easily walk in on them and discover them there, on New Year's Eve. They were making love in the long green grasses of a ridgetop field, at dusk, fireflies blinking on and off, off and on, in the air all around them, while the stars sizzled noiselessly overhead.

When they were done, they lay together on their backs, exhausted from the present, delirious from their return to the past, all of that lovely time travel.

27

He wanted to buy Jessie the world, but there is only so much for sale in most small towns. So, they arrived at her group home late in the morning bearing the bounty of a six-pack of orange soda, a box of popcorn, and a few packages of Reese's peanut butter cups. It would have to do, for just then.

Blueberry rode in the truck with them, one of Charlie's navy-blue bandannas tied dashingly around his throat. From the back seat, he poked his head between their seats, smelling of pet shampoo.

When they walked through the front door into a common area, Jessie burst from the soft depths of a Naugahyde recliner and hustled towards Vivian, wrapping her in a tremendous hug. He tried to imagine what that hug might feel like, but a moment later did not have to. When Vivian introduced him as Uncle Charlie, Jessie gave him a hug only slightly less enthusiastic.

He could not and did not care to stop the tears that ran down his face. She was shorter than him, and stockier, and he would have liked to press his nose into her hair and smell her, but he was crying so hard now that Vivian came beside them to wipe his face with a Kleenex. Now Jessie was rocking him side to side, like they were dancing clumsily at a wedding, and he could not believe that he had lived all these many years without her, without even knowing she existed, and then, if only briefly, there was a sharp pang of sadness, for he feared, and knew, that there was so much less time ahead of them than behind.

When Jessie quite abruptly stopped hugging him, Charlie worried that he had done something wrong, but it was only that she noticed Blueberry, he saw, as she dropped to the floor and pressed the big dog to her.

Oh, she kept saying happily, oh, oh, oh.

And that was all they did for more than an hour. They found a quiet corner of the common room and talked easily. Jessie held the dog. Patted the dog. Rubbed the dog's belly, scratched his ears, and the area beneath his mouth. Blueberry made a sound like a low growl, and she looked at Charlie, confused.

He only makes that sound when he's extremely happy, Charlie said. He must really like you.

Such a good dog, she intoned, lying down beside Blueberry as if he were her own dog, and Charlie supposed that he was, or could be.

They remained that way for some time, and through an open window came the smell of fresh-cut grass and the sound of wind rushing through new spring leaves.

On the ride back to his house, she said to him, You really aren't angry at me? For not telling you?

234

He pursed his lips tightly, glanced at her, then gripped the steering wheel tightly.

I've been thinking, he began, how long a time forty years is. More than half of my life. I've known people, from our youth, that didn't make it to forty. I don't know if you think about folks like that, but I do. Friends of mine, killed in drunk driving accidents, overdoses. I guess I've been feeling lucky to make it this far. That some people don't need all this time to mature, but that maybe I did. That maybe, if you'd told me even five years ago, I would have been angry. I would have been irate. I know I would have been. I would have felt aggrieved. The victim. Righteous in my, uh, newfound knowledge.

He reached for her hand.

But I never felt that, Viv. Not for one second. I'll remember that moment for the rest of my life. How many sixtysomething-year-old men get a present like that? A daughter. Out of nowhere. A chance to be someone's father. You gave me that.

28

On the final day of May, they moved her things out of the house she had lived in for so many years with Melissa and the girls. All her possessions, a lifetime of belongings, fit in the bed of his truck and one small trailer. On the curb, they left a pile of broken, sun-bleached, torn, stained, and rusted things. Old toys. Strollers. Threadbare furniture.

It was a matter of minutes before a neighbor stopped on the sidewalk and began sorting through the things, like a gull or a crow, scavenging the remnants of a misbegotten feast.

Moving on up? the old woman asked, pointing her chin at Charlie's truck.

No, Vivian said. Just out. My daughter and granddaughters moved to Saint Paul.

Looks like you landed on your feet then.

Maybe, she allowed. Then, with conviction, and some pride, Yes. Yes, I did, actually.

The grass in the spare little front yard was vastly outnumbered by dandelions shining yellow. She stopped there, on the broken sidewalk, the woman still noisily rummaging through the pile behind her. The house suddenly looked tremendously small and sad. For the first time she noticed how the whole structure seemed to slump just slightly to one side. She could hear Charlie inside, whistling and humming as he swept.

She felt resolved. And more than that, beloved.

29

They took so many walks together. Their first forays were only a mile or two. But within days, they'd begun stretching the distance, farther and farther, until they were walking five, six, seven, eight miles. Back roads, mostly. Blueberry trotting beside them, or just on ahead. Sometimes they drove to state parks, but more often than not, they left his house and just walked down the driveway. Sometimes they went right. Other times left. They held hands. He felt healthier than he had in many, many years—so many years, he could not pinpoint the last time he'd felt this euphoric blend of health and well-being.

Most days they visited Jessie. They went to movies together. Small-town cafés and diners. Baseball games: amateur baseball games played in tiny stadiums or well-maintained village diamonds. Cheap brown paper bags of popcorn all spotted in melted butter. Cold sodas in waxed paper cups. Admission was free or almost free, and Charlie settled right into that. That variety of small-town entertainment. The ways in which he had been raised, but had forgotten or ignored. All these families sitting together on the weather-beaten gray bleachers, with so little to their names, who still wanted to feel distracted from their jobs, their sorrows, their disappointments. Who still wanted to be entertained. Families who watched amateur baseball games with greater intensity than most fans at a major league stadium, those fans who might've shelled out a couple of hundred dollars, only to ignore the game on the field, right there in front of them, in favor of the nonsense on their phones.

He liked the evenings when they picked Jessie up and drove to the Carson Park baseball field, the green heart of Eau Claire. An old CCC-era baseball stadium. Henry Aaron had played here. Mature white pines embraced the field along the first base side. It was not uncommon to see an osprey soaring over the field as it returned to its nest above the banks of outdoor lights.

One day, when they had planned to visit Jessie, Vivian complained of a headache.

Well, would you mind if I visited her? Charlie asked. I mean, you're all right here by yourself, aren't you?

She was lying in their bed, the curtains drawn on the morning. Sure, I'm fine, she said. You two have fun.

All right, he said. Well, can I bring you anything?

No, no, no. Go on. I'll text if I need anything. Tell her I say hello.

When he arrived at her group home, Jessie was playing checkers with another resident. Charlie sat down beside her and watched the game. When her last checker had been removed from the board, she sighed and leaned back in her chair, intertwining her fingers behind her head. He noticed that her fingernails were painted neatly, a nice glossy pink.

Well, Jessie, he said, would you maybe like to go somewhere? Anywhere you'd like. My treat.

Her face broke into a wide smile. She leaned forward in her chair and rubbed her hands together, Anywhere?

Anywhere. Anything you'd like.

Anywhere? she repeated devilishly.

Anywhere.

———

Pushing her cart through the aisles of Walmart, Jessie made a point of saying hello to just about everyone she passed. She took her time. Scrutinized the shelves. Handled boxes and packaging.

My friends will like these, she said, dropping a dozen coloring books into the cart and as many boxes of markers. Also: construction paper, glittery glue, scissors, tape, pens...orange soda, popcorn, peanut butter, chips, beef jerky...

My cart is full, she said to Charlie. It's hard to push. She was stone-cold serious—clearly this was a problem, and his to fix, not hers.

Okay, he said happily, umm, let me think. Can you stay right here? I'll run and get us another one. Or would you rather come with me?

But she was already standing in front of the sugary cereals, pointing at the colorful boxes, and sounding out the words, frosted toasted oat cereal with marshmallows...

I'll be right back, he said to her.

He walked as quickly as he could to the front of the store. Walked past several gumball machines. A group of retirees was talking in front of the carts, and he stood there for longer than he would have liked before they noticed him and let him through. He snagged a cart and pushed it as quickly as could past other shoppers until he was back in the cereal aisle. But she wasn't there.

He felt sweat immediately bead on his forehead, felt his pulse surge. Don't worry, he thought, she couldn't have gone far. He turned the empty cart into the next aisle, but still didn't see her. He doubled back, glancing down the cereal aisle. She wasn't there. He looked in the next aisle over. She wasn't there either.

A panic seized him now, and he considered calling Vivian right then. No, no. That wasn't necessary. She must be nearby, he thought. He pushed the cart faster. Went through every food aisle twice. Began asking other shoppers. Any Walmart employee he could find.

What's her name? someone asked.

Jessie, he said.

Is Jessie a nickname?

Yes, he said, then, Her full name's Jessica...Jessica...

But he'd forgotten it. He was fumbling, fumbling around inside his own old head. His memory. He knew her name, of course, but he couldn't find it just then, couldn't put his finger on it, as if he were trying to mine for the name of some old actor or actress, the name of a movie he'd seen many decades before... He couldn't remember his own daughter's name. Jessie, he thought— she was just Jessie. But that wasn't enough. That wasn't what they were asking exactly. He felt as if he were standing before some great web of ropes, some intricate knot, and he could not untangle the mess, no matter how hard he focused.

And who is she?

Well, she's my daughter.

But you don't know her full name?

Wait—now he knew. Now it popped, like a bubble in his mind: It's Jessica. Jessica Ann Peterson. Please. Help me. She has Down syndrome.

Do you have a picture of her?

No, he said. No, I don't.

You don't have a single picture of your own daughter? Not even on your phone?

No, see I just... But it was no use. He couldn't explain everything. It was too much. Too complicated.

Sir, are you okay? You seem pretty confused.

He pulled away from that person, heard them talking to another customer.

He stopped pushing the cart and began to move through the clothing department, through all the racks of clothing, through aisles of cheap socks and cheap underwear. Calling her name loudly.

Sir, someone said, sir, please. Stop. Who are you looking for?

My daughter. Jessie. Jessica. Jessica Ann. Jessie Peterson.

242

Okay, sir, how old is she?

He stopped. A large bald man's hand was gripping his shoulder. A security guard. Or loss prevention. Some goon who foiled shoplifters. Charlie realized he was sweating profusely. His heart beating desperately. He wanted to cry. Can I just call someone? he asked. Can I call Jessie's mom?

The man crossed his arms.

Please, just let me make a quick phone call. He motioned with one finger in the air—one.

The security guard shook his head, exasperated by whatever this situation was. Fine, he said, be my guest.

Vivian's phone rang and rang but went to her messages. He tried his home landline too, but she did not pick up. He texted her, repeatedly, but she didn't answer. He wasn't sure how many minutes had gone by since he'd last seen Jessie. Ten, maybe twenty. He called her name again.

Hey, a woman said. An employee with a blue vest. I think I found her.

She was standing in front of a giant television screen, watching Snow White and the Seven Dwarfs. That beautiful old cartoon. The dwarves were singing as they walked, and Jessie was laughing, imitating them.

Jessie, he said, rushing to her.

She ignored him or seemed to ignore him. She didn't so much as glance at him.

Jessie. Jessica, he said. It's me; it's your uncle. Charlie. Remember?

She stopped marching and turned to regard him.

Jessie? Are you okay? Where is your cart?

She turned back to the television, mumbling the words of the dwarves' song.

Sir? I thought you said you were her father. Hey?

I am her father, he insisted. But it's complicated.

Maybe you should come with me, the big bald man said now, reaching again for Charlie's arm.

No, that's not necessary.

Yeah, well, buddy, I think it might be. The police are on the way. So, let's you and me just go to my office, and we can straighten all this out.

I can't leave her alone, Charlie shouted, his face burning red. Jessie, I have—

The female employee was standing beside Jessie now, touching her gently, asking her something in a tone so low Charlie couldn't make out any of the words. He checked his phone again. Nothing. No texts. No missed calls. The sweat was freely dripping off his forehead now, off his nose, soaking his armpits and his chest. He could see her, right there, but she was absorbed with the television. And suddenly he did not feel very well. His chest felt like it was tightening, like someone was cinching a corset around his ribs and stomach. He winced in pain.

Jessie, he said loudly. Jessie.

Her eyes never moved from the screen.

Sir, the security guard said forcefully, I don't want to have to put my hands on you.

Can I—

But he was slipping down to the floor, to the dirty industrial carpeting, below the T-shirts hanging from fixtures, his legs useless, like sand beneath him. He felt his head bounce off the thin fabric, and then more pain, shooting through him like electricity. There was a child looking at him. A small child. Shorter than the bottoms of those shirts. She was waving at him now, but the look on her face showed only concern.

Now he closed his eyes, but he heard the girl's voice saying, Mama, look—there's a man on the ground, sleeping.

30

No one would tell her anything at the hospital. Was she family? Well, no, not exactly but—

I'm sorry, they said. There are rules we have to follow.

But can't you tell me what room he's in? Or if he's okay? I'm his ex-wife. I'm the only family he has.

I'm sorry, ma'am.

She held her phone in her hands and waited. Every ten minutes she tried calling him until finally, someone answered.

This is Charlie Fallon's phone, a woman said.

Hi, hi, yes, this is Charlie's ex-wife, I'm here at the hospital, but no one will tell me anything. What room he's in or if he's okay. Please. He doesn't have any other family.

What's your name, ma'am? the nurse asked.

Vivian. Vivian Peterson.

Vivian—wait a minute. Class of seventy-seven?

Yes, but—who is this?

Vivian. It's Deanna. Deanna Avery. Oh, for heaven's sake,

the woman said. He's on the fourth floor. I'll meet you at the nurses' station. And listen, just tell everyone you're married. Okay? Come right up.

Minutes later she was following this old high school friend to his room. He had a heart attack, Deanna said. He's stable now but resting. There was significant blockage in one of his major arteries, so the doctors put in a stent, and I'd have to check his records, but I think they performed an angioplasty as well.

But is he going to be okay?

Yes, I think he should be fine. The treatment is so good these days that he'll probably be released in the next twenty-four hours. It's amazing, to be honest. Not quite as run-of-the-mill as a broken bone, but not too far off.

Before they entered Charlie's room, Vivian reached for Deanna. Do you know where my daughter is, Jessie?

I didn't know you had a daughter by that name. I thought it was just Melissa. I have that right, don't I? Melissa? Beautiful girl.

It's a long story, Vivian said. But—so you haven't seen her? Her name is Jessie, or Jessica. She's forty years old. Short. And, well, she has Down syndrome.

I haven't, Viv, I'm sorry. Have you tried calling her? Look, why don't you sit down in Mister Fallon's room? I'll bring you a glass of water. Call your daughter. Mister Fallon isn't going anywhere. He's very safe here with us. Okay? And we'll catch up later. It's great to see you.

Vivian called Jessie, who answered immediately, apparently

unperturbed, and back at the group home. They had just finished lunch.

How did you get home?

Oh, the nice policeman gave me a ride.

Vivian shook her head. The police. Well, that was kind of them.

Yeah, they let me turn on their lights and sirens. Okay, bye, Auntie. As sometimes happened, Jessie hung up the phone without any further ado.

Vivian exhaled. One lost soul found. Now to check on the other.

She walked into his room. His head was turned away from her and toward the light of the window. The machinery beside his bed beeped and hissed. A television on the wall opposite his bed was showing an afternoon game show, the volume lowered to a level of utter pointlessness. The room was peaceful but severe feeling. This wasn't some kid who had broken their arm skateboarding. Or endured a tonsillectomy on the way to several days of chocolate milkshakes. As she sat on the bed beside him, she reached for his hand just as he tried to pull himself up, but then put her hand on his chest, on the thin nightgown they had provided him with, and silently urged him to stay as he was. His white chest hair stuck out from the flimsy garment, and she ran her fingers through it now.

Jessie, he said, is she all right? She wouldn't respond to me, Viv. Like I was a stranger or something. I was so scared.

It's okay, she said soothingly, Jessie's fine. She just—listen, she just forgets sometimes. Especially if someone is new in her life. And she's easily distracted.

She began laughing quietly, knowingly as she reached towards his face. Let me ask you something: Where were you?

He glanced out the window, then down at his hands.

Actually, she said, let me guess. Walmart?

How'd you know?

It's her favorite place. Can I have another guess?

Okay.

Did you lose her near the TVs? Or was it the gaming stuff? Maybe the frozen food aisle? Near the ice cream?

Now he smiled.

The thing with Jessie, she explained, or really anyone for that matter, is that she tends to do the same things. She has patterns. Behaviors. You didn't know those patterns. And you didn't lose her. She just does this. At Walmart, she goes to the TVs. At the mall, she goes straight for the food court. Every single time. You never had any children, but it was actually the same with Melissa. She liked to play hide-and-seek in the changing rooms, but the thing was, I didn't know we were playing. Used to drive me crazy.

You're not angry? he asked.

No, she said, still touching his face. I was worried about you.

They sat that way for a while. Looking straight at each other. Holding hands. Breathing deeply.

I was afraid, he said. I was afraid for Jessie, but…I also thought, at one point, I was going to die. I don't want to die. I'm not ready for that.

You're not going to die, Charlie. Not now, anyway. You can't. Look at this as a wake-up call, don't you think?

I know, he said. No more smokes. No more drinking. I get it. I just want to get home.

Me too. But you have to listen to them. The doctors. Take the medications. Exercise. I like our walks, but we could do more.

I like our walks too.

Anyway, it sounds like you'll be released tomorrow. They might not want you to drive because of your surgery. We can figure out how to get your truck home later. Don't worry about that.

She looked out the hospital window. The land was growing ever lusher and greener, fragile leaves widening, elongating, unfurling on tree branches, new grass already inches high, pushing past and through last year's old khaki-colored grass. She stood and cracked the window. Birdsong. The steady drone of distant traffic. A train whistle, far off. Mournful and plaintive. Like a hymn for sunset, for dusk, for the soft appearance of the first evening stars. It was a common enough sound on that edge of town, but no less welcome for it.

Do you ever miss it?

What's that?

Trains. Do you miss trains?

He nodded. Yeah, sometimes. It was a simple life. I was outside all the time, moving. But it isn't a job for an old man.

Can I tell you something? she sighed.

Anything, he said, sitting up again, regarding her with a measure of concern.

You know when we helped Melissa move into her apartment? That was the first time I'd left Wisconsin since before Addison was born.

Come on. Really?

Yeah. It's about four or five years. And even before that, I'd occasionally visit Melissa when she worked in Minnesota, sure, but I never got any farther than that.

But you never left? In those four or five years? Not even to go shopping in Minneapolis? Or up to Duluth? To see Lake Superior?

No. There was too much to do and, frankly, never enough money. To be honest, it never even dawned on me, any of this, not until we were driving west, until we crossed the Saint Croix River. Isn't that funny? I never thought of other places. I guess it was...unimaginable. She reached for his hand. Promise me something?

Okay.

We'll travel, won't we? It doesn't have to be anything exotic. It could just be how we used to travel. Camping. I just—I think I realize now what I was missing.

Anywhere you want to go, my love.

They held hands. Looked out the window as the dusk burned on the horizon like a dirty light bulb. She stayed until night fell complete over the land, and then kissed him goodbye and drove back to the house, where she let Blueberry out to do his business before visiting Shelby in the barn.

31

He was released from the hospital just before noon. Vivian was right there waiting for him and drove him over to Walmart to get his truck.

Sure you're okay to drive? she asked.

Absolutely, he said, nodding.

I wish I could come home with you, she said, but Melissa has a busy few days coming up, and I offered to stay in Saint Paul and help with the girls. But I'll check in with you. Please watch your phone. I don't want to get worried. I just want to know that you're okay. And if you're not, let me know. I'll be there as soon as I can.

I'm fine, I'm fine, he said. Go on. Give everyone my love.

That first night, he slept deeply. So deeply in fact, that it was Blueberry who woke him up, whining to be let outside. Charlie took the stairs slowly and let the dog out into the sunlight, then checked his phone for messages. There were two texts, already, from Vivian.

You still alive? the first one read.

Then, after an hour had passed without a reply, Seriously, let me know you're still alive.

He smiled and typed, I'm still here.

Instantly, his phone dinged: Thank god. You had me worried for a second. I wouldn't have to worry about this sort of thing with a younger boyfriend.

He laughed, then typed, When will I see you again?

Thursday morning, she replied. Can't hardly wait.

But Thursday was three days away. They hadn't spent that long away from each other in weeks.

———

By Wednesday night he was still recovering, still a bit sore. Still taking naps when normally he might be out, doing chores. He should have been exhausted, but he hadn't let himself fall asleep. Would not allow it. He had been waiting for this moment for years, maybe decades, even if he hadn't quite known it.

To keep himself awake, he had written her a letter. The words did not come freely, even though he had been rehearsing and rehearsing in different iterations exactly that which he now sat at the kitchen island, desperately trying to record. Blueberry trotted over and set his muzzle on Charlie's thigh, aimed his eyes up and at Charlie's face.

Dear Vivian,

I know the doctors would be furious. They'd want me to be resting. But I can't sleep. Because I hope that by this coming morning, we will be engaged. I was thinking about it, and no one gets engaged in the morning. It seems to always happen in the evening. At dinner, say. Or after dinner, when both people have surely had a drink. But I want you to know that when I ask you to become my wife, I am not in the least bit drunk. I haven't touched alcohol in many days. My mind is clear and excited. Even before this recent episode, this heart attack, I was thinking about time. How much time I've wasted. And what I want to do with the time I have remaining, however long that is. What regrets I have. What mistakes I've made. How I might still make things right. Everything that I think about comes back to you. How much I love you. I've never looked forward to a sunrise as much as I've looked forward to my next one. And the one after. And the one after that.

Love,
Charlie

It had taken him five hours to write less than a page. He had filled a garbage bag with balled-up drafts. It was important to him that the letter was handwritten. That this was his handwriting. His cursive. He tucked the letter into an envelope and licked the flap. Wrote her name on the flap of the envelope.

Two hours until dawn. He could not chance sleep, but now he was tired. And sore. His chest was sore but so were his knees, hips, and shoulders from that fall in the Walmart. When he closed his eyes, he thought of that moment: the panic of losing Jessie.

Of disappointing Vivian. When he imagined himself dying, he imagined his bedroom, his heavy blankets, simply slipping away. Forced to choose his own ending, that is what he would choose. Home, his dog beside him, the window open, the radio on. Maybe classical music. And maybe the moon, big and yellow and low outside his window, shining his way forward. The last place he wanted to die was on the floor of the women's clothing department in a Walmart, with strangers looking on, like he'd just fallen through the roof.

Fresh air, he thought, let's get some fresh air.

A week or two ago, he might've grabbed a pack of cigarettes from the cupboard, but now, he just wrapped himself in a thick blanket, opened the door for the dog, and they went out onto the back porch. The night was very still. A fog clung close to the ground, like a congregation of ghosts. Near the pond, he could see the dim forms of two cranes, nosing their beaks slowly through the silty shallow water. The air felt vaporous in his nose, in his lungs, and he settled into a teak chair. Blueberry flopped down beside him. Close enough that Charlie could reach down and rest his hand on the dog's skull or backbone. He allowed his eyelids to close, and he fell asleep.

He dreamed he was riding the train again. Somewhere in New Mexico or western Texas. He leaned out of the locomotive and the wind was in his hair, rustling his clothing. The air smelled of sage and piñon pine and clean, dry dust. The sun was setting over the flatlands, and it did not matter where he was, only that he was traveling in the right direction. Someone was calling his name, repeatedly, a sweet voice, and now the dream fragmented and seemed to dissolve, and he was aware that he was between sleep and reality.

When he opened his eyes, dawn had come and gone, and Vivian was kneeling in front of him, the letter in one hand, her other hand resting on the dog's head.

Good morning, he said, attempting to sit up but suddenly feeling incredibly stiff along with slightly nauseous. He groaned and rubbed his eyes. Was aware that his breath was awful. That he had overslept on the most important morning of his life. He rested his head against the back of the chair.

This is not how I imagined it, he said, closing his eyes against the disappointment. This morning. You were supposed to show up, and maybe we'd take a walk or something, and I would be there, by your side, and then we'd come back here, and I'd make you breakfast... He sighed. Never mind. Did you read the letter?

She nodded and smiled. My name was on the envelope, so...

Well, okay. What do you think?

Is that your proposal?

No. Well. I mean. Oh, Vivian. Can we—

But she was already sitting in his lap, and they were quiet, holding each other. Not quite swaying, but—rocking. The way he imagined you might rock a baby to sleep. He had never actually held a baby. The only children he had ever held were Ainsley and Addison, mostly as he carried their sleeping forms into their beds.

He allowed himself a moment to breathe in the scent of this morning. The flowers and dewy grass. The spice of the meadow. The coffee in her kiss.

Did you already make coffee? he asked.

Of course, she said. I couldn't find you. I tried your phone, but it was up in the bedroom. I thought it was a little strange that you'd leave a declaration of love on the counter and then leave, but then it occurred to me maybe you were afraid of what I'd say.

I love you, he said. Would you like to get married, Vivian Ann Peterson? Would you marry me, Vivian, please?

Again? she smiled.

An encore, he suggested. Then he frowned. Shoot, I don't have your ring. I mean, I have it, but it's upstairs.

I'm not worried about it, she replied. Anyway, I've got the first one. She held up her hand to show him.

But—how? he asked. You never got rid of it? And how'd you know? That I'd ask?

I kept it, she said simply. Honestly, I hadn't thought about it in years, thought I'd lost it. But then, when we were cleaning out my house, I found it. In the girl's room, of all places. I must have given it to one of them, as play jewelry, and then forgotten all about it. There it was, on the floor. I almost vacuumed it up. Anyway, I've been carrying it around with me for weeks. I don't know why. Like a good-luck charm, I guess.

Unbelievable, he said, holding her hand. But still, I'd like to give you a new ring. I don't know. That ring wasn't much of a good-luck charm at all. Or maybe I bought a lemon.

Or maybe it was, she said, looking at her fingers. Because here we are.

Near the pond, out in the fenced-off meadow, the horse was running freely. Shelby. As if playing. In the air, low over and around the pond, dragonflies were flitting, their gossamer-thin wings glinting in the early slanting sunlight.

Maybe it was, he admitted.

32

On a Sunday evening, they sat on a couch with the girls watching episodes of Abbott Elementary.

This show is fantastic, Charlie said.

Can we watch another? the girls asked, huge toothy grins spreading behind poorly camouflaging fingers. It was clear to see that they thought Charlie an easy mark, and they were right. Long before they arrived for this babysitting gig, he'd been researching the Twin Cities' best ice cream, doughnuts, pizza, and hot dogs, and most of the day had been spent driving from one restaurant to the next, sitting outside in the June heat while they clumsily ate. The girls had already changed out of two outfits today and were now wearing their pajamas; they were all tucked into the couch, cuddling, and she could see that Charlie was having as much fun as she could ever remember.

Yes, Charlie said emphatically. But first, let's pop some corn.

Nobody says that anymore, Ainsley said. They say, Let's make some popcorn.

Charlie, Vivian said, your heart. Haven't you had enough junk food for one day?

He looked at her as if he were crestfallen, his smile dissolving into a pronounced frown. Girls, he said, have we had enough junk food for one day?

No, they sang in chorus.

I didn't think so either, he said, rising from the couch to wander into the kitchen, humming as he did so. As he rifled through the cabinets and cupboards. Minutes later the apartment filled with the smell of buttered popcorn, and they all happily readjusted their positions on the couch while Charlie dispersed paper napkins and held out a large bowl for them to share.

Just as the episode began, Addie looked at Charlie and asked, Are you my grandpa?

Yeah, Ainsley chimed in, still focused on the television. We've never had a grandpa.

He glanced down at her, kissed the top of their heads, and said, I don't know. What do you think?

Well, if you're marrying my grandma, Addie reasoned, then you must be my grandpa.

I can't argue with that logic, Charlie agreed.

So can I call you Grandpa?

Vivian noticed that he could not immediately answer. After a moment, he passed the bowl to Ainsley and excused himself before walking to the bathroom.

Vivian rose and followed him.

Charlie, she said, her lips pressed close to the door. Charlie, are you all right?

His voice, when it returned to her, sounded strained. I'm fine, he assured her. Fine. Be out in a minute.

Are you feeling okay? Charlie?

I'm fine, Vivian, he said. I'm just—can I have a moment? Please?

Not if you're going to have a heart attack, Charlie, then, no, you can't.

I'm not going to have a heart attack. I took my pills. My heart feels fine.

Well, I'm just going to stand here then, she said. I'm sorry, but I'm not going to sit on a couch eating popcorn, while you have a stroke and bang your head on the—

The door opened a few inches, and she slid inside the small bathroom. He was sitting on the floor, his hands over his face.

Are you okay? she asked. Charlie? Do I need to call an ambulance? She sat down beside him. Took his wrists in her hands. Ran her fingers through his hair. Charlie?

He moved his hands away from his face, and now she could see that he had been crying.

I never thought I would be anyone's grandpa, he said. You know? You get older and your friends start to become grand-parents. They show you photos of their grandkids. They talk about their grandkids all the time. It used to annoy me, he said, wiping his face with a hand towel. But now...I get it. They're just so miraculous and perfect. And they like me. I thought I'd be invisible to them or something. I didn't think they'd even really notice me.

She smiled. Of course they like you, Charlie. They love you. You're really good to them. And they've never had that. They've never had a steady male presence in their lives.

Oh, he said, taking a deep breath. What a day. What a day this has been.

You know, you don't have to hide in the bathroom when you're happy, she said, kissing his ear. It's okay for people to see you cry.

I was worried they'd think I was croaking. You know, dying. Or in pain. I think if they'd hugged me that might have been too much for this old heart.

Do you still need a minute? she asked. Can I get you anything?

No, no, no. I'll be out in a second.

She kissed him again, this time on the lips, and then slipped out of the bathroom.

Is Grandpa okay? the girls asked.

Oh, he's fine. Too much junk food's what I think. Grandpa has an upset stomach. You know, that's what happens.

She sat on the couch and reached for the bowl. Ainsley passed it to her, but it was empty. Just a dozen or more unpopped kernels, rolling around the ceramic. What they used to refer to as old maids. Just a few tiny pools of congealed butter.

Did you finish all this? Just while I was in the bathroom?

Neither of her grandchildren could speak. Their mouths were full of popcorn.

Long after the children went to sleep, she and Charlie walked down to the first-floor front porch and sat on the stoop, drinking ice water. The sides of the street were lined with parked cars, the windshields shining opaquely beneath streetlamps. The air was heavy with pollen. Heavy, too, with the promise of impending rain. Lights from a baseball diamond pushed back ominous scudding cloud banks, and the moon was impossible to find. The ice cubes calved quietly in the glasses, and to the west came the low sound of thunder. They didn't say a thing. She leaned against him and sighed.

The rain came on quickly. Fat raindrops slowly pounding the roofs of the cars. Then the storm intensified, and they were forced off the stoop and away from the rain. Her skin was wet, and with the rain came a dramatic fall in temperature. The air was cooler now, and fresh smelling. Deeper under the porch's protection sat two crackly, aged wicker chairs and they rested there, rubbing their shoulders for warmth.

I'm going to grab us some blankets, she said. Is that okay? It's just so nice here, watching this storm.

Thank you, he said simply. Oh, and if there's any coffee left in the pot, could you bring me a cup?

Of course, she said, rubbing his shoulder lightly.

She walked up the stairs, listening to the old house creak and groan beneath her feet. She poured the last inch of coffee from the pot into a mug and set the mug in the microwave for a half minute. While she waited, she walked to the window, and from that vantage she could see Melissa and another person standing on the corner of the block, perhaps a hundred yards away.

Vivian stood motionless, for some reason aware that she might be noticed, spying. But Melissa was oblivious. The person she was standing with moved closer until they were near enough to take Melissa's face in their hands and kiss her, deeply, while Melissa wrapped her arms around their waist. The streetlight was a spotlight upon them, upon that soft corner of concrete. The person, Vivian realized, was another woman. They kissed and kissed, the two of them, slowly, in the rain. She watched as their clothing grew darker; they were soaked through, and oblivious to it.

The microwave sounded. She felt both sizzling excitement and happiness, but also a kind of confusion. A woman. Did that make Melissa gay? She supposed it did. And how did she, herself, Vivian feel about that? Did it matter to her? Was she surprised? Well, she was surprised, yes. Now Vivian forgot entirely about the blankets and the coffee and all but ran down the stairs eager to meet this person, her daughter's friend, her girlfriend. She banged through the screen door, startling Charlie.

No coffee? he asked.

She looked down the street and Melissa was running toward them, at first, hand in hand with her friend—her girlfriend. Then, as they came closer, they dropped their hands, pounding through puddles, screaming against the rain and the lightning, a passing car that curled a wave of water directly at them. And then they were on the porch, gasping for breath but smiling, and laughing too, holding their own shoulders, slicking their hair back and away from their eyes, tucking hair behind their ears, pink with the new wet cold. It had been so long since Vivian had heard her daughter laugh.

Well, Vivian said, aware of her own motherly tone, how was dinner?

Come on, Vivian, Charlie said first. Let's get these gals inside. They must be freezing. I'm Charlie, by the way, he said, rising a bit stiffly from the chair to shake Melissa's friend's hand.

Jill. Then she turned and offered her hand to Vivian. It's really lovely to meet you. You know you're Melissa's hero, right?

Oh, come on, Vivian said, let's get you two dried off.

They stood in the kitchen, drinking hot cocoa, the silence wooden and awkward. Jill in the bathroom, the sound of the shower.

Your friend seems nice, Charlie said to Melissa.

Vivian felt her daughter's eyes on her. She wasn't quite sure what to say, which troubled her, because she knew that she didn't have to say anything. That this didn't really concern her. She wasn't, in fact, quite sure how she felt, and that troubled her too, because she knew that the only thing that mattered was that she loved Melissa and wanted her to be happy. And yet, this was a surprise. And at least a short-term secret, but maybe something withheld for much longer too. It was natural to feel confused when such a thing burst forth, revealing the truth.

Mom, Melissa said quietly.

Yes.

I didn't know this was going to happen. Jill, I mean. I'd never really had these feelings for a woman before. Or if I had,

I didn't really consider them, you know? I just thought…they were occasional fantasies. Oh my god, this is too much. I can't believe I'm telling you all this. Okay. Here's the thing. She is really, really, really nice to me. And to the girls too. She doesn't ask for anything either. She just, you know, supports me. Makes me feel good. It's easy with her. To be with her.

That word, easy, resonated, like a sacred musical note in Vivian's heart. She felt she understood immediately, even if part of her was resistant, stubborn, even—she could admit—hard, mean.

We have the best time. We really do. Doing absolutely nothing. It could just be baking. Or taking a walk. Cooking together. We laugh all the time.

The shower suddenly hushed. The sound of a plastic curtain pulled back. A towel rustling.

I haven't told her anything, Mom, but I think I love her. She makes me feel safe. And here's the other thing—she doesn't drink. Never has. She's straight edge. Totally straight edge.

Straight edge? Charlie asked.

She was a punk when she was a teenager. Some punks are straight edge. It means no drugs or alcohol, no cigarettes. She's as clean as a Girl Scout. She doesn't even like pop or juice or candy. Mom, I've lost ten pounds since we started dating. She pulled up her shirt and squeezed a pinch of belly fat. See? We even work out together. It's bananas.

Not even any sweets, huh? Charlie asked, confused. What about ice cream?

Vivian bit her lip and closed her eyes. This needed to be celebrated. Encouraged. Blessed. Or maybe it didn't need to be; it just could be. But she wanted to celebrate this. From the bathroom, she heard the toilet flush, and the sound of water splashing in the sink. She went to Melissa, wrapped her daughter in a strong, strong hug.

Listen to me, she whispered. Don't ever let her go. You hear me? If you really love her, then don't ever let her go.

She kissed her daughter and squeezed her harder still.

Thanks, Mom.

Oh, and I guess I have something I need to share with you as well, Vivian said, but...let's wait a few days. Nothing will change, okay? I'll call you. Tuesday night? It's good news.

Good news?

Great news.

Of course, Mom. And—

Just down the hallway, the bathroom door opened, and Jill looked at the three of them and smiled.

Thanks, she told them simply. This really means a lot to me.

————

The streets and highways were largely empty when Charlie pointed his truck east for the drive home. They were quiet. Held hands. She stared at the lights of downtown Saint Paul, the humble skyline of a city that'd seen its zenith many decades before. She glanced quickly at Charlie and was pleased to see that he was just focusing on the road, his face utterly content. It didn't seem to matter to him—Melissa and Jill. She liked that. He didn't seem to care as long as Melissa was happy. He certainly didn't seem surprised. She squeezed his hand, and he peered over at her.

What? he asked.

Nothing, she said, shrugging her shoulders and smiling.

The rain had abated, and now the streets shimmered with headlights, brake lights, streetlights. She felt tremendous relief. A relief she'd never experienced before. In one evening, it felt as if her daughter had finally and safely learned to swim, to navigate the waters of life. And now, Vivian didn't have to hold on so tight, or watch so vigilantly. Her work was complete.

33

The chairs were more comfortable than he imagined. There were fewer people than he imagined, too. Four other men. About his age, maybe a little bit older. They didn't even sit down at first. Just stood in the church basement like a service had ended and they were avoiding their wives.

I'm Charlie, he said, introducing himself.

They welcomed him warmly. Samuel, Stanley, Evarist, and Holling. Introduced themselves. The basement smelled of burned coffee, though from outside, the air carried in the smells of earthworms and wet asphalt; irises were blooming.

We could sit outside, Stanley offered. The church has a little courtyard. Nice and private. It's too beautiful to be inside anyway. C'mon. Grab your chair.

Outside, they asked Charlie questions. About his working days on the railroad. All of them were real curious about that. His retirement and his new life here. Holling knew Vivian; he'd been a high-school history teacher and had taught Melissa so many years back.

How is Vivian? he asked. She getting along all right?

Oh, I think she's doing well, Charlie said. Real well, I hope. We just got engaged, in fact.

Well, now, Holling exclaimed. Good for you. Good for you both. She's had a hard go of it, I know that. Her husband's health. She stood by him—no offense—like an angel. Everyone recognized it. She was so beautiful, and a young mother, and she kept that garage going and was a good wife to him, all that time. I heard that her husband didn't say a word, those last three, four years. He wasn't catatonic, but he'd just stare at you, no matter who you were, like you were a stranger. Like he was looking right through you, past you. Must've been tough. Well, anyhow, good for you. She's a keeper.

I'm happy as I've ever been, he said to those four men, who held their paper coffee cups in both hands and looked at him expectantly, waiting for the confession they knew was bottled inside him.

You don't have to say anything, son, Evarist said. But is there a reason you're here today? Here with us?

Charlie nodded his head and looked at his feet. Birds were singing from the maple boughs and overhead, leaves were gently waving with the evening wind. He took a deep breath.

I need help, he said. I do. I'm an alcoholic, and I want to be free of it. I don't want to drink anymore.

Well, Charlie, Stanley said, taking a deep breath. You see that tree over there? That big old oak?

Yessir.

You see its shadow—stretching toward the fence?

I do.

You're that tree, Charlie. And that shadow, that's your relationship with alcohol. You can't ever shake it. So don't think that you will. You come to these meetings, and you bring your shadow right with you. But at least now, you're acknowledging it. You're acknowledging that you have this shadow, this dark side. We all do.

Okay, Charlie breathed out.

Stanley set his hand on Charlie's shoulder. When was your last drink?

A week ago, Charlie said.

How do you feel right now? Do you want a drink?

Charlie looked up, at Stanley's face. At his kind eyes. At the watch on his wrist, crowded by white arm hair. At the other men, leaning towards him, as if he might reveal some hot investment tip. He looked at their old scuffed shoes. The pleats in their well-ironed pants. He looked at their thick work-worn hands. The sunset was hot against his right cheek, like a warm palm, and he closed his eyes and said, Yes.

That's okay, son. That's okay. We all do. We all understand. We're here to help you.

34

All the clothing she'd found at garage sales, auctions, and resale stores—the entire inventory of Violet Vintage—they'd moved all of it into Charlie's basement. It was dry down there, and mostly empty except for the wine cellar. She opened a door off the kitchen and flicked on a light switch to lead her guest down the old wooden stairs.

Six racks of clothing, each garment's price indicated by a small paper tag attached to a length of pink string. When the reality that she would never open a storefront presented itself years ago, she'd had the intentions of someday organizing at least a garage sale. Sell all these clothes and put them toward the girls' college or something. But somehow, she could never find the time even for that. And so, these beautiful garments just hung there, waiting to be worn once more.

But now she wanted to be free of these old things that were weighing her down. And more than that even, she wanted, for the first time in her life, to splurge.

You're selling it all? Diane asked.

Yes, all of it is for sale. One lot. I'd prefer it if you took every-thing. So I can stop moving all these clothes around.

You're ready to make a deal then?

I'm ready to make a deal.

Diane's fingers parted the garments, considering each one, before moving on to the next rack. Rack to rack. Occasionally she peered at her phone, Vivian suspected, to check compara-ble prices on eBay. It took her twenty minutes to peer through everything.

Look, I'm not going to add everything up. So let me just make you a flat offer.

Vivian had, in fact, already added up the total sum of all the garments, as tagged, and that number came to just over six thousand dollars. She figured if she could get half of that, she'd spin a little profit. I'm all ears, Vivian said.

Four thousand. Diane reached into her purse and showed Vivian a thick wad of cash. I've got the cash right here actually. I'll take everything for four.

Vivian suppressed a smile, crossed her arms, and said, Four thousand five hundred.

Forty-two fifty.

Deal.

Deal?

Deal.

The two women shook hands.

Can I help you load all this into your van? Vivian offered.

Absolutely, Diane said. And oh, here's your money.

Vivian accepted the cash, slipped the bills into her pocket, and felt light as a breeze. A sailboat suddenly and smartly discovered by a gust, the canvas billowing, that lightness, she imagined, of wind guiding a boat across a body of water. Her life was surging now, gaining speed, and she could hardly wait to see what was out and ahead of her.

35

There were mornings now when he woke up to find the bed empty. But this did not fill him with fear or uncertainty. He knew where she was, and the thought of her absence from the bed was not a sad sensation but simply the knowledge that she was happy. So happy that she would wake before dawn to begin chores that were hardly work for her at all.

He would rise contentedly. Visit the bathroom. Then downstairs. Sometimes Blueberry stood by the door, looking for her. Other times the dog remained sacked out on the floor, legs moving with unknowable dog dreams.

The coffee was always made, and he would stand at the kitchen window and look for her through the window, out there in the new sunlight of the day. Out there in the pasture. Sometimes leading the horse, reins in hand. Other times sitting on top of the new Western saddle she'd bought. She spent almost as much time with Shelby as she did with him. She was even trying to convince him to buy another horse. His horse.

That's the thing about horses, he said, one horse leads to another horse. Soon you've got a whole stable full.

I'm not sure I understand what the problem is, she said playfully.

Hayburners is what my dad used to call them, Charlie said wryly.

He gave her space. Time too. Time, it seemed to him, to play. To do the things she had dreamed of doing for over four decades. Maybe her entire life. Her hand on the horse, whispering to Shelby, or pushing the creature into a gallop just after dawn, as the sun began to burn through the fog just like a welding torch.

And then her face, shiny with sweat when she returned to the house. Smelling of leather. Of horse sweat. Her own sweat. Hay. Dewy grass. Fresh summer air. Wrapping her arms around him. Kissing his lips, the sweat there, just above her upper lip. He loved that best of all.

A few weeks later, they drove slowly south down the Wisconsin Great River Road—the Mississippi River to their right, like the grandest handrail. They stopped in small towns. They took little hikes. In Prairie du Chien, they crossed the river, America's vena cava, and entered Iowa near Marquette.

I didn't know Iowa was so beautiful, she said.

Hills and bluffs and coulees and hollows. Oak forests. Hilltop vistas of cornfields riding ridgelines. Little farms. Sandstone buildings. Rivers and creeks. The world moving at a slower pace.

Honestly, Vivian said, this is so gorgeous.

Well, thanks for agreeing to come with me, Charlie said. I

2222222

can understand how this might feel awkward for you, but…it's important to me that you meet my friends. That you meet Mona.

Decorah looked like the set of a Jimmy Stewart movie. A quaint downtown. A beautiful college campus. Little boutiques and stores. They pulled to a stop beneath mature oak trees whose canopy stretched over the street, and in front of a perfectly refurbished Victorian, its pristine paint job like that of a dark blue dollhouse, all accented in white and burgundy and pale blue. From the wraparound porch, he saw his friends rise out of two rocking chairs, Mona moving quickly, then returning to Nathaniel's side to steady him. Now they came down the steps towards him and Vivian, and they were holding hands.

Welcome, Mona said, taking Vivian's hands in hers, and congratulations. Come inside.

———

They sat on that porch all evening, not a bottle of alcohol in sight. Mona asked about their wedding plans. Charlie asked about Nathaniel's health. Vivian asked Mona about her retirement. They talked about Melissa, Jessie, Ainsley, and Addison. They talked about Shelby and Blueberry. Nathaniel said he was hungry for dinner, and they moved inside to eat a fresh green salad topped with a thick salmon fillet all drizzled with a soy sauce and maple syrup reduction.

Do you miss it? Mona asked Charlie. The drinking?

He took a sip of water and then nodded his head. Yes, he

277

admitted. Sometimes I really do. I've had a wonderful evening. But in my mind, I'm still thinking that everything would be made better by a bottle of perfect Oregon pinot noir. That the wine would magnify every taste.

I'm proud of you, Mona said, in the way only a teacher can. In the way only a friend can. I didn't think you had it in you, she admitted. You proved me wrong.

Charlie reached for Vivian's hand.

I finally had someone to live for, he admitted. People to live for.

Well, Nathaniel said, we don't have wineglasses, but I think water will suffice. He stood, a little awkwardly, raised his water glass and said, Cheers. To the newlyweds. May the second time be the charm.

They touched glasses, said, Cheers.

Really, Vivian put in, it's the fourth time for Charlie. But who's counting?

Charlie wrapped an arm around Vivian's shoulder, and they sat that way. Tired, comfortable, content.

And Charlie tells me he's even a father, Mona said, shaking her head in wonderment. I always knew he was a slow starter, but this takes the cake.

Here she is, Charlie said, offering Mona his phone, where he proudly stored dozens of photos of Jessie, Melissa, Addison, and Ainsley. He couldn't believe it himself. Suddenly, he was a father, and an honorary grandfather to boot.

Oh, let me take your picture, Mona said, fumbling with the phone. You two look so cute together.

And they posed that way, leaning into one another, smiling, so happy.

Later that night, after Nathaniel and Vivian had retired for the night, Charlie and Mona sat on the porch, listening to the neighborhood's night sounds. They were quiet, and he knew something was wrong. Mona was rarely this subdued.

Is everything all right? Charlie asked.

She shook her head and began gently crying. He stood and rested a hand on her shoulder.

The cancer has spread, Mona said through tears. This is the last time you'll see him.

I'm so sorry, Mona. There isn't anything to be done then?

No. And he's tired. He's been through the treatments already. He hated chemo. I thought about asking him to keep fighting, if only for me. But—

Mona's voice caught and she allowed herself a few moments to regain her composure.

That wouldn't be fair.

I wish there was some way I could help, Charlie offered. Please let me know if I can help, okay?

I don't know what I'm going to do, she said. I don't know what I'm going to do without him. I don't want to think about it. This house? How can I live here without him?

Charlie sank to his knees, and they held each other for a long time.

I'm here for you, he said. Like you were there for me. Anything you need. We'll be here.

Thank you, she said bravely. The irony, she laughed darkly. You live a roguish existence for sixty years. Breaking hearts and riding the rails. Then, in your sixties, you find love, a daughter, grandkids, a farm… We aren't that far from our fiftieth, but when Nathaniel dies…I won't have a thing. Isn't that something?

She took his face in her hands. It all goes so fast, she said. I don't understand where all that time went.

He wanted to say, There will be more time. But he didn't. He said, I'm so, so sorry.

———

Two mornings later, they stood on the front stoop while a neighbor took their picture. Four of them, arms balanced on each other's shoulders. All smiles. Then they hugged one another, and as Charlie and Vivian were walking back to his truck to leave, Mona said, Let's go to Spain. Next spring. The four of us. San Sebastian. What do you say?

Charlie turned back to look at his friend, his old professor, his second wife, and he could not control the moisture beading across his eyes. But he said, as cheerfully as he could, We can't wait. I love you both. Goodbye.

36

He sat in the passenger seat of his own truck, eyes closed. She sat in the driver's seat and strapped the seat belt into place. Then regarded him, sitting there, like a kidnappee. She reached over and squeezed his thigh. Then ran her hand up a bit higher and gave another squeeze.

All right now, he said, his voice cracking, what are you trying to do to me?

She allowed herself a little laugh.

Now put the blindfold on him, Jessie, Vivian said. There you go. Make sure it's tight. Can you see anything, Charlie?

I can't see a thing.

Are your eyes open? Melissa asked.

Yes.

And you're sure you can't see anything? Vivian asked.

Yes. Well, maybe a little. I can see my legs. The seat. Sunlight.

Take it off him, Jessie. Now Charlie, close your eyes again. There you go. Make it wider, sweetie. Slide it over his nose too. There you go. Melissa, can you help her?

Over my nose?

Shhh, Jessie said, taking her task very seriously.

Okay, open your eyes. Now, can you see anything now?

No. It's completely dark. I can't see a thing. You've blinded me. Are you happy?

Excellent.

You do know how much I love this truck, right? Charlie asked.

What are you saying? You trust me enough to marry me, but not enough to drive your truck?

Charlie paused for longer than he might have intended. Yes, I guess I am saying that, somewhat.

You think I'm a bad driver?

Just maybe not as attentive as say, I am.

Well, this will be a real trust exercise for you then, Vivian said, slapping his thigh, before adjusting the rearview and side mirrors. You buckled in back there, ladies?

Yes, I am, Jessie said. Did you bring my pop?

In the cooler beside you. But, Jessie?

Yes?

One bottle, okay?

Got it.

She can be mean sometimes, can't she? Melissa asked.

Like when she blindfolds someone, Charlie put in.

Okay, here we go.

And Blueberry will be okay? he asked. And Shelby? You've got a plan for the animals?

Yes, I told you, Jill and the girls will be here late afternoon, as soon as she can get out of work, and they'll stay all weekend. It'll be a nice break for them, out of the city.

She pulled the truck slowly out of the driveway, the blinker's steady rhythm throbbing. Any sense where we're going?

West, he said tentatively. West for the moment. But I don't know how long I'm going to be able to keep the compass steady in my mind.

And Jessie didn't spill the beans? She didn't tell you where we're going?

I didn't, Jessie cried out.

No, look, I told you. I tried. I even attempted bribery. She wouldn't say a word. Poor thing, you must have scared the bejee-zus out of her.

I did nothing of the sort. Vivian smiled.

And Melissa? She didn't tell you? These days I swear she likes you better than me.

Well, he shrugged, what can I say? We're simpatico. Aren't we, hon?

Melissa reached out from the back seat of the extended cab and rubbed his shoulders. I'm sorry, C, we've got to keep it a secret. But I think it'll be worth it.

Fine, he said, I think I'll just close my eyes then and get a little shut-eye while I'm getting my shut-eye.

Yeah, Vivian said, peering in the rearview mirror to where her two daughters were talking to one another. Good luck with the peanut gallery back there.

She imagined him settling into a cozy kind of darkness.

Trying his best to relax into the role of passenger. Feeling invisible hills roll beneath their tires and slide away. Feeling the gravity of valleys. Smelling the manure of passing farms. The cool fresh air blown off a no-name stream gurgling over fieldstone riffles, and sun-bleached fallen cottonwoods and box elders. Birdsong. Cranes and red-winged blackbirds. Low-country birds. Feeling them slow at four-way stops. Hearing the air brakes of eighteen-wheelers wheeze and shudder. Listening as she and Jessie talked about lunch, about what Jessie would eat for lunch, and then, then drifting off again... She could hear his breathing relax into something just lighter than a snore.

When he awoke, she wondered if he could feel the commerce, the activity of a highway pulling them towards a city. Her hands tensed on the steering wheel. This wasn't as bad as driving in Saint Paul or Minneapolis, but it wasn't like home either, not at all like Chippewa Falls. Could he sense traffic surrounding them on the roads? He pushed himself up in the seat and was just about to remove the blindfold when her hand was on his and she was saying, We're close but not quite there yet.

Where are we?

I can't tell you yet, she said.

La Crosse, Jessie put in from the back seat.

Jessie, Vivian said.

Oh, sorry, Auntie.

Home of the Bodega bar, Melissa sighed. What a wonderful place to drink a cold beer. Or, like, eight cold beers.

I do love La Crosse, he said. So can I take the blindfold off now?

No, Vivian said. Absolutely not. And Jessie, don't you say another word, do you hear me, girl? If you spoil this, I swear to god…no more soda. Ever.

He stifled a laugh, freezing his face into a mask of seriousness.

Ever? Jessie squeaked.

Ever, Vivian said. I mean it.

Mom, Melissa said, a little harsh maybe?

They exited off the highway, slowing by degrees as they matriculated to smaller roads. They drove closer and closer to the Mississippi River, to the old buildings of downtown La Crosse. She rolled her window down and felt the summer air against her face, blowing her hair around her face.

Eventually, she pulled them to a stop in a wide parking lot. People milled around the truck. Walking toward the central gravity of the train station. People of all ages. Old people shuffling and young children plodding along holding on to their parents' hands. Luggage rolling and scraping. Car doors banging shut. Talking. Excited talking. There was a thrumming of excitement in the people she heard. An anticipation of something. Something collective.

Vivian felt nervous, nervous in the best possible way. Nervous about doing something totally new. Something unexpected. She'd never been on a train before and always wanted to. Always wanted to ride along with him through countryside she'd seen, never imagined. Wondered if he was the same man while he was working, or if he presented himself differently.

Where are we? he asked.

She loosened his blindfold and ran her fingers along his jaw while he blinked his eyes to see that it was now late morning, the sun high above them and bright. They were outside a train depot, and from far off they heard that whistle, that huge shrill whistle reverberating between the bluffs of the river and off the wide flat face of the blue-green river. The air shivered and vibrated with the encroaching immensity of the locomotive and all the cars stretched out behind it.

Are we going somewhere? he asked. On a train?

She nodded then, her eyes shining with the joy of the surprise.

Chicago, she said. Now come on. It's all taken care of. I'll just need a little help with the bags.

Wait, on the train? We're taking the train? We're taking the train to Chicago?

She nodded again.

I've never ridden Amtrak. All my years on the railroad, and I've never been on Amtrak. Always wanted to, but I...

Well, she smiled, that makes four of us.

Is there a caboose, Charlie? Jessie asked.

Charlie turned in his seat, smiled at her, I hope so, he said, though he knew the likelihood was incredibly small. There weren't many cabooses left on the rails except those owned by the extremely wealthy. Then, looking at Vivian, he said, You didn't have to do this. Please, let me pay for everything once we get there. I can't let you—

Can I tell you something, Charlie? she said, interrupting him.

She wanted him to note that. The use of his name. Her tone.

She even suppressed the smile she still felt inside. A reprimand was coming. A good-hearted reprimand.

I'm serious now, she said. I mean this: Can you stop talking about money, please? I hate it. Everything is fine. We're not staying at the Peninsula, or whatever, but we're not staying at Motel 6 either. The ratings were good, and they have a free breakfast. It's for two nights. One room, two beds. Now I've saved money for this. My money. Please don't ruin this for me. I mean that now. Do you understand me?

He nodded.

You never talked about money when we were first married, she put in. Ever.

Well, I didn't have any.

I still don't, she said. So there.

Me either, Melissa echoed.

Me either, Jessie said, nodding.

You're right, he said, I do talk about it too much. I can even hear myself when I'm doing it. It's terrible, I know.

I just want to be comfortable, she said. That's all I've ever wanted. I don't need fancy restaurants or hotels. Because then what? What comes next? Expensive clothing? I can't walk into a nice hotel in old shoes. Someone staring at me while I eat dinner because I'm wearing a dress from Target. I certainly can't walk into the Four Seasons this way, with my roots growing out and my nails looking like a farmer. Does that make sense, Charlie? Do you understand me?

I do, he said, and he meant it.

Are you fighting? Jessie asked, somewhat nonchalantly.

No, Vivian said sweetly. Charlie is just learning something important.

You're teaching him?

That's right. I am. I'm teaching him. Although sometimes, certain lessons seem to take longer than others.

Is Charlie slow? Jessie asked.

He might be, sweetheart, Vivian laughed. But I still love him.

You two are a hoot, Melissa said, rolling her eyes.

They stood away from the edge of the platform as travelers began saying their goodbyes. Lifted their luggage up off the ground. As students shouldered backpacks. Something about a train slowing. Something about a train coming to a stop. Such power. Such vast, thrumming power. There was an occasion about it. An opportunity. This machine and its constituents were moving somewhere, and if a person only climbed aboard, the train promised new terrain, new perspectives, new towns and cities, new faces. She was nervous. Nervous that the tickets would somehow be unreadable on her phone; she didn't like the fact that she didn't have paper tickets, something to safely stow in her purse.

She helped him haul their bags up and onto the train, stowing them in a storage compartment, while Melissa held Jessie's hand. The train jolted beneath her, and her body felt electric with anticipation. Travelers jostled, shouldered past, finding seats or moving from car to car. The train car's ventilation system whispered on, and the space was filled with new fresh air purifying the scent of diesel, body odor, and fast food in grease-splotched paper bags.

She gently directed Jessie into a seat and pointed at a space across the aisle for Charlie and Melissa. This felt familiar: marshaling a family. This she could do.

I get this seat, Jessie said, by the window.

Vivian leaned across the aisle and kissed him lightly. The kind of kiss that was commonplace between them now, though even a year ago it had been the stuff of dreams, or old memories. Sometimes she tried to record one of their kisses in her mind, the way a mundane day is nevertheless still documented in a diary, still essential to the record.

Can I tell you something? she asked. I've never been to Illinois. Never been to Chicago. I'm nervous. Excited. She bit her lip. I didn't think...for years, I didn't think this was something I could do, or ever would do. And I guess what I want to say is... that I wouldn't be doing it, not without you.

Thank you, he replied. Thank you for this beautiful trip you've planned. Honestly, I'm astonished. I'm excited too, I really am.

She allowed herself a small laugh, and realized they were flirting, holding hands, tiny sparks popping in her hands, palpable electricity. Like the moments when a roller coaster lurches up its track, just before the great stomach-twisting fall.

Honestly, you two make me sick, Melissa laughed. You know? Like, get a room already.

Chicago is one of my favorite cities, he said to Vivian, squeezing her hand. You'll love it. I don't want to say too much about it. You should experience it for yourself. But I can't wait to see your face.

The train rocked, and rocked again, and then they were moving. Slowly, to start. The river off to her right. Jessie's face pressed against the window. She was singing something, some song Vivian recognized, but not immediately. She was singing the same line, over and over again, and it took her a moment, but then she recalled it. I see your true colors...

How do you know that song? Vivian asked.

Everyone knows it, Jessie said casually.

You know that song was on the radio all the time a couple years after you were born?

Was it?

Jessie had lived with her for a little more than two years. A little more than two years before she passed her sweet baby to the Stapletons. But during those first months, they had often sat in the front yard of her aunt and uncle's house under the generous shade of a great cottonwood tree. She remembered that cottonwood tree now. How it moved with the wind. How she used to sway and rock Jessie in time with pendulous tree branches' languid movements. The sunlight dappling down. Just Vivian and her little baby and the brief time they had together as mother and daughter. She said a silent thank-you to those relatives of hers that had helped her, aided her in a time of need, reached down and lifted her up. Sometimes, she realized, it is too late to properly acknowledge the good fortune of generosity and kindness, but it is never too late to try to duplicate such acts, to multiply them, like a family growing larger, like a grand old tree branching out to embrace the sun's good light.

Strange, but just then Vivian was thankful for that summer weather of that long-ago time. For those days of benevolent breeze and long sunlight. It might just as easily have been winter, dark and cold, and they would have been cooped up inside some bedroom not her own. Buried beneath warm blankets to ward off the cold that accompanied those howling winds of a Montana winter. Or it might have been raining. But that wasn't what she remembered. She just remembered her beautiful baby daughter and that cottonwood tree. She remembered grace and kindness. And she remembered those two old people who shepherded her across the vastness of the country.

They rode and they watched. Watched the countryside sweep by. At first the bluffs buffering the Mississippi River. Long barges burdened with coal. Freight trains idling. Small towns of brick buildings and narrow streets. Fishermen. Then away from the river. Gentle hills. Fields of corn. Fields of grass. Fields of beans. Forests and barbed-wire fences. Sparsely trafficked roads. Then power lines and telephone lines. Poles marking the miles. Bigger towns now, more stops.

The anticipation was back. That they were moving toward something big, something grand. People adjusted and readjusted in their seats. Organized bags. Folded newspapers and magazines away. Checked makeup. The roads and highways were now flush with swiftly moving traffic. If Chippewa Falls moved at a certain speed, Chicago moved a hundred times faster, a thousand times faster. Frenetically so. Passengers were checking their phones now, making last-minute calls.

She glanced over at Charlie, but he didn't seem nervous in the least. He reached out for her hand.

Hey, he said, the great thing about a big city is that you're invisible. Nobody cares. You just do your own thing.

She nodded her head.

Can I tell you something else?

Okay, she murmured.

This might surprise you, but I think the two friendliest big cities in America are Chicago and New York. People there, they put on these, you know, gruff masks. All business. But if you get lost in New York and need directions, and you're brave enough to ask someone, next thing you know you're surrounded by New Yorkers fighting to give you the best directions. It's happened to me. Same with Chicago. You ask someone where to find a good hot dog, and then suddenly, a cop is flashing his lights and asking you to follow him to his favorite place.

Really?

Sometimes, yeah. I mean, they can be jerks too, of course, but most of the time not so much.

Now, the skyline came into view, like a bookcase of the gods. Towers hulking through the smog and sunlight. Jessie fell silent, her mouth slightly open, as they lumbered closer and closer to the heart of the city. Passengers stood and shuffled towards the entrances of the cars.

Vivian reached out and touched Jessie's thigh. We're in no hurry, sweetheart. We can take our time. She knew she was talking as much to herself as to her daughter. Across the aisle, she saw Melissa pop a piece of gum into her mouth and then check her hair and makeup on her phone. A person didn't even need a mirror anymore, she thought.

They let the other passengers disembark and then stood up to gather their own bags. She and Jessie held hands as they stepped down from the train. Charlie and Melissa handled the luggage. The air, thick with exhaust, seemed to pulse with energy.

I don't know where I'm going, Vivian admitted.

Come on, he said, follow me.

Inside Union Station he paused to allow them to take in the great barreled skylight above them, the polished terrazzo floor, the soaring walls of pale stone.

You've been inside this building before? Vivian asked.

It's been a while, he admitted, but I have seen The Untouchables.

Then they moved out onto Canal Street, and she gawked up into the sky at one of the world's great skyscrapers, a building she'd always read about or known on TV as the Sears Tower. Stray paper rode on gusts of wind, and elevated trains tumbled by down some unseen tracks. It was all dizzying, dazzling.

Glancing at her watch, Vivian said, We should check into the hotel. I do have one thing planned for this evening.

37

One evening, weeks before Vivian had moved out of her house and into his, Charlie was sitting on the porch, drinking a glass of ice water with a wedge of lemon. Trying to drink more water, he noticed that he actually felt better, had more energy, was less lethargic in the morning. Dusk settled over the fields and forest surrounding his house. From the barn, he heard the neighbor girl, Maddie, talking to the horse. Warm light issued out of the open barn door, smudging a rhombus of yellow over the gravel just outside. He felt anxious to see Vivian again, even though they'd taken a walk that very same morning. Summer had that effect on him: he couldn't stop moving, working, walking, tinkering.

He climbed into the truck and drove to her house. He just missed her. Was curious as to what she might be doing. He wanted to talk to her. It was a long drive, but even if she lived four hours away, the distance would not have stopped him.

He parked on the street and knocked on the front door. No answer. He tried the door: Unlocked. Called her name. Edged into the house. Called her name again. Withdrew his phone from a pocket and texted her: You home? From the kitchen counter, he heard her phone vibrate. He walked into the kitchen, and through the window above the sink he spotted her, out in the last of the failing light.

She was kneeling in the backyard grass in a pair of old gym shorts. The soles of her bare feet dirty. The width of her pale thighs. Her hands were working, digging. From time to time, she swatted away a mosquito. On the telephone line overhead, a mourning dove cooed.

Hello, he called out the window.

She startled a moment before realizing it was just him. Then turned and sat down. Blew hair away from her face.

Are you trying to kill me?

What?

You can't sneak up on a person like that. You'll scare them to death.

I knocked on the front door, he said.

Well, I didn't hear anything.

What are you doing?

Digging up bulbs, she explained.

What?

Flower bulbs. Tulips. Some lilies. I thought I'd bring them to your house.

You look beautiful, he said, smiling.

I do not. I'm a mess. I'm filthy. And sweaty.

Forty years ago, he would have taken off his shirt and pants, walked into the backyard, and made love to her there in the grass. But now he just leaned against the counter, marveling at her.

My lord, you're beautiful, he said.

Forty years ago, she might have said, Oh yeah? Come prove it then. But now she said, Make yourself useful. Put these in your truck, will you? And maybe, just maybe, if you're lucky I'll come home with you.

Sorry, he said, grinning, but did you say I might get lucky?

Don't push it.

Back at his house, he drew her a hot bath. Removed her clothing. Then helped her step into the old claw-foot tub. He opened the window so they could listen to the frogs and night insects. He lowered himself to the cool tiled floor beside the tub. Then he stood, turned on the radio, and scanned the FM dial until he settled on a signal. He sat down again. She hung a foot over the edge of the tub with a satisfying little splash, and he held her foot to massage the sole, the arch, the toes.

Who is this? she asked. This music?

Bill Withers, he said, smiling. I think. Isn't it Bill Withers?

It's nice, whoever it is.

Yeah, it really is.

Whole years of my life. I don't think I listened to any music. Isn't that terrible? But it was like triage. Years of triage. Or fighting fires. I never even thought about music.

Can I get you anything? he asked. Something to drink? Or read?

No, she said, stay. Just stay with me here, please. This is so, so nice.

38

When they were first married, he used to play on a softball team, with other men from the railroad. Young men, effortlessly slender and muscular. Many of them wore their hair long. Mustaches were in vogue. Older men too. Forties, fifties, and sixties. Men who kept their hair cut a little tighter, men who had filled out across their chest and stomachs. Almost everyone smoked cigarettes. Those who didn't chewed tobacco. They played from May until October. That was what they did on summer nights.

He wore tight polyester pants and an even tighter T-shirt, and they drove together a little ways into the countryside where there was a softball diamond illuminated by tall lights. She sat in the stands and mostly ignored the proceedings. Read a book. Crocheted. Sometimes jotted on a postcard to her cousin, then living on an Air Force base in Germany. Or chatted with other wives and girlfriends. Sometimes the women talked about the challenges of being married to a railroader. The constant moving, the days and weeks away from home, the injuries.

Listening to other wives during those games could be a sort of therapy for her.

She always watched him when he came to the plate though. Those moments filled her with a strange swirl of emotions. He was essentially alone out there, and she felt nervous for him. Afraid of failure. But thrilled too. Thrilled and proud when he made contact with the ball.

The last spring they were married, he said something offhandedly, about how he had never been to a Major League Baseball game. Never sat in a real stadium. It wasn't like him to talk about things he wanted or dreamed. Even when she prompted him. Even when they were lying in bed together, the lights out, their heads resting on pillows. Most of his desires were uncomplicated. When he came home from work, he wanted a cold beer or dinner; sometimes they made love, or he'd take a long shower, or just walk out to the garage to tinker on their old Ford truck.

She remembered that one time though. The time he had actually wanted something. So she called the Wrigley Field box office. Bought the cheapest tickets she could find. Two seats in the left field bleachers. They weren't as expensive as she had expected, but then again, the Cubs were awful. Even the employee from the box office told her so. Then she waited every day thereafter, checking the mail with the intensity of someone expecting their lottery winnings, a check for a million dollars.

When the tickets arrived, she hid them in her underwear drawer. Then she wrote him a love letter. A survey of where they had come from, where they were, and where she hoped they might someday be. She didn't hold back either. She wanted him to quit drinking. She wanted him to quit the railroad. She wanted to start a family. She believed in him. She loved him.

She never had the chance to give him the letter. Or the tickets. He was gone. And forty years' worth of time seeped into her life, at first like a slow leak, and then, increasingly, like a lifeboat full up to the gunwales and sinking fast.

But now he was back. Now they were getting married all over again. And if he hadn't quit his drinking, he certainly had slowed it, practically to a stop. He was done with the railroad. Retired. And not just retired—successfully retired. He was around for her family. In ways she never might have known to want, much less expect. He was more patient with Melissa than she was. Spoiled her grandchildren. Was fiercely defensive of Jessie and doting upon her. And though she believed in him, and loved him, the man he was now did not seem to need that kind of approval. Didn't need anyone to believe in him. He believed in himself with a degree of certainty and hard-won wisdom that was more attractive than the man he had been forty years earlier.

She looked at him now. Standing in front of the hotel window of their tiny room, his arms around Jessie and Melissa as they peered down into an alley of Dumpsters, parked cars, and hotel staff out for a smoke. He wore nice boots—Blundstones, she had read on the label—and crisp, dark jeans she knew he'd ironed that very morning, before stepping into the shower, topped with a pale blue dress shirt. His hair was cut as neatly as ever. But it wasn't his body or his face. It was his confidence. His spirit.

He wasn't afraid of anything. Except maybe—and this made her blush; she couldn't even quite accept it, but—he was afraid of losing her.

Charlie, she said, I want to give you something.

Okay, he said, turning to her. Now Melissa and Jessie were examining the nearby buildings that surrounded their hotel as they stood at the window, peering into other hotel room windows, peering up into offices, watching custodians empty wastebaskets or vacuum.

She reached into her purse and gave him the envelope. From 1980. Inside was that old love letter. And the two tickets to Wrigley Field. She sat down on the edge of one of the beds, unsure whether to watch him or not. Or to excuse herself to the bathroom.

After he opened the envelope, the two tickets fell onto the carpeting, like long white feathers. He looked at them, confused. Then read the letter.

He rubbed a hand over his face, and she knew he was smoothing his emotions away. He covered his mouth. Reverentially, he folded the paper. Then he carefully unfolded it again to slide the tickets inside, tucking the works gingerly into the envelope itself, by now soft as old linen.

He sat down on the bed beside her. Took her hands in his and kissed them. The backsides of her hands, where she could not hide her age, or the work she had done, the labor. Then he kissed her soft palms, the places of her hands that she moisturized with lotion many times a day, the softest spot on her body. He kissed her palms and pressed them to his face. She could feel moisture on his cheeks. He laid his head in her lap, and she ran her fingers through his hair. She did not know how much time passed.

She observed her older daughter contentedly peering down. Eight stories down. A view that to any business traveler, most any tourist, would have been desolate, was to Jessie a fascinating urban diorama—this magical city somehow exposed. The working city; the city working.

He looked at Vivian. His left hand holding her right thigh, kneading it slowly. Then he set his head back down, and she ran her hands through his hair for a time.

Hey, she said, look at me. You see my purse over there? Why don't you go grab it for me?

He stood, took the purse off the bathroom counter, walked it back to her, and sat on the bed.

She reached into the purse now and produced a second envelope. A newer one. Handed it to him. He opened the envelope and inside were four tickets.

This is for tomorrow's game, he said in wonderment. Then he reached for the old envelope and peered at those original tickets. Wait, these are the same seats. Well, two extra seats, but…these are the same seats.

She nodded. The Cubs are maybe a little better, but I guess sitting in the bleachers is kind of the thing to do these days. Anyway, the weather should be nice. He glanced down at the tickets again.

Thank you, he said. All these years and I've still never been to a game. Always wanted to. But at some point... His voice snagged. I didn't have anyone to sit with.

Well, now you do. Now you can sit next to your fiancée. And two beautiful young ladies, for good measure.

———

That night they walked Michigan Avenue, window-shopping. They strolled Navy Pier. Rode the Centennial Wheel. Took photos in front of Cloud Gate at Millennium Park. Then more photos in front of the Art Institute's big verdigris lions. By nine o'clock, Jessie was exhausted, unaccustomed to all the exercise.

They returned to the hotel, and Jessie fell onto one of the two queen-size beds. They helped remove her shoes and socks. Vivian laughed while she stood Jessie up and helped her into the bathroom, then tucked her back into bed. Melissa crawled in beside her half sister.

They shut off the lights and listened to the building groan and breathe. Listened to other guests making their way down the long carpeted hallways. They held hands and listened as Jessie snored and snored.

She sounds like an outboard motor, he whispered.

She always has, Vivian whispered back, then began giggling.

Forget earplugs, Melissa said quietly. I might go sleep in the bathtub. She waited a beat. Or maybe the hallway. Two floors down.

They laughed quietly and for a long time. Vivian leaned her face against Charlie's shoulder, held his arms.

Thank you for today, he said.

You're welcome, she said, rubbing his chest.

Hey, before you go to sleep, I have something for you, he whispered.

Charlie, she said somewhat loudly, honestly? Not the time.

Keep it down, Melissa grumbled, or pay for another room.

Are your eyes closed? he asked.

Charlie?

Are your eyes closed?

Yes.

Good. Open your mouth.

Then there was the exquisite taste of chocolate. A regal, smooth chocolate that gave way to a luscious raspberry center.

Oh my god, she said, what was that?

Mom, Melissa said, I swear to god.

From my favorite chocolatier, Charlie whispered. Candinas, in Madison.

I love you so much, Vivian said. What a day.

And then they all happily succumbed to sleep.

39

He woke to Vivian tapping him on the shoulder, saying his name, and beyond her voice and touch, the rude sound of someone banging on the door of their room. Loud, heavy fistfalls, battering the door.

Charlie, Vivian said, her voice rising above a whisper, Charlie. Wake up.

Now he was wide awake, his bare feet on the carpeting, his heart pounding. The knocking was incessant, almost violent. Beyond the door a voice, hoarse and belligerent, slurred, My room. This is my room. This goddamn key.

In the neighboring bed, Jessie said, an edge of fear in her voice, Auntie? Auntie? Are we okay?

Just some drunk, Melissa murmured, wrapping her pillow over her head. He'll go away eventually.

But the stranger did not go away, and now the knocking rose in volume and intensity.

Charlie, Vivian said, should we call the front desk?

But Charlie was already rising from the bed, dressing quickly, irritated that he couldn't find his shoes in the darkness.

Charlie, you're not going to—don't confront this guy. Charlie? What are you looking for?

My fucking boots, he said, my shoes.

Charlie? What do you need your shoes for? Charlie? Call the front desk. Charlie?

He wasn't frustrated by Vivian exactly, but his temper was flaring. And something new. A defensiveness. His family was in the room, and his daughter was scared. Vivian was scared too; he could hear it in her voice. There wasn't time to have a discussion about confrontations, poor behavior, or fighting. About the fact that he wasn't going to open that door without his shoes on. He felt his heart pumping, not with love or excitement or even fear, but pure adrenaline, just jet fuel. The knocking persisted, and from far outside the door and far down the hallway, he heard plaintive voices, to which the drunk only answered, Yeah, yeah, yeah. Fuck off.

He used to live for these moments of conflict. Years ago, he would even go to a bar looking for fights, looking for these dark moments, moments of violence and release. Nights culminating in parking lots or bathrooms. Bloody knuckles, cut lips, black eyes, a line of stitches melting into a new scar. He liked to fight on Fridays, then heal over the weekend before heading back to work on Monday with a new story he'd rehearsed and edited like an article about a boxing match. For some of the men he worked with, fighting was a sport, a hobby. It was one of the things Vivian detested most about his job and coworkers.

Charlie quietly unclasped the chain locking the door and snapped the door open.

There before him stood a young man in a well-tailored dark blue business suit, his burgundy tie loosely unknotted over a pale collared shirt that showed blotches of perspiration or perhaps spilled alcohol. The man certainly smelled of alcohol. His thick dark hair was swept back off a sweaty face, and his dull eyes looked lost behind drooping eyelids. He wore expensive shoes and a heavy silver watch that seemed to tug the left side of his body down, as if a toddler were pulling at his sleeve. The young man wiped his nose with the back of his hand and steadied himself.

That's my room, he declared.

From several doors down the hallway, a huge man stepped out into the hallway, which his wide body seemed to practically fill. This man wore flip-flops, athletic shorts, and a white tank top.

Wrong room, Charlie rumbled, unconsciously clenching his fists.

What'd you say to me? the man down the hallway called.

What I said, the drunk man slurred, is—fuck off. Now, if you'll excuse me, he continued, slowly trying to brush past Charlie.

But Charlie stepped in front of him and, with his left arm, blocked the young man from moving forward again. C'mon guy, he said, go sober up.

Fuck off? the big man called. Fuck off?

Charlie? Vivian said. Please.

Hey old-timer, the drunk continued, you must be confused. Pronouncing that word, confused, took him considerable effort.

Fuck off? the big man repeated, this time as he pounded a great forearm over his chest, making an audible thumping sound. Fuck off?

Charlie? Vivian said louder, I'm calling the front desk.

He could hear Melissa trying to calm Jessie, and something in him cooled. The jet fuel that seemed on the brink of combusting dissolved, and he realized he didn't want the temperature to rise one degree more. That he didn't want to fight, not at all. It was their voices behind him. He was no longer who he once was. He turned back to Vivian and said, I've got this. And then he stepped forward and shut the door.

The moment he turned his head from glancing at this hand on the doorknob, the young man slapped him hard across the face. The slap left Charlie whiplash dazed. He shook his head and stared at the drunk, who suddenly took a step back. There wasn't any violence in his heart at that moment, but he knew his eyes were aflame.

You gonna let him punk you like that? said the man down the hallway, who moved steadily closer to them.

Charlie held his hand in the air between him and the drunk, his other hand massaging his face. What's your name? Charlie asked.

Huh?

Your name? Charlie asked again.

Cooper, the drunk said.

Cooper, Charlie repeated. Okay. Cooper, I need you to stop talking and sit down. Right there. Can you do that for me? Charlie's voice was low and commanding, and he felt the power in his words, in the restrained volume. Sit down, and try to relax.

The young man retreated slowly until his back pressed against the wall of the hallway, and then he incrementally collapsed to the floor until his head hung between his knees.

Now Charlie moved towards the big man. He allowed his limbs to loosen, and although he rubbed at his face, he tried his best to smile. He could feel other travelers cracking their doors, eavesdropping. He could hear quiet voices, no doubt on the telephone, talking to the front desk. He hoped he had the time to make everything right.

That was my nephew, he said casually. Kid can't hold his liquor, am I right?

He's lucky he's alive, the big man said, no longer moving forward, but crossing his arms over his massive chest.

He didn't mean any offense, Charlie said, offering the man his hand in peace. But I'll tell you this, if the cops get called, he's going to lose his job. So can I ask you a favor, brother?

The man said nothing, just glowered at him.

Let's all go back to bed.

Charlie slung one of the young man's arms over his shoulder and half carried him as quickly as possible into one of the awaiting elevators, propping him in a corner.

I'm going to go through your pockets now, Charlie said quietly.

Wrong room, the drunk managed.

Yeah, you went to the wrong room all right, Charlie said, as he found the plastic key card tucked inside a small white envelope. He flipped the envelope over and read out loud: Eighteen oh eight. Cooper, your room is eighteen oh eight. Guess which floor we're on?

Eighteen? Cooper slurred.

Not quite, Coop. Nope, we're on eight.

Charlie pressed eighteen, and they rode the elevator up, Cooper's chin now resting on his lapels. When the elevator door opened, Charlie moved out into the quiet hallway, but Cooper stood there, in the corner of the elevator, quite like a mannequin, except for the puddle forming around his shoes.

Come on, buddy, Charlie sighed, and lifted one of the man's limp arms over his shoulder, navigating him towards his room. He knew the man wouldn't remember it, wouldn't remember him, these steps, his words, this night, but what he said next, he said in the manner of a prayer or a mantra, hoping that somewhere, the words took hold, found purchase, like a windblown seed clinging to a cliff crag. He said, I don't know you, son, but I know this wasn't who you've always been, and you don't have to be this person, if you don't want to be. I've been to the place you're at. There are better places. I'll be thinking about you. And I wish you luck.

At room 1808, Charlie pressed the key card against the door, and heard the lock relax and open. With his arm holding Cooper upright, he pressed a shoulder against the door and eased into the room.

The lights were on, and immediately, a young woman dropped her phone on the bed and raced towards them. Beyond her, he could see two children sleeping on a separate queen bed, their heads resting on pillows. She had been crying; she was obviously relieved, but still frantic, still upset, and as soon as she saw Cooper, she helped ease him onto the bed, and then, just as Charlie was about to reverse course, she hugged him, her arms around his neck, like she was clinging to a pier, a riptide pulling at her legs. Charlie returned her embrace very lightly, then more firmly. The young woman was crying against his chest. They stood that way for a few minutes, until her breathing evened, and then she let her hands run down Charlie's arms until they caught his hands, which she squeezed.

Where did you find him? she asked.

He tried... Charlie began. He was lost. Wrong floor. It can happen to anyone.

She was shaking her head in the negative. I don't know how to thank you, she said. I looked everywhere. I called his friends. His family. I called the police. I've been looking for him for three hours. Two of his friends have been walking along the lake. One of his coworkers is following the river. He could have drowned. Or been mugged. I don't know...

Her voice trailed off.

I don't know if I can keep doing this. What am I saying? She laughed darkly, dropping Charlie's hands and wiping her face. Thank you. Thank you for being so kind. I wish I could repay you, honestly. Thank you.

There was so much Charlie wanted to say, but he didn't. He was tired too, though his body was still jagged with adrenaline. Good night, Charlie said, drifting towards the door, which he shut gently.

Now he stood in the hallway, in the darkest hours of the night, and he knew that even if he would have preferred a walk or a cigarette, there was only one place for him to go. So he rode the elevator down to the eighth floor and felt tremendous relief when he reached into his pocket and discovered a key card. He slipped into the room, welcomed by the sounds of Jessie's snoring, and then gently slid into bed beside Vivian.

Oh, she sighed, there you are. Is everything okay?

Everything's fine, he said, kissing her shoulder. Everything's fine. But for a long time, he merely stared through the darkness of the room towards the curtains cloaking the glow of the city, and as the minutes and hours passed, he thought he perceived the sliver of light between those curtains grow brighter and brighter.

He thought of all the times when he had been drunk, belligerent, violent, cruel, loud, or dangerous, and all of the times someone had talked him down or picked him up out of some gutter. The countless times some bartender had asked for his keys, or some friend had driven him home. The nights when Vivian had made him drink glass after glass of water, when she'd guided him to toilets, or helped him into a comforting shower, and later bed. All the weddings he could not remember because he had blacked out. All the dinner parties he'd spoiled by lighting a cigarette in someone's house, or the hosts he'd offended with some crass joke. He closed his eyes against the memories. He had missed the birth of his daughter, her entire childhood. His daughter had been raised by another family because he could not be troubled to part from his drinking, his bottles. He shook his head and wanted to be free of those things he'd done.

The tiny room was filled with the sounds of his family breathing, sleeping, and he closed his eyes and said in his mind, Please forgive me, please forgive me, please forgive me.

He woke hours later to the rude sounds of the television squawking and a blow-dryer's steady drone. He opened his eyes, and the curtains were parted. Jessie stood at the windows, her palms on the glass. She was humming a song he couldn't quite place, but it made him smile. His heart felt overfull in a way he now recognized was only possible for those people who understood that their second chance was as good as or better than heaven. And then Viv was there, kneeling down beside him, smiling too, and touching his face gently.

Are you okay? she asked quietly.

He nodded and fought back the happiest of tears.

Are you sure? Did someone hit you? Your face...it looks swollen.

I'm all right, he managed.

You helped that man last night. Was he okay?

He'll be okay.

He was lucky you were there, she said, running her fingers along his earlobe. Do you know that? What if you hadn't helped him?

He could imagine the spectrum of outcomes, all of them disastrous, some of them even deadly, and he thought of the man's wife, up there in that hotel room, calling everyone she knew, asking for help, and all that implied.

He nodded his head.

Hey, she said, taking his face gently between her two hands, I love you.

I love you too.

And guess what?

What?

It's a new day. And we're in Chicago, can you believe it?

He shook his head no, because he couldn't, he couldn't believe it.

Come on, she said, leaning down to kiss his forehead, let's go find some coffee.

40

The game began at 1:20 in the afternoon. A beautiful early summer day. Green leaves shimmering on the trees like so many sequins. Flowers blooming in the planters along Michigan Avenue. Sunlight reflecting boldly off Lake Michigan, where lines of waves broke gently on the beaches or concrete embankments. Children played on the shore. Seagulls wheeled above. They spent the morning drinking coffee, walking, and eating pastries. They weren't as ambitious today, and that was okay. They sat down frequently. Jessie people-watched behind huge sunglasses as she ate a croissant. Melissa called Jill and talked to the girls.

At eleven thirty they took the steps down into an L station and bought tickets for the Red Line.

Do you know what you're doing? Vivian asked.

Not really, he admitted. But we've got time.

Anyone from the city could see that they were out-of-towners. Charlie struggled with the order of operations at the turnstile. But someone helped him, and he pushed through. Vivian could see the sweat beading on his forehead. But then that same person helped Jessie and Melissa. By then, Vivian had the knack and joined them beyond the turnstiles.

We want to go north, Charlie said.

Are you sure? she asked.

Positive, he replied. The White Sox are the South Siders. Cubs are the North Siders. There, he said, pointing at the Red Line map. We need Addison, I think.

They waited for a train to roar into the station. Jessie plugged her ears with her fingers while Melissa crinkled her nose. The air was hot and still under the wail of a saxophone from far down the platform. The train arrived in a rush of wind and noise, and when it came to a halt, they waited for other passengers to board before pressing forward themselves. Viv held Jessie's shoulders and kissed the top of her head. The doors closed, and the train moved forward. Their eyes widened. This was not Chippewa Falls. Or Spooner. The farther north they rumbled, the more riders pushed into the car, most of them wearing Cubs hats or jerseys, more than a few of them wearing Pirates gear.

When I bought the tickets, Vivian said, they told me the Pirates weren't a good team.

She leaned closer to Charlie. They have some player named Andrew McCrutchen? He's supposed to be very good. At hitting.

He leaned back into her, kissed her lightly on the lips, and said, McCutchen.

Who?

Andrew McCutchen.

Whatever.

At every stop, more and more people boarded the train until it seemed unimaginable that they could fit even a single other person amongst them. And yet they did. People squeezed themselves into corners. Sat on rails. Sat on laps. Held their arms up in the air or tightly pressed to their sides. Some young men were happily, drunkenly chanting, Let's go, Cubbies, then clapping their hands five times in quick succession. This delighted Jessie, who began chanting as well, much to the delight of the rest of the train.

The train labored forward, north. The day was bright, and sunlight slammed into the graffitied windows of the train. Even though she didn't care for baseball, Vivian perceived that they were suddenly part of a tribe, a people. All moving in the same direction, all unified by a common experience. It wasn't so different from all those afternoons and evenings of watching Charlie play softball, except on a much grander scale. A sensation multiplied by thousands of people, tens of thousands of people.

The train came to a stop at the Addison platform, and when the sliding doors parted, passengers spilled out into the daylight and the steady breeze blowing off the lake. Their own little group accounted for what seemed the very last four people off the train, moving awkwardly together, as a single unit. It was slow walking down the steps to street level, into the deep shadows below the platform where pigeons maddened the air and street musicians pounded drums, blared horns, and sang nearly as loud as the vendors, who howled and barked, hustling their wares.

Vivian glanced at Jessie to see how her daughter was managing with the crowd, the city, all the hullabaloo. But she seemed perfectly content. Or happily dazed. From time to time, she leaned her weight against her half sister.

It's a lot to take in, isn't it? Charlie said to Jessie.

Yeah, she agreed. But everyone's happy.

A child walked by, holding on to his father's hand while also clutching a pink nimbus of cotton candy up to his mouth.

Jessie swiveled her head, said, I want one of those.

To which Charlie said, Then you shall have one, my dear.

Suddenly, the stadium, so massive on television, was right there. Right there in front of them, beside them. It seemed the epicenter of the neighborhood, in the way some colleges are, or cathedrals. WRIGLEY FIELD HOME OF THE CHICAGO CUBS, read the great sign over the entrance.

Do you want your picture taken? Vivian asked Charlie.

He looked around, a somewhat pained expression on his face. She sensed that he did, he did want a picture, but was embarrassed to say as much.

Jessie, Melissa, Vivian said, you two and Charlie get together. In front of that sign. There. Perfect. Now smile.

She glanced down at her phone, and there they were: father and daughter, smiling broadly, arms around each other, while Melissa clutched on to him as if he were her favorite uncle. Charlie sidled over to Vivian, peered over her shoulder at the phone, and she knew from his silence that he wasn't just pleased; he was truly touched.

Come on, she said, touching his arm gently. Let's get Jessie a hat. She's always getting sunburned. And that cotton candy she asked for.

They strolled around Wrigleyville. Bought souvenirs for Ainsley, Addison, and Jill. T-shirts, sweatshirts, and hats.

We're going to a baseball game, Charlie said, but it looks like we've been to the mall.

You're traveling with three women, Melissa snickered. What did you expect? That we're here to watch baseball?

You're right though, Vivian said. Enough trinkets. Shall we find our seats?

There was a gravity to the stadium, pulling fans in off the street, out of Ubers and taxis and Lyfts. Away from the Red Line. Out of businesses and taverns and restaurants. Hundreds of fans drifted to the stadium, thousands of them—holding out phones, processing past security guards, turnstiles, and then the easy distance between gate and field, between concrete and the greenest grass imaginable.

They moved as if riding an easy current, flowing, spinning even, as they looked this way and that. All people, every kind of person, what seemed the whole of humanity—walking, jumping, running, singing, dashing, galloping, skipping, dancing, hugging, holding hands, pointing, praying, rejoicing, lamenting, hoping that no matter what might come, this was the year, their time, the moment of their glory and faithful reward. She couldn't help but smile. No matter how little Vivian herself was invested in the Chicago Cubs or baseball in general, she loved seeing Jessie this ecstatic. All that might have been too much was just a little bit more than all right. Such smiles and laughter. The kind of laughter and glee that Vivian did not see enough of in Jessie's life. At the group home. Or at the jobs she occasionally worked. Even with Vivian herself, she thought with some sadness. But no, this wasn't sad. Here was her Melissa, an arm wrapped around Jessie's shoulder, smiling. This was just spectacular. A day among days.

They sat in the bleachers. Pressed in among happy strangers. The air smelled of beer and ketchup, hot dogs and mustard, popcorn and salted nuts and nacho cheese and french fries. Everyone was drinking, and she chanced a look at Charlie, but if he noticed, or was tempted, he wasn't letting on. He had an arm around Jessie as he pointed out various players to her and brought her attention to the dated pennants flapping in the wind. They walked to the very edge of the bleachers now, as close to the field as they could get. Charlie pointed to the ivy along the outfield wall. Vivian drew closer, trying to listen to him. Her fiancé. Her once and future husband.

Hey, Charlie was calling to a man out on the field. A player. Hey, number seven. Swanson. Hey, Swanson, number seven. This is my niece, Jessie. She loves baseball. But you're her favorite. Maybe you could get her a ball? Whaddaya say? And sign it for her? C'mon, buddy. This is her first time at Wrigley.

She could hear a rising in the crowd surrounding them. More than mere murmurings too. There was a collectively rising volume of encouragements, a small group chanting, Swan-son, Swan-son, Swan-son. Melissa held her arms over her head, clapping loudly, whistling, screaming, Swan-son, Swan-son, Swan-son. And then she saw the player, number seven, smiling and laughing, catching a ball thrown from a teammate, and then catching a Sharpie thrown to him by the fans. He signed that baseball, and then lobbed it gracefully to Charlie, who duly caught it, and then, after passing the ball to a delighted Jessie, bowed to Swanson, bowed like he had just been granted a magic wish, and Swanson placed his two hands together, in the seminal pose of gratitude, before turning his back to flash that number seven and resume the pregame loosening up as if nothing remarkable had happened at all.

The crowd cheered. Vivian saw all this from a distance of maybe thirty feet. Which, she thought, was another way of seeing it all perfectly. Everything specific and close, however small a detail, in the vast entirety of the bleachers, the stadium, the city. The crowd on the bleachers surrounding them, not just witnesses to this feat, but accomplices, as they applauded Charlie and Jessie, tipping plastic cups of beer towards the sun.

And then the national anthem. Sung by a blind man, very old. But he stopped everything with his voice. Stopped traffic. The jets in the sky overhead. The very clouds seemed to dissolve in the waning wind, like sugar in warm water. Vivian felt her hand on her chest as the man sang. The heat of her skin, the sun there. Then they applauded. Everyone was happy. It was summer, glorious summer, in this grand lakeside city she had just discovered. Here, at Wrigley Field, with her family, she was happy, and amongst Chicagoans, who seemed to welcome them as their own.

The game settled in now. Smart pitching. Crafty baserunning. Bunts begetting stolen bases, and brave runs. Stellar defense. A ball hit to the warning track, run down before the ivy, and then absolutely rocketed to second base where a tag was applied, neat as can be. The crowd lived and died and was born again.

Before the bottom of the sixth inning, he leaned towards her and kissed her. It was a slow kiss, in no hurry to finish. Eyes closed, she sensed they were being watched, then heard a wave of noise surrounding them, and when she opened one eye, she saw that everyone sitting around them was standing and pointing at them, and at the giant screen just above them, and on another screen beyond right field. The whole stadium, it seemed, was cheering for them.

Then, just as quickly, their faces were gone from the stadium jumbotrons. But he was still kissing her, and now she turned fully towards him, and wrapped her arms around him, her hands in his hair.

There was booing now, riotous booing, a righteous booing. Thirty-five thousand fans broadly booing. Not near them, no. Near them, people were simply talking and drinking. But a few were booing right here as well. Someone on the jumbotron was wearing a Yankees hat; he looked like a broker, skipping work for the afternoon, not a care in the world. Louder booing. She opened her eyes again, and now a young couple was on the board, disengaging from a kiss.

And then it was them again. Her and Charlie. Up on the jumbotron. Still kissing. The crowd roared. Then roared louder. She smiled and laughed into that never-ending kiss and squeezed him tighter and tighter still, kissing him passionately; she wanted everyone to know. That they were in love. That love was still possible, still something a person could have.

Yay! Jessie yelled. They love you!

Melissa jumped up and down, up and down, cheering.

They kissed and kissed and kissed, and the crowd made such a joyous noise. And there was applause. Louder and louder; it was thunderous, that applause. People yelling and cheering. Still, the ovation continued. Applause and applause and applause. Stomping feet, clapping hands. She imagined the applause ringing through the city, from block to block. It sounded like that. Like people opening their apartment windows and applauding. Honking car horns. Traffic cops blowing their whistles. Chefs and cooks and servers and dishwashers banging on pots and pans. Cymbals crashing outside the symphony hall. Louder and louder and louder still. Such cheering, such happiness. No one wanted their kiss to end.

READING GROUP GUIDE

1. Have you ever considered reconnecting with old friends, romantic or otherwise? What might cause you to reach out or not?

2. Do you think it was presumptuous of Charlie to message Vivian after so long? Are some things more acceptable the older you get?

3. Was Vivian right to keep the secret of Charlie's child from him? How would you react to a revelation like that?

4. In a dark moment, Vivian describes children as vampires, sucking the life from the parent. Would you consider this a harsh description? Or accurate occasionally?

5. When someone is entering a relationship with existing children, when is it the right time for children to meet a significant other?

6. Charlie and Vivian's first marriage was fraught with troubles, leaving scars for both of them, yet Vivian is willing to look past this. How willing are you to forgive the sins of the past? Does it depend on the sin or how far in the past?

7. Do you dream about your loved ones? Are the dreams more often negative or positive?

8. Both Charlie and Melissa struggle with alcohol throughout the novel. Why is alcohol so difficult for them to break from, and how does Charlie eventually determine he has to leave it behind?

9. How is a relationship (romantic or platonic) different when you're a teenager or in your twenties versus when you're middle-aged or older?

10. Melissa, upon encouragement from Charlie, writes a list of "Top Five Things I Want for My Life." If you were to create such a list, what would you put on it?

11. What's it like to come from a small town and enter a city for the first time? Or the opposite: a city-dweller going to the countryside?

12. Can people truly change from their past selves? What might cause such a change? What might stunt any potential growth?

A CONVERSATION
WITH THE AUTHOR

How did you approach writing love between an older couple? Was it different from how you might approach love between a younger couple?

So much of the writing of this novel really stemmed from an actual encounter I had with an older couple at a bar who seemed to be on a date or possibly considering rekindling an old flame. I listened (and took notes) on every word they said, and I really metabolized everything they said and heard. Yes, writing an older couple is different than writing a younger couple, absolutely. Everything about aging, about being a thoughtful human being, about regret and learning is an accumulation of experiences, mistakes, and lessons. One reason I'm so proud of this novel is that I think both characters changed (developed) in their time apart and even later when they are reunited. But they needed each other for forgiveness, for redemption.

Why did you choose to write from both Charlie's and Vivian's perspectives?

There was never any question as to how the novel would be told. I think the alternating points of view build a nice rhythm in the book that will (hopefully) encourage a reader to turn pages. And I think that alternating perspectives also allows for a measuring of narrative information. In other words, as a writer, I can withhold certain information, certain secrets.

This book started with inspiration from an older couple in a bar: How do you expand a story beyond a scene to a whole novel?

As a writer, you just get a feeling—I don't know how to explain it; maybe it's inspiration or insight or some sort of unexplainable transmission from without—but *I knew* who these people were. I don't mean that literally. But I do mean that I had met people like this before. They weren't just people at a bar to me. I could feel that they were passionate people and that life hadn't always been kind to them, and I felt a deep curiosity and compassion for them. I don't know what happened to that couple, but the moment they left the bar, I was cheering for them.

How does location factor in to how you write certain characters? Why is it so important that this book is set in Wisconsin?

I don't really set out to plot my books in one place or another, but it is very necessary to me that I know enough about a setting to get things right. And clearly when I write about Wisconsin, I am not worried about getting things wrong. The Tomahawk

Room in Chippewa Falls, Wisconsin, is absolutely one of my favorite places to have a cold beer or brandy slush anywhere on the planet. So, the question then becomes, how do I communicate that affection for place throughout the novel. Certainly, this *plot* could work in Manhattan or SoMa or Palm Beach, but the characters would be decidedly different. Vivian, for example, has never really had the privilege of leaving her hometown, and I wanted that to come through in the novel, because her life is so different from Charlie's in that way.

Considering your thoughts on people-watching for inspiration for stories, how do you know something you've seen or heard will make a good book? How do you know when there is enough substance for a novel?

When I first started publishing books, I would have answered this question differently. And the funny thing is, I don't know how I would have replied. But in the case of *Godspeed* and *A Forty Year Kiss*, both books sprang from conversations I had or conversations I was eavesdropping on. I have this theory that people tell writers their best stories because they know that's what we do, and in some way, they hope their stories are repeated and treasured. But lately, I have to admit that I think there is something very magical, very mystical about being a writer. Sometimes, I have to say, the universe puts me in a spot at a certain time, and my obligation is to pay attention and listen. I know that some people may not understand that, but the older I get, the more I really believe it.

What kind of research did you have to do for a book like this?

Many nights at the Tomahawk Room. I kid, but I also gave the novel to some close family friends who provided some needed insight into one of the characters (I don't want to give anything away here). In short, I tried to practice due diligence.

What did you enjoy most about writing this book?

Honestly, I loved everything about writing this book. It's a very positive novel full of love, family, second chances, redemption, kindness. My prior novel, *Godspeed*, is about late-stage capitalism, meth addiction, greed, and the illusion of the American dream. I'm of course proud of that novel as well, but I can testify to the fact that the writing process was much, much different. So, writing this was a dream.

ACKNOWLEDGMENTS

On September 22, 2022, I was sitting at the bar of the Tomahawk Room in downtown Chippewa Falls, Wisconsin, working a sudoku puzzle and sipping a beer. I did not expect to find the inspiration for this novel. In fact, at the time, I was suffering from my first case of writer's block and had been since the beginning of the COVID pandemic. But then I heard a man, two seats down from me, say, "I still dream about you. I dream about the mornings when we were lying in bed. I dream about kissing you. Can I kiss you?" In that instant, I knew what the story for my next novel would be. To those star-crossed lovers who unknowingly gifted me their story, I offer a profound *thank you*. I felt as if the cosmos had handed me a great opportunity, and no matter what I had thought my literary plans might be, I suddenly had no choice but to write this book. Thank you also to the owner of the Tomahawk Room, Rob Kiefer, a man so generous he once offered me a wooden tray so I could more comfortably write handwritten letters at his bar. Thanks to Nathan Berg, my favorite bartender at the Tomahawk.

Choosing a title can be a contentious decision, and sometimes, the writer isn't the one making the choice. I had a tough time naming this book, but one night, I was sitting in the Fox Head Tavern in Iowa City, with my old roommate from the Iowa Writers' Workshop, Adam Soto (read his excellent fiction), and I described to him the plot of this novel. He said, "That sounds like a forty year kiss." Several days later I asked his permission to use that title, and he graciously said yes. For that grace, I cannot thank him enough.

A debt of gratitude is owed to Katie Yee, who published an early incarnation of this novel on LitHub and whose enthusiasm was deeply edifying and reassuring.

Thank you to my friend, the great novelist Matthew Quick. Matthew and I have long been fans of each other's work, but in the past few years, that fandom has evolved beautifully, sensitively, generously into a friendship that I am deeply grateful for. Matthew does not need my help, but do yourself a favor and find his books; you'll be grateful you did.

Thank you to my fellow Royaleer, the visual artist Andy DuCett, whose wise musical counsel led me to relentlessly listen to Willie Nelson's "Christmas Blues," the soundtrack and touchstone of this book.

For inspiration, I must acknowledge the poet Sam Reed, whose work influenced a scene near the beginning of this novel.

This book would not have been possible without the best

literary agent in the world, Rob McQuilkin, who has been with me since my Iowa City days. I do not have the words or eloquence to properly thank this man, who has so changed the fortunes of my family. Thank you to everyone at Massie & McQuilkin, including Maria Massie, Max Moorhead, and Ellie Roppolo. Thank you also to all my foreign agents and editors.

Thank you to the Wallace family of Eau Claire, Wisconsin, in particular, Ruth and John Wallace, for reading an early manuscript of this novel. Thank you to Simon, for also being an early reader and friend. Thank you to Ian Wallace, for howling at the moon from my backyard.

Thank you to Shana Drehs, for believing in this novel from the very start. Your editorial suggestions were right on the mark. Thank you to Liv Turner, for additional editorial input. Thank you to everyone at Sourcebooks Publishing.

Thank you to my family. To my wife, Regina, who has supported me in so many ways for so long. Thank you to my children, Henry and Nora, who keep me grounded in, as Jimmy Durante sang, "the real stuff of life." Thank you, Mom and Dad. Thank you to Jim and Lynn Gullicksrud. To my brother, Alex. To my uncle Jack and aunt Judy. My late aunt Carol.

Thank you to the innumerable independent bookstores and booksellers who have supported my career from the beginning. Thank you to the critics and journalists who have covered my career over the past six books.

For their early support, Leif Enger and Ash Davidson—thank you.

To my friends, Royaleers, teachers, and neighbors: Brad Baumgartner, Jenna Blum and A Mighty Blaze, Tim Brudnicki, Marcus Burke, Mark Cecil, Sam Chang, Drew Christopherson, Guia Cortassa and Giulio D'Antona, Chris Dombrowski, Doug Duren, Peter Geye, Anita and Rajesh Girdhari, Chanda Grubbs, Nicholas Gulig, Bill Hogseth, BJ Hollars, Tracy Hruska, the Iowa Writers' Workshop, Brian Joseph, John Larison, Michael "Swayze" Link, Chris and Sara Meeks, Nik Novak, Ben Percy, Michael Perry, Dustin Price, Ed Roberson and his *Mountain & Prairie* podcast, Josh Swan, Hilary and Mike Walters, Dave and Jaci Welke, Tim and Jen Wilson, Eric Zimmer and his *The One You Feed* podcast.

Finally, thank you to all my readers.

Nickolas Butler

Stanley Lake—Iron River, MI

ABOUT THE AUTHOR

© JIM IVORY

A graduate of the University of Wisconsin-Madison and the University of Iowa Writer's Workshop, Nickolas Butler is the international bestselling and critically acclaimed author of four previous novels and one collection of short stories. He is also a prize-winning poet and essayist. Butler lives in rural Wisconsin on sixteen acres of land adjacent to a buffalo farm with his wife, two children, their dog, and chickens.